CRAZY LIKE A FOXE

CRAZY
LIKE A
FOXE

A Skyler Foxe Mystery

Haley Walsh

Foxe Press

Cover design by Jeri Westerson

**Sign up for my newsletter at
SkylerFoxeMysteries.com**

Foxe Press
PO Box 799
Sun City, CA 92586

To my Long Suffering Husband
for loving me even as crazy as I am

"The fox's greatest enemy is its tail." —Tajikistani Proverb

CHAPTER ONE

SKYLER FOXE GLANCED ACROSS THE FOOTBALL field. The day was already becoming a scorcher even at ten in the morning and the hot, grassy scent of the lawn almost overpowered in the shimmering heat.

The field was jam-packed with young teen boys vying for a spot on the varsity and junior varsity football teams, running scrimmages, ramming into the tackling dummies, and listening avidly to…

Skyler sighed. He couldn't help it. He always thought he had his feelings under control. No need to look sappy all the time where Keith Fletcher was concerned. Okay, yes, he was in love with the guy. Everyone knew it and they had moved in together just nine months ago, but he supposed he never had a clue about what being in love would entail. Sure, he'd had lots of hook-ups. *Lots* of them. But he'd never fallen before. And with Keith, well. Skyler had fallen all the way. Just watching him across the field in his tight shorts with those strong-muscled thighs, that polo shirt taut over his brawny chest, made his heart thump and his stomach twist in a strangely pleasant way.

Jeez. I just saw him only a few hours ago. He shook his head at the absurdity of it all.

As head football coach, Keith directed the boys and the other assistant coaches in a ballet of sorts that was well beyond Skyler's ability to understand, but just seeing his man in charge made him glow with pride.

And then Keith spotted him. If his heart had thumped before it gave a victory leap this time. Keith's face broke into a truly melting smile and he waved. Skyler lifted his hand to return the wave and then ducked his head with embarrassment as nearly the whole field turned to look at him. He adjusted his hat and slipped behind the chain-link barrier and up into the stands.

Up a few tiers he spotted Rick Flores, the lanky Hispanic teen who had a boyfriend of his own out on the field, the stocky Alex Ryan. Rick sprawled his tall frame back against two rows of seats. His tanned skin shined with perspiration in his white tank top. His canvas shorts reached down to his knees.

For the umpteenth time Skyler cursed his own fair skin that had to survive this time of year under layers of sunscreen and long shirt sleeves. His blond hair seemed blonder, if that were possible, and his head and nose were protected under a brimmed hat.

"Hey, Rick," he said.

The teen looked up, shielding his eyes under a large hand. "Hey, Mr. Foxe. What are you doing here? Isn't July teacher's time off?"

"I wish. Do you mind if I sit with you?"

"Pull up a bleacher."

Skyler sat and jumped up just as quickly. Metal seats in the hot sun! He stuck his leather satchel under him and sat on it. "Most people don't know that teachers have a lot of meetings to go to before school starts again. I'm here most days."

"That sucks."

"Yeah. It does."

"So are you waiting for Coach Fletcher to get done? He's looking mighty fine out there."

Skyler was certain that his cheeks were blushing a furious red under the sunscreen. "Coach Fletcher is none of your concern," he said airily. "After all, don't I see Alex out there?"

Rick offered a lazy smile. "My big, handsome football player."

"That's *right*. So keep your eyes on *him*, mister." He grinned. "Hard to believe you aren't my sophomores anymore. You'll be my *juniors* in two weeks. So Alex moves up to varsity, right?"

Rick beamed. "He's official. Or will be when they pick the team."

"Have you been here every day for tryouts?"

Rick scanned the sweating boys, some in pretty plum condition. "Just supporting the team, right Mr. Foxe?"

"Go Polk Panthers!"

Rick relaxed back again. "Yeah. I've been watching the process. And do you see that player over there, hitting the tackling dummy?"

Skyler looked. A broad-shouldered teen—looked like Samoan or some other Pacific Islander in sweats and a baseball cap—kept slamming it with excessive force while some other teens, obviously already on the team, looked on with what Skyler could only describe as disdain. "Yeah. What's with him? Why are the others giving him such a hard time?"

"Because it's not a *him*. It's a *her*."

Skyler looked again. Wide shoulders, strong stance, but…yes. There was something different about how she moved now that he looked carefully. "Wow. Are we about to make history at Polk High?"

"She's pretty good, actually, despite the shi—uh, crap she's been getting."

"Do you think she's good enough to be on the team? I mean...some of those guys can really do some damage."

"If a girl tries out they usually end up being the kicker. They don't end up in the pileup."

"Oh." Skyler watched her more critically. He certainly was all for Title IX but he didn't want to see a student get hurt unnecessarily either. He'd have to ask Keith about it when he was done. Which would be—according to his watch—in five, four, three, two, one...

Whistle blow. The teens all trotted toward Keith. He talked to them, looking them all in the eye and gesturing, and then dismissed them. He watched them go, conferred with his coaches for a good ten minutes, and then nodded in finality. Tucking his clipboard under his arm he moved purposefully toward the bleachers where Skyler was making his way down the steps to greet him.

"Hey, babe," said Keith. "What are you doing here? I thought you had museum duty today."

"I'm on schedule in half an hour. Since I'm finally done with my meetings, I thought I'd pop over to see what you were up to."

"Walk with me to the gym?"

Skyler's least favorite place but he said nothing as he tried to keep pace with Keith's longer strides. "It's been pretty interesting, especially today."

"Yes, I saw the newest recruit. *She* looks pretty good."

Keith frowned. "You saw that, did you? It was only a matter of time."

"Is she good enough for the team? Will she be kicking?"

"Actually, she doesn't want to be a kicker. She wants to be in the scrimmage."

"Oh. Is she good enough for that?"

His frown deepened. "I have to tread carefully here. I have to give her an equal chance out there but I know the guys are going to be extra hard on her. And she really is good. Smart. Fast. To tell you the truth…" He stopped and looked around to make sure no one was within earshot. "I think she'd be good on the team. But I am going to get shit from everyone, including the district."

"Why? Don't you have to give her a chance? And if she qualifies…"

Keith released a sigh. "Skyler, I've been wrestling a lot with the new guidelines on concussions in high school kids. The statistics are pretty clear. I've been inundated with materials and parents' complaints. I've got a lot to do changing attitudes about how we play the game itself, let alone attitudes about women on the team. And just between you and me…I feel uncomfortable with the idea of a girl getting hit and tackled. It's pretty brutal."

"Why Keith Fletcher!"

He made quieting gestures with his hands. "Keep it down, Skyler. I know that sounds sexist but it was the way I was raised."

Skyler folded his arms over his chest and lifted a brow. "You played football with your sister. I saw you at New Year's."

"That's different. That was flag. I wasn't out for blood." He hurried on.

Skyler raced to catch up again. "I think it would be great for the school. It's still good publicity, isn't it?"

Keith nodded reluctantly. "It would be, yes. As long as she didn't get hurt."

"You can't guarantee that. And I'm sure if she's played before—and it looks as if she has—that she knows that, too. Have you talked to her parents?"

"Yeah. Her dad is over the moon. They just moved here from Hawaii and though she tried out at her other school they wouldn't put her on the team. He had higher hopes for California."

"Are you going to do it?"

Keith slammed open the gym double doors and barreled on through the locker room where most of the teens were busy showering and getting dressed. He and Keith climbed the metal staircase to the coach's glass-walled office overlooking the locker room. The stairs still gave Skyler pause. After all, the coach before Keith had tried to kill Skyler on those very stairs and he still had flashbacks, something he had yet to mention to Keith.

Once inside the office Skyler took a deep breath and looked down at the rows of lockers, benches, shower stalls, and towel cupboards below. "If she's on the team, where will she…?"

"Exactly," said Keith, dumping his thick binder and clipboard on the desk. "There will be a lot of logistics to work out. The girl's locker room is farther away from the field, as inconvenient as it comes. But you know what? I think I'm going to go for it."

He grabbed Keith's arm, caught up in the man's excitement.

"Keith, that's fantastic! What a great opportunity for you and the school. I'm really proud of us."

The man chuckled. "Well, one thing's for sure. It's going to be an interesting year."

Skyler beamed. August began in a week and a half and with it the start of the new school year. And in a few short months it would be the one year anniversary when he met Keith. He had instantly gravitated toward the handsome coach and biology teacher, even when he hadn't known he was gay.

The thought of this important anniversary when he'd never spent more than a week with hook-ups before, gave him pause.

There was a warm presence directly behind him. "What's the matter, babe? You got all pensive there."

"Oh, nothing." He sidled away. It was too tempting having Keith so close to him.

Keith shrugged and dug into his binders, settling into his seat. "Oh by the way. I'm signing you up for a self-defense class."

Taken aback, Skyler stared. "No you're not."

"Yes I am."

"Keith, you don't have to do that. I told you. I'm not going to go solving any more crimes."

Shuffling papers Keith smirked. "Yes you are."

Folding his arms over his chest Skyler postured. "Well…then you don't know me very well."

"Yes I do."

"Stop that! I don't need the classes."

"You're taking them."

"Why do you think you can order me around?"

"Look, Skyler, I love you. I don't want you getting hurt. I want you to protect yourself. You're a gay man in a redneck county. It wouldn't hurt to do this anyway, don't you think? Now please. For me?"

Keith blinked his baby blues. He wasn't doing it on purpose but those eyes with their long lashes got Skyler every time. "Well…if you put it like that…"

Smiling, Keith concentrated on his papers again. "Good. The first class begins tomorrow night. If you like, I'll go with you."

"You don't need to escort me," he grumbled. But on thinking of it, he thought it might be a good idea after all. Maybe he'd call Jamie. They could take the class together. He brightened. "So I'll see you later. Redlands Bowl tonight."

"That's right. Our usual spot?"

"The blanket will be ready and waiting. Congratulations on the team."

"Thanks. Love you."

"Love you, too," he muttered and then, before his face completely burst into flame, he made a hasty exit down the steps and out of the gym.

Skyler did a quick clean-up, donned a white linen shirt and tan cargo pants, and hurried down to his Bug. It wasn't far to the Lincoln Shrine. It was a 1932 museum of Civil War and Lincoln memorabilia created in memoriam to a fallen World War I vet. As Skyler slid into his seat, he got on his phone to Jamie.

"Hey Skyboy, what's up?" Skyler could hear the quick tapping of Jamie on his laptop keyboard in the background, no doubt inputting lines of codes for his website designs.

"Keith signed me up for a self-defense course beginning tomorrow night and I wondered if you want to do it with me."

"Hmm. That's probably not a bad idea what with our Scooby Gang activities and all."

"We won't be doing that anymore."

Jamie laughed. "Oh sure we won't. Whatevs. Just tell me when and where and I'll be there."

"No, seriously, Jamie." Skyler started his car. "This crime-solving is getting in the way of lots of stuff, so it's over."

"Sure, you just keep telling yourself that."

"Hey! You know what…never mind. I'll call you tonight with the details."

"You guys going to the Bowl tonight?"

"Of course. I'm on collection duty."

"Dave and I might join you. Your usual spot?"

"Yeah. See you."

Putting the Bug in gear, Skyler pulled away from the curb. With the air conditioning blasting, he made his way down the wide avenue, took a quick left, and found a parking spot on the street behind the museum. An unassuming building resembling an armory with its hard angles in blocks of stone, the museum had been home to Skyler every summer since he was thirteen.

"Good afternoon, Skyler!" The director Lester Huxley waved from the doorway. An African American man in his seventies, Huxley was definitely slowing down. His gray hair had receded up his wide forehead and wrinkles teased at his eyes.

Skyler smiled. "Hi, Mr. Huxley. How's it going?"

Skyler waited for the familiar reply of, "Slower but gettin' there" and wasn't disappointed. "Were your meetings just as boring as yesterday's?"

With a sigh, Skyler shut the front door, checking again to make sure it was unlocked. "Yes. I don't know why they have to be. Really, a lot of this stuff can be emailed to us. Why we have to suffer through lectures day after day…"

Huxley nodded. "Same in my day. One of the reasons I retired early. And the fact that the wife made a good living." He winked. "But I do miss the classroom. Kids giving you problems?"

"No, I wouldn't say that. I really enjoyed my first year. Looking forward to my second."

"Good, good." He patted Skyler's hand. "I'll miss you when school starts. That's any day now, isn't it?"

"About a week and some change," said Skyler, flipping on lights.

"August! It's earlier every year, isn't it? Whatever happened to summer vacation? I don't know what I would have done without you during summer vacation."

"That seems like a long time ago."

"Not that long. You were a tiny thing when you started here. Twelve, weren't you, all wiry arms and legs."

Skyler smiled. "Thirteen. And such a history nerd. Nothing like adding that to being a gawky teenager."

"But look at you now! You're a teacher, Skyler. I'm proud of you."

"Couldn't have done it without your encouragement, Mr. Huxley. I appreciate what you did to help me get through school."

"Now, now. Water under the bridge. You paid me back. You're a good man, Skyler. The place is always quieter without you."

"Quieter without whom?" A young African American man walked through the front door, looking boldly at Skyler.

"Without Skyler, Jerome," said Lester.

Skyler smiled over his shoulder as he adjusted a shelf of books. "Jerome, I was about to tell your uncle that you can take over my duties for the rest of the summer just fine."

"That so? I may be doing more than that."

"Don't jump the gun, Jerome," hushed Lester.

Skyler looked from one man to the other. "Jump the gun on what?"

"Uncle's gonna retire this year. I'm slated to replace him."

"What? Retire? Oh no, Mr. Huxley. The Lincoln Shrine wouldn't be the same without you."

"I've been here a long time, Skyler. Since before you were born. No, I've paid my dues. I'd like to think I left my mark taking good care of this place." His lips tightened to a straight line, and he tilted his head from one corner of the octagonal rotunda to the other. "But it's time to go. If you weren't so dead-set on being a teacher I'd have recommended you for my replacement. You have to know I trust no one more than you, young man."

Skyler's heart warmed. "Mr. Huxley…"

Jerome grunted.

"Don't worry yourself, boy," he said to Skyler. "You will always have a place here. No one knows it like the back of your hand like you do…except maybe me."

"And me," said Jerome a little huffily.

"Sounds like a deep conversation going on," said a man walking breezily through the door. He had dirty blond hair, a frat boy polo shirt, and white running shoes. His docent nametag read "Ron Harper."

"Nothing much," said Lester.

"Only that he plans to retire," said Skyler, feeling a pang in his heart at the prospect.

Ron stopped. "Who's going to retire? Not you, Lester."

"Now everyone, just calm down. It isn't happening tomorrow. Just...soon. Now if you all don't mind, I have work to do." He turned to his nephew to speak in low tones while Skyler brooded and raised his face to the familiar rotunda; to the bookshelves in their closed glass cabinet doors; to the art deco paintings on the curved walls around the domed roof; of painted Depression-era stylized angels bearing the legends under each one of "Patience", "Tolerance", "Courage", "Faith", "Loyalty", "Wisdom", "Justice", and "Strength". Skyler felt at home among the books, the glass display cases, the dummies with Civil War garb. He and the others sold souvenirs from the little nook in the far corner to tourists and their kids, and explained about what visitors were viewing in the cases. He made sure the two TV monitors showing Civil War documentaries were up and running, and he glanced into the cases to make sure all was in order.

So it took him a few seconds to do a double take when one of Lincoln's stove pipe hats that should have been behind glass was conspicuously absent.

He hurried to the display cabinet and looked for the little tag he and the other curators placed there when an exhibit was removed for repair or study, but none was there.

"Excuse me, Mr. Huxley?"

Lester had finished with his nephew and was almost to his office when he turned.

"Um...what happened to the stove pipe?"

Huxley's eyes widened for a moment and he waddled toward the cabinet Skyler was standing in front of. He seemed to chew on his cheeks a moment before he grunted and turned away. "It's, uh...it's out for repair."

"Oh. It's just that..." Skyler grabbed the clipboard from behind the main counter and perused the pages. "No one made a note of it."

"I probably forgot," said Ron. He hurried behind the counter and grabbed the clipboard. "I'm sure it's here somewhere."

Skyler shrugged. But he couldn't help but notice Lester narrowing his eyes at his nephew who seemed to be studiously ignoring his uncle.

The old man seemed frail to Skyler, now that he thought about it. Oh he had always seemed old to Skyler. After all, Skyler had started work at the museum when most adults had seemed pretty old, but Mr. Huxley didn't have gray hair then. His eyes had been bright, his features smooth and free of wrinkles. Now the whites of his eyes were yellowed, his hair was in gray tight curls, and lines scored his face at eyes and forehead. He seemed weary and fragile. Maybe it *was* time for him to retire.

Lester said nothing more as he clutched his ever-present coffee Thermos in his large hand and retreated into his office.

Skyler would have let him go (he noticed that the man sometimes napped there now in the late afternoon) but he needed to talk to him.

Lester was just settling in to his desk when Skyler knocked on the door jamb. "Knock, knock," he said as Lester looked up. "Sorry to bother you, Mr. Huxley, but I have these receipts..." He pulled out his wallet and took out the papers, unfolding them. "This is the receipt for the repair to the electrical wiring. It's kind of a lot because there was a rat infestation and here's the other receipt for the exterminator. They both needed payment so I paid them myself. This is for a reimbursement."

Lester took the papers and looked them over. "Damn rats. They did this much damage?"

"You know how the wiring is in this old place. One thing leads to another and then there's plaster than needs to be cut and repaired."

"This old museum. It's a wonder it's still standing." He unlocked the middle desk drawer and pulled out the large checkbook binder and laid it on his desk. He opened it and examined the ledger. He seemed to stare at it a long time before he slowly closed it. "I'm…uh…out of checks for now. But I'll hold on to these and get one to you as soon as I can. Will that be a problem for you, Skyler? I could pay you myself…" He reached for his back pocket and Skyler waved him off.

"There's no rush, Mr. Huxley. It can wait."

"Are you sure? That's a big amount. And you on a teacher's salary."

"I have Keith. I won't starve, I assure you."

"Okay then." His hands seemed to shake as he closed the binder and placed it back in the drawer. He rubbed his chin and stared off into the corner as Skyler shut the door softly behind him.

Weird. Because it looked to him as if the binder was full of checks.

They had more tourists than the day before, and when Skyler closed and locked the doors at five, he did a cursory dusting, vowing to be more thorough tomorrow when he had more time.

"You're running off to the bowl tonight, aren't you?" Huxley shook his head with a grin. "I forgot it was

Tuesday. You sure keep yourself busy. Don't you leave time for having fun?"

"I can assure you, Mr. Huxley, I do. Why don't you come to the bowl tonight? It's the orchestra."

"I just might do that. Your young man will be there?"

Skyler blushed as he always did at mention of Keith. He had thought that coming out last fall would be one big hullabaloo and then the dust would quietly settle. But what he hadn't counted on was that coming out was a continual process. Each old friend, each new person he met, he'd have to come out all over again. And he had worried about it, especially to older people like Mr. Huxley. But he needn't have. The old man had known all along anyway and he greeted Keith with the same warmth and charm he'd always shown to Skyler.

"Yes, he'll be there. In fact..." Skyler checked his watch. "I'd better go out there now and leave my blanket in our spot or I'll lose it."

Lester waved. "Then go! What are you messing about here for? Get out of here."

Skyler headed for the door. "See you tonight?"

"I'll be sitting on the benches. I leave the picnic blankets for the younger folk."

"Okay, then. See you there. Bye Ron, Jerome!"

Skyler hurried out, got to his car to get the blanket, and ran across the street to the park with its ninety-year-old amphitheater surrounded by spiring cypress trees. Known as the "Redlands Bowl," it was "America's longest continuously running summer music festival at which no admission is charged." He quickly spread out the blanket on the edge of the lawn where it met the sidewalk under a cypress, and rushed off to meet with the other volunteers.

Already people were staking out places on the lawns on both sides of the 5,000 seat benches in front of the pastel-lit bowl, where on the stage, the chairs for the orchestra were being set up. Lighting techs focused lighting instruments and spots, while the sound engineer took his usual spot in the center of the bench seating that curved around the stage. He adjusted toggle switches and checked gauges on his board. When he noticed Skyler he waved and Skyler waved back.

Skyler loved that his hometown played host to this free concert series. He had enjoyed it every year since his childhood when his parents took the walk to the bowl from their house, the place where his mother still lived. And where Skyler's long ago absentee father seemed to be spending an inordinate amount of time.

He shook the thought loose. He had his duties to concentrate on. He had to sit at the information booth and hand out programs. He used one to fan himself. The heat was still vigorous, even in the shade of the trees.

As the sun slowly made its way over the bowl and visitors began filling the seats and the lawns, Skyler was temporarily released from duties to set up his own picnic area. A quick change in the nearby bathrooms finally got him into shorts, and then he made his way to the car for his picnic basket.

He was setting it up just as Keith arrived with their sand chairs.

"Hey, babe," said Keith with a huge smile. He leaned in and kissed Skyler. Redlands was becoming more tolerant and even though Keith eschewed the looks they still got, Skyler could never quite get over his embarrassment. He ducked his head, ignoring those around him, and set up their fare.

"So are we celebrating?" asked Skyler, scooping crab salad onto leaves of endive and passing the plate to Keith.

"Yup. It's official. Polk High has a girl on the football team."

Skyler paused, wine bottle in hand. "That's awesome! You won't be sorry."

Keith shook his head, but his smile was evident by the deeply grooved dimple in his cheek. "Well, I might be at some point. Just waiting for the backlash."

"Backlash nothing." He uncorked and poured the Sauvignon Blanc into their acrylic stemware. He handed Keith one and raised his glass. "Here's to the Polk Panthers making it to the CIF!" They clinked and drank. Skyler settled in and crunched an endive leaf.

They chatted, ate, and drank. And even through the heat, Skyler relaxed, forgetting for a time about his mother, Title IX, and Mr. Huxley's retirement.

They sang golden oldie songs along with the Community Sing, neither able to carry a tune. They belted it out anyway, laughed, and then settled in — sand chairs close together so Keith could hold Skyler's hand — as the lights dimmed and the concert began.

After an hour of enrapturing music, the park lights came up, intermission began, and Skyler leapt to his feet to get his "red bowl" to wander around soliciting donations for the concert organization. He waved at Randi who seemed to be there with a girlfriend. Seth was there as well, lolling on the benches, listening to something on his phone. Skyler wondered if he was even listening to the concert. He noticed Ron buying ice cream from the Soroptimist's booth, but he didn't seem to notice Skyler. Even Jerome showed up, but he wasn't sitting on a bench or at a picnic. Just standing on the path that arced around the benches, arms crossed tightly over his chest and staring at the stage as if it had done him some harm.

In his wanderings, making his way through the picnickers to take donations in the red bowl he carried, Skyler noticed a few of the museum board members scattered hither and yon, but he didn't want to interrupt them with their friends and family. Yes, Redlands was like any small town in America, he supposed. Smiling, he enjoyed his "The Music Man" moment.

His last stop before intermission ended was to walk the edge of the bench seating, and passed the bowl down row after row...and came upon Mr. Huxley. "So you made it," he said to the older man. He kept half an eye on the red bowl as it marched down the benches. Another volunteer stood at the far side, ready to pass it down to the next row so it would end up back at Skyler's end.

Lester glanced up to the stars. "It's a lovely night and the music is enchanting. Claudine and I really used to enjoy the orchestra especially. I do miss her."

"I do, too. She was a lovely lady."

"She was that and more." He sighed and sat back, continuing to gaze at the stars. "And, I suppose, she *is* here, looking down."

Skyler smiled wistfully and couldn't help looking back at Keith relaxing on their blanket and sipping his wine. Lester and Claudine Huxley had been married over fifty years. He wondered how that was, being with one person that long. She'd died only last year.

Huxley unscrewed the cap of his Thermos and poured more coffee into the plastic cup. "I know you had to rush off to get here tonight, Skyler, but tomorrow, I'd like to talk to you about something. Something...important."

"Mr. Huxley, you know I have my classes to teach. I can't possibly take on more—"

"I know that, boy. It's about something else." He frowned and sipped his coffee.

"Is everything all right?"

"Well...I need to tell someone before it gets out of hand. I don't know how it got so..." He suddenly looked up as if remembering Skyler was there. "Now don't you worry," he said, shifting his eyes away. "We'll talk tomorrow. You go on. Enjoy yourself." The donation bowl came his way again filled with crumbled bills. He added some of his own and handed it to Skyler. "Here you go, Young Mr. Foxe. Keep on doing good work."

"Are you sure, Mr. Huxley? I can take a few moments now to talk."

He offered a weak smile. "Don't be silly. You have donations to collect and your young man to share this warm summer night with. Go on, now."

Skyler moved on to the next row, looking back. But Lester simply sat, sipping his coffee.

The lights flickered once more signaling the end of intermission. But before Skyler could return to Keith and their picnic, a man, nearly Skyler's twin, stepped in front of him. He was slight of frame as Skyler was, just as tall, perhaps a little taller, with golden blond hair.

"Are you Skyler Foxe?"

"Uh...yes."

The man stood back and insolently appraised him. "Of course you are. My, my. He sure knows how to pick 'em."

"Excuse me?" A distinctly unpleasant vibe poured off the guy and Skyler took an involuntary step back.

"Believe me, dude, you're only one in a long line of them. What did he tell you, I wonder?"

"Who? What did *who* tell me?"

"Keith, of course. Keith Fletcher? That *is* your boyfriend, right?"

A shiver crept up Skyler's spine. "What about him?"

"Ah you're so sweet. Just like he likes them. I'm afraid I wasn't the sweet type. But I was blond enough. And you! Wow. Pretty fucking blond. Is it natural?"

"Listen." Skyler took another step back, feeling suddenly dirty under the man's smirking scrutiny. "I'm gonna go now." Was this one of Keith's old boyfriends? "Whatever deal you had with Keith is over. So I suggest you just leave us alone."

"Whatever 'deal'? Oh my friend, it's far from over. Just tell him Ethan says *hi*. Ta ta!" He waved his fingers and turned on his heel.

Chapter Two

SKYLER CLENCHED HIS HANDS. HE HAD NEVER wanted more to grab someone and slam their face into the ground.

He gritted his teeth, stomped back over to their blanket, and threw himself into his chair.

Keith shifted toward him. "Skyler, what's wrong?"

"Nothing." And then he realized he was clenching his arms over his chest. He tried to relax, smoothing his hands over the chair arms instead. "It was just...someone..." He turned to face Keith and took a deep breath. "I was told to tell you '*Ethan* says *hi*'."

Keith's face fell. "Ethan? What did he look like?"

"What did he look like? He looked like *me*!"

"Oh shit." He snapped to his feet, looking around, searching, when the lights suddenly dimmed.

Slowly he sat as the orchestra leader strode onto the stage amid the audience's applause. "I'm...I'm sorry about that," he said to Skyler's ear.

"I take it he's an ex," whispered Skyler.

"A very *ex* ex," said Keith softly.

"Boy, he sure looks like me."

Blowing out a breath, Keith leaned his head back. "I told you I have a type."

"I know. I just didn't realize how...*typey*...it is."

"Skyler, I am not with him anymore. I'd *never* be with him again. I'm with you. End of story."

A woman behind them hissed a "Shhhhhh!"

Skyler whipped around. "Do you mind? I'm having an important conversation."

"Yes, I *do* mind," she said. "I can't hear the music."

"Really? A full orchestra and you can't hear it?"

An arm grabbed him and yanked him from his seat. Keith marched him up the path away from the picnicking audience and to the street. "There's no need to make a scene, Skyler."

Feeling embarrassed he looked away. "I know. I'm sorry. He just...came out of nowhere with this kind of...slithering attitude. Who is he anyway? Is he the one who..."

"Yes. He's the one."

Skyler recalled Keith's telling him about his other boyfriends. Even his family made fun of Keith's predilection for young, blond men. But there was one who had cheated on Keith and Skyler was guessing it was this guy. "What's he even doing in Redlands?"

Eyes still scanning the crowd, FBI senses no doubt kicking in, Keith shook his head. "No idea. What else did he say?"

"Just a lot of snarkiness. 'You know how to pick 'em', that sort of thing. Even asked me if I was a *natural* blond."

"That asshole," he muttered.

Skyler drummed his fingers on his crossed arms. "I hope you weren't with him very long."

"I wasn't. I can't believe I fell for him at all."

"Neither can I. I thought you had better taste than that."

"I thought I did, too. I do now," he said, staring pointedly at Skyler.

"What do you suppose he wants?"

"I don't know." He resumed scanning.

"He knew my name."

Keith halted his search and glued his gaze to Skyler's. "He what?"

"Called me by name. Knew we were together."

"Must have caught all that stuff on the internet."

"Lovely. Is he going to get all stalkery?" Yup. Self-defense class was looking better and better.

"He'd better not," Keith all but growled. "Look, don't worry about it. I'll have my friends at the Bureau check it out, find his local address, if he *has* moved here."

Skyler's arms were still tight across his chest. "I don't know what you saw in that guy."

Keith's slow smile replaced the stoic expression. "You're jealous."

"I am not!"

"You are." Keith moved closer and enclosed Skyler in his arms. "But you don't need to be. I love *you*. There's no one else in my heart."

"But you loved *him* once." He could have kicked himself for the petulant way that came out. He squirmed against Keith's chest.

Keith hugged tighter. "No, I don't think I did. I'd remember *this* feeling."

Skyler looked up. Keith's blue eyes gazed down tenderly at him.

"Oh." He let Keith hold him a moment longer before he gently extricated himself.

Well wasn't *that* nice. *Had* he been jealous? He felt suddenly ridiculous. An old snarky boyfriend? He was pretty sure Keith would have gotten over *that*. And he really looked nothing like Skyler when he thought about it. Sure he was blond, but a fake sort of California surfer blond. Maybe *he* wasn't the natural blond.

Speaking of snarky.

But on thinking of Keith's words he did feel better. "I'd remember *this* feeling." It made Skyler's belly squirm in a good way. Keith loved *him*, dammit, not this other guy. He raised his chin, doing some looking around himself. *What an asshole.* But he wasn't thrilled with the idea that someone might be stalking Keith...and then it just as quickly occurred to him that this Ethan might be stalking *him*.

He took out his phone. "I, uh, have to make a call..." He hit Jamie's number even as Keith slipped back into FBI mode to search the grounds.

"Skyler, are you at the concert?"

"Yes. Are you?"

"Yeah, we just arrived. Left a little later than we planned."

"It's already the second half."

"I know but Dave and I sort of lost track of time...know what I mean?" He giggled.

Rolling his eyes, Skyler switched the phone to his other ear, trying to be as quiet as he could at the edge of the crowd. "Yeah, I know. So where *are* you?"

"We're making our way to your blanket. But where are *you*?"

"Coming right back." He cupped the phone and tried to keep it down so Keith wouldn't hear. "I have stuff to tell you...after the concert." He shut down the phone and slipped it back into his pocket. Keith was still straining to scan the crowd. "Let's get back to our blanket. Jamie and Dave are joining us."

They stepped carefully through the lawn chairs and other picnic blankets and returned to their seats. The woman behind him made an exasperated sound. He couldn't stop himself from turning to her and saying,

"It's the William Tell Overture. I *know* you've heard it before."

"Skyler," warned Keith, and Skyler sat just as a lanky man with bright acid orange hair and another taller muscled man with dusty blond hair, wended their way toward them. They shuffled, making room for their guests, and Keith offered them wine from two more glasses.

Skyler ignored one more shush from Shushing Lady and settled in, trying to enjoy the music. But Jamie sidled closer and in his ear said, "So what's going on with the self-defense class?"

Glancing back toward Shushing Lady, Skyler motioned to him with a finger to his lips. Jamie sighed, sipped his wine, and leaned his orange-haired head against Dave.

A little after ten, the orchestra took their final bows, the lights in the park came up, and the audience began cleaning up their picnic areas.

"So what's this about a class?" asked Jamie. Dave and Keith were folding chairs and packing up their cooler.

He pulled Jamie aside. "You'll never guess who I ran into tonight."

"Who?"

"Keith's. Old. Boyfriend."

"No way."

"Way. And he looks *exactly* like me."

"Wow. Keith's personal Stepford wives."

"No kidding."

"Wait...what's he doing here in Redlands? I thought his former beaus were in Colorado or Washington or someplace like that."

"Exactly! He made a point of coming up to me to say hello. Knew my name and everything. He's up to something."

"Oooo. Shall I call the Scooby Gang?"

"No, no." He pulled Jamie farther away from Keith and Dave. "I'm going to keep an eye out though, that's for sure, but no funny business. Though now I'm really gung-ho for this class."

"Right! So where and when?"

"At the community center at seven. Will you go?"

"Sure. Dave thinks it's a good idea, too. Everything's been rainbow flags lately but there are still homophobes out there."

"Yeah, okay. Good. I feel better going with a friend."

"So do you guys want to catch a drink at the Shakespearean?"

"I still have my duties here. But if everyone is going, I'll catch up."

Jamie turned to their respective boyfriends. "Hey, guys. Want to hit the Shakespearean?"

Keith rolled up the blanket in a lump which Skyler tugged out of his hand and folded neatly instead. "I have an early call on the football field, but I could go for *one*."

Dave nodded. "I'm still off this week. Might as well party while I can."

"My fire-fightin' man," cooed Jamie.

Keith grabbed the chairs while Dave took the cooler. "I'll take this stuff to the car, okay Skyler?"

"Okay. I should be done in around twenty minutes." He watched them go. The park was clearing out in record time. In twenty minutes no one would be left. He began picking up trash left behind. "No matter how many trash cans you have, there are people who are just ignorant slobs," he muttered. He dumped the glass bottles and cans into the recycling bins, waving to the other volunteers across the lawn doing the same.

Once or twice out of the corner of his eye, he thought he saw a blond head nearby, but every time he whipped around, they had disappeared into the crowd. "Stepford creep," he murmured.

After twenty minutes, sure enough, the place was deserted. He waved his good-byes to the rest of the staff and was making ready to leave when he noticed a lone figure still sitting in the benches.

Coming closer, he realized it was Mr. Huxley. The man had obviously fallen asleep. Skyler approached and knelt beside him. Gently he shook his shoulder. "Mr. Huxley? The concert is over. Time to go. Mr. Huxley?"

But when the man slid over and fell to the bench, Skyler could see the froth at his lips, his bulging eyes, and the fact that he was *not* sleeping at all.

Chapter Three

THE AIR WAS WARM BUT SKYLER SHIVERED. Flashing red and white lights strafed the dark lawns and mute cypresses. The EMTs had worked on Mr. Huxley but not for very long. He was plainly dead. Skyler shivered again.

Keith had wrapped him in their blanket with an arm tightly around him. Skyler was grateful for it. Dave was talking to the EMTs while Jamie stood by, fidgeting and plainly not knowing what to do.

"I'm so sorry, Skyler," he said for the umpteenth time. "You've known him forever, haven't you?"

"Yeah," he said, swallowing past a warm lump in his throat.

"He was an old man," Keith muttered.

"I know. And he missed his wife."

Keith squeezed tighter.

A familiar figure was walking toward him and his heart lightened. "What are you doing here, Sid?"

"I was on duty," she said, tossing her shoulder-length curls out of her face. She wore her detective's badge on a chain around her neck over a cap-sleeved t-shirt and linen slacks. "Wanted to see what was up, just in case you were here. And lo and behold."

"It was Mr. Huxley. He just…died. Right there, in his seat."

"Ah Skyler, I'm sorry."

"Yeah. It's kind of shocking. I mean I'm in shock."

Sidney looked up at Keith. "But you're being taken care of, I see."

Keith smiled grimly. "He'll be all right."

"I know." She reached out and closed her hand over the one Skyler used to clutch the blanket to him. "You should go home."

Skyler glanced toward the EMT's now wheeling the covered body of his longtime friend toward the ambulance. No need to hurry. "Should I...should I...?"

"You should go home, Skyler," she repeated more forcefully. "We'll contact his next of kin."

"I think it's his nephew Jerome. Jerome Williams. He's in Redlands."

"Okay, sweetie. You've done all you can. Keith, take him home."

Keith turned him and they headed for the car. Dave and Jamie followed silently behind. "You know," said Skyler suddenly, "I think I would like to go to the Shakespearean. Have a toast to Mr. Huxley." He looked at his friends and they brightened.

The Shakespearean, a British pub on State Street, wasn't exactly bustling on a Tuesday night, but tables were occupied, someone was playing darts in the back, and the TVs were showing a soccer tournament playing somewhere in the world.

They mutely slid into a high-backed wooden booth and stared at the table. A waiter came by and took their drink orders and returned with them in little time. Skyler raised his pint glass and the others followed suit. "Here's to Lester Huxley. A fine human being and a wonderful boss." They drank.

Dave curled his hands around his glass. "How long have you known him, Sky?"

Skyler sat back, toying with the beer mat under his glass. "Gosh. A long time. He gave me my first job. When I was thirteen I asked him if he needed anyone to do odd jobs around the museum. I thought it would be cool to work there. And he hired me on the spot. I worked every summer after, and when I got to high school I even worked there after school during the year. He was a good mentor, like a father to me. He and his wife Claudine would invite me over for dinner all the time." He grabbed his glass and took a sip. "She died last year, and Lester was never the same. But in those early days…" Skyler smiled, remembering. "He used to tell me stories about all the things in the museum, how they were acquired, the people behind them. He was big on African American studies. He had a degree in history, used to teach at James Polk, but he retired before I got there. He could tell you anything you wanted to know about history and make it come alive. He was just one of those people."

"Sounds like a great guy," said Keith.

"Yeah. I'll really miss him. It's funny how you think the people in your life will always be there, don't you?"

Jamie scooted his glass back and forth on the table between his hands. "But that's life, Skyler. Change is inevitable. Change brings good things, too."

He shrugged. "I guess."

"I mean, look at all of us. Look how we all came together to be friends…from what we once were. And look at me and Dave. I never would have met him if it wasn't for you. And look at you and Keith. If you hadn't changed and let him come into your life, how sorry and sad *that* would have been, right?"

Frowning, Skyler drank. His life wasn't exactly "sorry and sad." Different, but not sad. He hadn't been lonely. He'd made it a fine art of hooking up and he wasn't sorry for that part of his life either. He wouldn't have the Skyler Fuck Club, or as Jamie called it, the SFC, if he hadn't hooked up with that much frequency. These were now his bosom friends...like Jamie, Dave, Philip, and Rodolfo. He supposed being with Keith changed him in ways he was yet to discover.

He took a sidelong glance at Keith and his handsome features. Yup, he was pretty glad to have him in his life. Not that Skyler ever lacked for love, but the kind of love he felt for Keith and Keith for him was...different. Special. Deep.

He licked his lips. "I guess I can't feel sad for Mr. Huxley, then. He really missed his wife. I hope he's in a happier place. With her."

Jamie lifted his glass with a bright smile. "Then let's drink to that." They clinked glasses, drank their beers, and settled down to subdued conversation.

After an hour, Keith looked at his watch. "I hate to break this up, but I have to get up early."

"And when he says 'early'," said Skyler, "he means five."

"Yikes," said Jamie. "That's far too early in the morning to deal with kids."

"Have to. Any later and it's too hot for the students out there on the field."

"Better you than me."

"We should go, too, Jamie," said Dave, already sliding out of the booth.

"Okay. It's been a little bit of a downer anyway tonight. Oh not that reminiscing on your boss was a bad thing, Sky. I'll see you tomorrow night at that class, then?"

"Oh yeah. Almost forgot. Tomorrow night. Be on time."

"I'm always on time. It's Dave that makes me late."

"Hey, don't blame that on me. You're the one who wanted to try that thing—"

"And just *look* at the time!" said Jamie, shoving Dave toward the door.

Skyler chuckled. He knew hanging with Jamie would make him feel better.

When they got home, arriving in their own cars, Skyler dragged himself upstairs and flopped back on the bed. His fat tabby cat Fishbreath came to investigate and nose-bopped him. He stroked the cat's soft fur with both hands while Keith readied for bed in the bathroom.

"What a day!" Skyler sighed. "I still can't really believe it."

"I know, hon."

"Oh God! I'm going to have to contact the board of directors. They're going to need a new museum director. Oh this sucks so much!"

"You told me he was going to retire anyway, right?" Keith leaned in from the bathroom doorway, a towel in his hands. "They would have had to replace him soon enough."

"I know. Shoot." He sat up. The cat yowled in protest. "He wanted to tell me something, too. Looked kind of serious. Now I'll never know what it was."

"It's just as well, sweetheart. One less thing to worry about."

"What do you mean?"

"You get so invested in these things. You wear your heart on your sleeve, you know that. Time to step back a little."

"That's all going to be over in two weeks anyway. When school starts my summer job is over."

"I know. But you need to let the board of directors handle it. It's up to them now."

"I wasn't going to do anything."

Keith crouched down to look at him. "You have that gleam in your eye. Let it go, Skyler."

"I don't have a gleam," he muttered as Keith retreated to the bathroom to turn off the light.

"Yes, you do!"

"No I don't!"

Skyler rolled out of bed to begin his own bedtime routine. *Besides*, he thought soberly, *it wasn't as if it was a murder.*

Chapter Four

IN THE MORNING KEITH HAD ALREADY LEFT hours earlier and as Skyler readied for another tedious day of meetings and endless lectures, he grabbed his phone and called the president of the museum board, Denise Suzuki.

"Hello, Skyler. What can I do for you?" asked the female voice on the line.

Skyler maneuvered his Bug into traffic and talked into his Bluetooth. "Hi, Denise. I hate to ruin your morning, but last night...well, last night Lester Huxley passed away."

"Oh no! Oh God. What...what...?"

"I think he just gave out. He was watching the Redlands Bowl concert and died right there."

"Oh my God, that's terrible. Does Jerome know?"

"They were supposed to contact him last night. I'm still going in today at one, but I don't know who else will be there. I think Ron and Randi are on the schedule with me. I don't know about Jerome."

"Listen, I'll talk to the other board members and as many of us who can will be there today. I think you might have to close for the day."

"I don't think Lester would have wanted that."

"Hmm. You may be right. You knew him best. Well, we'll do what we can, but we all really need to talk. Perhaps a meeting after hours?"

"That sounds better, though I will have to leave a little before seven. I have a class I need to attend."

"You're always so busy, Skyler. I wish... I wish you could take over for Lester."

"That's just not possible, but I appreciate your confidence."

"Let's plan on a five o'clock meeting then. Can you let the other docents know?"

"Sure thing."

Boy, this was set to be a pretty tough day. Not that he had any illusions it wouldn't be. He hit the first contact.

Once he got to school and parked his car, he headed toward the auditorium where the other teachers had gathered in the rows of theater seats. He found an empty place between the art teacher Ben Fontana and Kate Traeger, the girls' volleyball coach. Down in front he spotted Keith and the other coaches but he didn't want to bother them. They seemed pretty deep in conversation.

"Glad I could catch you, Skyler," said Ben on his left. He was leafing through the pink Xeroxed pages of the new school schedule. "Looks like you're going to have a sixth period class."

"Yeah, I've been meaning to talk to you about that. I've been assigned Junior Comp for that time period. What are we going to do about the GSA meetings?"

The Gay-Straight Alliance had been meeting in Ben's classroom during sixth period on Fridays and now that Skyler had gotten up the courage to attend last year he didn't want to miss them.

"That's what I wanted to talk to *you* about. Just like last year, I won't have a sixth period."

"Oh. Soooo…"

"Yeah. I was thinking that maybe you should take over the GSA and have it in your classroom."

"Ah, but Ben, you're the one who was brave enough to sponsor it in the first place. I'd hate to cut you out of it. And the kids really like you."

The man blushed under his beard. "I appreciate that. But they really relate to you and it's important you continue with them. I won't be a stranger. I can drop in from time to time but it just isn't all that convenient now."

"I understand. And really, if there is any way to accommodate you…"

"I'm just glad it's as successful as it has been. The summer field trip was a great hit."

"You are so invited to that next summer. And anything else we devise for this year."

"You got it, buddy."

Kate elbowed him on his right. "Hey, I saw in the news about your boss at the museum. I'm sorry to hear that."

"Thanks. It's gonna be a tough afternoon."

"Tougher than this?" She gestured toward the front where Mr. Sherman the principal was making his way across the stage, a clipboard thick with papers in his hand. The movie screen creaked downward from the stage's flyspace.

Skyler slid down in his seat. "Oh no. A film?"

"Wanna sneak away to The Bean?" she whispered as everyone began to quiet.

He shook his head. "You are a bad influence on me."

Rachel Kerner, assistant librarian and major homophobe, was glaring back at him a few rows ahead. It reminded him of Shushing Lady from last night. But instead of giving her the finger as he wanted to do, he offered up a syrupy smile instead. She turned away and squirmed in her seat. *Probably from that stick up her ass*, he thought with a genuine grin.

Just as he suspected, Mr. Sherman droned on. The film was some dumb production on "Educating for Today's Teens" full of bullet points and slightly outdated advice. He looked at his watch with a sigh of relief. Almost lunch time. God, now he knew how his students felt.

Kate kept making fun of the film in his ear with some fairly raunchy jokes and he had to stifle the giggles more than once. And sure enough, Rachel swiveled back to glare at him.

That's right, beyotch. I'm laughing at you!

But that wasn't very nice. Even though she gave him a hard time he was determined to keep his relationships civil at school. After all, he had survived coaches who had actually tried to kill him. After that, he figured he could get along with one snippy librarian.

Finally they were released for the day. Skyler decided to hurry over to The Bean to grab some lunch before heading to the museum.

He parked in front and made his way under the friendly green awning by the rainbow flag. Cashmere Funk, Philip's Rasta barista, was in fine form. His dreads swung as he practically danced behind the counter. His long arms stretched to retrieve a coffee jug here, a flavor bottle there. But ducking under him just as furiously and with the same amount of aplomb was Philip's newest barista, Jesse. Pale-skinned, short, shaved head with a nose ring, dark purple lipstick, and emo vibe, she was a distinct counterpoint to Cashmere's Jamaican cool.

She came up to Skyler when he made it to the counter. "Hi, Jesse."

No reaction.

"H-how's it going?"

Still no reaction.

Oookaaaay. "I'll have a turkey avocado on sourdough, please. And a medium chai."

No words, but she did turn to go at it efficiently.

Philip came up behind him, pushing his rectangular glasses up the bridge of his nose. "Hi, Skyler."

"Hey." He got in close. "So how's it going with Miss Emo over there?" he said quietly out of the side of his mouth.

"I couldn't be happier. She's extremely efficient and no-nonsense. I wish she could teach Cash some of that."

"But it wouldn't be The Bean without Cashmere and his style."

"Hey Sky-ler!" said Cashmere, waving long-armed. "Weh yuh up to, man?"

"Nothing much. And you?"

"Mi aright!"

Skyler turned to Philip. "See?"

"Still. I think Jesse adds a certain something."

"A zombie something?"

Philip chuckled. "Well...she is quiet, I'll give her that."

"So is she...you know?"

"Is she what?"

"You know. A lesbian?"

"How should I know? It's not like I put that on the job application."

"But you did talk to her, right?"

Philip fussed with his green apron. "*I* talked, yes. *She* did very little. And that's the way I like it."

Skyler shrugged. "It's your place."

Emo Girl slid his plate across the counter. "Turkey avocado and chai." Her voice was husky and, he supposed, a little sexy.

"Thanks, Jesse. See you."

She narrowed her eyes slightly before turning away.

Skyler exchanged a look with Philip and the man threw up his hands. "All right, I get it. Still." He walked with Skyler to a café table and sat in the other seat. "Not everyone has to be a ray of sunshine to do their job. She keeps Cash in line when I'm not here and that is worth gold."

Skyler dug into his sandwich but he suddenly remembered all the things he wanted to tell Philip and it spilled out when he mumbled it with his mouth full, "You'll never guess what happened last night!"

"Good grief." Philip whipped out a napkin from somewhere and wiped the table. "No need to sprinkle the joint."

Embarrassed, Skyler covered his mouth with his hand and swallowed a big lump of food. "God, Philip, last night my boss died at the Redlands Bowl!"

"What? What happened?"

He shook his head and placed the sandwich back on his plate. He toyed with a crinkle cut carrot slice. "Died of natural causes. Heart attack or something. No one noticed. I found him."

"You are a death magnet."

Skyler drew back. "No, I'm not! That's a horrible thing to say."

"Well, you have to admit, you do find dead bodies."

Thinking about it critically he frowned. Just because he found a few didn't mean he was some sort of albatross.

"Be that as it may," he said indignantly, "at least it *was* me. A friendly face. I mean, I don't know that I believe in an afterlife but I'd like to think he'd rather have someone he knew find him than a stranger. I guess. Some comfort in that at least." He slurped his chai but then set it down hard. It sloshed and Philip rolled his eyes as he mopped that up, too. "But that wasn't all. I was also confronted by one of Keith's old boyfriends."

"Last night? Wow. Busy for a Tuesday."

"No kidding. And he threatens me, subtly. And Philip, he totally looked like me."

"Really? So that is a thing with Keith?"

"Yeah. Makes me feel...I don't know. Like I'm interchangeable."

Philip laughed. "Honey, there is no one like you, believe me."

"Still, though. It does sort of cheapen Keith's affection."

"No it doesn't. Where are you getting this? Keith loves you."

"But he easily could have loved *Ethan*. And whatever lookalike it was he loved before *him*."

"But he doesn't. Oh you are so paranoid."

"You didn't meet him. He was real oily. Like some comic book villain. I don't see what Keith ever saw in the guy."

"What did Keith say?"

"He said he didn't know what he saw in him either. Ethan was the one who cheated on him."

"Well there you are. You're not jealous, are you?"

"No! That's stupid. Why would I be jealous of *him*?"

"Then you're jealous of the *memory* of him. That Keith wasn't yours and yours alone. Now I guess you know how Keith feels about your...um, past."

Skyler sank back in his seat. *Was* he jealous? "Oh God, Philip. That *is* what I'm doing. I'm jealous of his past. That's ridiculous." He looked up, horrified. "Oh poor Keith. That is a hideous feeling. Oh man. I feel like I owe Keith a ton of apologies."

"You don't. You aren't ashamed of your past. I mean, look at us. We never would have met if you hadn't been such a slut. I mean player." He smirked when Skyler gave him a withering look.

"I know. It's just…this jealous feeling. And Keith must have it multiplied by… hundreds."

"Thousands."

"*Hundreds.*"

Philip shrugged. "Whatever. What did the guy want?"

"That was the mysterious part. He has no business even being in Redlands so what gives with that? He made a point of coming up to me. He could be a stalker."

"But how long ago was he with Keith? That's a rather delayed reaction."

"I don't know. I didn't ask. But I'm taking a self-defense class tonight with Jamie. Want to come?"

Philip frowned. "Are you that scared of this guy?"

"No, it was something Keith signed me up for before all this happened."

"Oh. Well, no thanks. Not interested."

Skyler picked up his sandwich again and took a bite. "Seriously, Philip. You should consider it."

With a disgusted look, he wiped at the table again. "I'm fine, thanks. I really don't worry about it. No one's ever bothered me."

"But you never know."

"What makes you think I *can't* defend myself?"

He looked Philip over. He wasn't slight, like Skyler. He was taller. Most men were. And fit. Philip exuded a confidence that seemed…well, masculine. But he also didn't seem particularly straight, and being perceived as gay made one a target.

"Suit yourself." He looked at his watch again. "Boy, I do *not* look forward to today. I told the other docents about Mr. Huxley but the board wants to meet with us after work. This is going to be one craptastic afternoon."

"I am sorry, Skyler. He was a sort of mentor to you, you said."

"Yeah. And he helped me with some of my college tuition. I paid him back but it was seriously nice of him to do it. He knew my mom couldn't afford it and all I had was my job at the museum."

"He didn't have any children?"

"No. His closest relative is his nephew, I think."

"Well, try to have a good day. And I want to hear all about your self-defense class. Take pictures of Jamie if you can."

He smiled. At least there was that to look forward to.

He arrived at the museum just as the other docents arrived. He unlocked the door, switched on the lights and air conditioning, and stared at the chair where Lester usually sat.

"Boy, it's weird being here without him," said Randi. She was a perky twenty-two-year old in her last year at the University of Redlands. Her dark, shoulder-length hair seemed to sit lankly today, like a mood barometer. "I can't remember a day when he called in sick."

"Me neither," said Seth, another docent. His long hair was swept up in a man bun. He had tattoos up his arms and he wore a Mala bracelet on his hairy wrist. "I don't think he ever did."

Ron, the third docent, toyed with the business cards on display on the front counter. Mr. Huxley's business cards. Ron was blond, wearing his usual polo shirt and tan slacks. "Man, what do we tell people?"

Skyler sighed. "Well, if they ask, we can tell them the truth. That he passed away yesterday. But we are going to honor his memory by keeping this place ship-shape, right?"

"Right!" they chorused.

"Now." Skyler reached behind the counter and grabbed the clipboard. It had a list of things to check. "The TV monitor in the east wing is on the fritz again. Who wants to take a look at it?"

"I'm on it," said Ron, "but I think it's time to call Bill the Tech Guy."

"He was here last week working on the other one," said Skyler.

"I know, but he never got around to this one."

Skyler jotted it down on his clipboard. "I'll call him later this afternoon. That leaves the rest of us to give everything else the once over." They all spread out. It was the custom upon entering the facility to make sure all was in order. No broken windows, no stray birds, nothing fallen over during the night.

Skyler went, too. He couldn't bear the idea of going into Lester's office anyway. But he did wonder where Jerome was. Shouldn't he have been here first thing this afternoon?

Skyler perused the books behind their glass case and saw right away that one was missing. It was a rare edition of a book of army flags from the Civil War from 1887. He flipped the pages over on the clipboard, looking for it on the list of borrowed books. Sometimes they lent them out to vetted students and reputable historians, but there was no listing of that book having been checked out. A small knot of panic burned in Skyler's chest, but he decided to check all the shelves just in case it was miss-shelved. But no such luck.

"Hey guys." He cleared his throat and held up the clipboard. "We're missing the 1887 *Designating Flags of the United States Army*. Does anyone know where it is?"

Everyone stared at him with blank looks.

"It's a pretty big book. Hard to miss."

"You know it's funny," said Seth. "But it seems a lot of things have gone missing recently. I mentioned them to Lester."

"Like what?" said Skyler, thinking of the stove pipe hat.

"Some military medals. The gloves that belonged to Mary Todd Lincoln."

Randi cocked her head. "*Those* are gone?" She turned to where the gloves had been displayed and put her hands on her hips. "That's not right."

"And the stove pipe," said Skyler. "Hmmm. Have you noticed…those are items that are irreplaceable?"

"And worth a lot," Ron piped up. "Hey, I know we're all thinking it. They'd get the most money if someone stole them."

Skyler raised his hands. "Whoa, whoa, Ron. No one's accusing anyone of that."

Seth scratched his bearded chin. "Does anyone know…if Lester was hard up for money?"

"Seth!"

"Skyler, it's a possibility. I pointed out something missing last week and he nearly bit my head off."

Skyler recalled his reaction to the missing hat. It was something of an under-reaction he had thought. "Well...that's just not... Mr. Huxley took good care of everything here..."

"No one's saying he didn't," said Randi, "but doesn't it strike you as peculiar? And now that rare edition. I know that's worth at least $600. The gloves and the hat are worth far more."

"Okay." Skyler wiped his face with his hand. "Here's what we're going to do. Today, let's make our own lists of things we think are missing without a reason or excuse. We'll take a look at it and start doing some investigating."

They all nodded. One at a time, they went to the front desk and got a notepad and a pen and spread out to the various rooms.

The front door opened and everyone paused, looking in that direction.

"What's everyone looking at?" asked Jerome, holding the door before he closed it, keeping the August heat outside.

"Nothing," said Skyler, giving everyone a meaningful look. No need to bother Jerome with this unpleasantness.

But Jerome waved his hands at everyone. "Why don't you all gather here for a minute?"

Silently, everyone ventured forward, standing around Jerome in the domed rotunda.

"Listen, I'm sure you all know what happened last night. Skyler, I understand it was you who found my uncle. And I just want to say...thanks for being there. It's...been a difficult twenty-four hours for the family. My Uncle Lester was an institution here, no question about it. And...I hope to continue the good work he accomplished in the Lincoln Shrine. Um...the funeral is this Saturday at Hillside Memorial Park. If any of you can come, the family would appreciate it."

Skyler stepped forward and clutched his arm. "Of course, Jerome. I'll be there."

"I knew I could count on you, Skyler." His eyes were shiny as he glanced across the others. "Well, I understand the board is going to meet with us after hours. I hope you all can stay."

Everyone nodded. Jerome gave them a small smile and retreated into the office. That took Skyler aback but he supposed that was going to be the natural order of things. Jerome was the likeliest to be in charge. The others didn't seem to notice and went back to their note-taking.

After several hours, one by one, the docents brought their lists to Skyler. It was worse than he thought. How had they missed these things? He decided to double check everything before he brought his findings to Jerome.

His head was so buried in files and ledgers that he failed to notice when five o'clock rolled around. But when the first of the board members arrived, he stuffed the books and notes away behind the desk. Randi and Seth brought chairs out and everyone took their seats. Denise Suzuki was there, her black shoulder-length bob streaked with gray. She always dressed smartly in fitted suit and skirt ensembles. Her bangle bracelet of charms—three, one for each of her children—always seemed to be there on her wrist clattering next to her watch.

There was also Dean Short, a portly middle-aged man in an outdated loose-fitting suit in gray; Jeanette Stone, one of the younger board members in a silky cap-sleeved top and linen pants; and the bearded John

Rawlinson in a more stylish shiny blue suit. There was a Marine Corp tie-tack right in the middle of the skinny tie.

Skyler took his seat along with everyone else and waited until they were settled.

Denise, the president of the board, spoke first. "It's such a shock. We were devastated on hearing the news of Lester Huxley's death. He touched so many with his staunch dedication to the Lincoln Shrine. I think it's fair to say he *was* the shrine, and brought it the care and attention of a dedicated scholar and archivist. He will be sorely missed."

Everyone murmured in agreement.

"Jerome, I want you to know that we all realize we are the recipients of your uncle's legacy. Redlands is all the richer for his years of dedication and devotion to this institution. It's going to be very hard to replace him."

Jerome sat up at that. His brows furrowed.

"To that end, I would like to ask Mr. Foxe in these last two weeks before the school year starts, to take over the duties of running and maintaining the museum before we transition a replacement."

Skyler's head shot up. "Wait! What about…what about Jerome?"

The board exchanged glances with one another. Clearly they had discussed this previously. "We are under advisement at this time to choose a permanent successor. Jerome Williams is certainly in the running, but we feel that we must open the field to more prospective candidates."

Jerome's chair skidded back as he launched to his feet. "In the running?"

"Mr. Williams, this isn't the time to talk about it…"

"Then when is the time? Look, I've been working hand in hand with my uncle here for years. He's been grooming me. We had every expectation that when he retired, I'd..."

"Mr. Williams, I really think we should discuss this at a later date. In private."

"Well I want to talk about it now!"

Denise glanced at her colleagues. "Jerome, I realize you may have anticipated a different outcome, but I assure you, Lester made no such recommendation."

"That's ridiculous!" He cast about toward the other docents. "Everyone knows this."

"Truth be told, Jerome, Lester...well. Lester told me the opposite."

"What? That's bullshit!"

"Now Jerome!"

"What is everyone trying to pull here?"

Skyler stood. "Jerome, calm down. Let's everyone take a breath. And once the funeral is over you can talk in private to the board and..."

He yanked his arm from Skyler's grasp. "You've always been trying to take this job, usurp my place."

"Jerome! That's absurd. You know it."

"I'm not listening to any more of this white-ass bullshit." He stormed toward the door, cast open the lock, and threw the doors open.

Everyone froze until the doors snicked closed again. Denise and the other board members stood. "Well, that went well," she muttered.

"Ms. Suzuki," said Skyler. "I can't..."

The others were all talking and she moved closer, looking back to make sure the others weren't listening. "Skyler, Lester Huxley was explicit that he didn't want his nephew to take over and he levied some damaging charges concerning it. As a valuable and trusted employee, Mr. Foxe, you are the best replacement."

"But I have school…"

"Not for another two weeks."

"But that doesn't mean I don't have work. I have a lot of prep to do…"

"And an office here in which to do it. Please, Mr. Foxe. The museum needs you. And I daresay, Lester Huxley was counting on you."

The weight of the world suddenly descended. But the museum was a beloved haven. It was a place to escape to when his parents were divorcing; a research bonanza when it came to writing history term papers; a place where a veteran teacher and an aspiring one had befriended one another.

Damn. He nodded. "Okay, Denise. But honestly, this is really—pardon my French—fucked up."

"You don't know the half of it."

He glanced at his watch. He had just enough time to head over to the community center. "I have to go. But…well, email what I need to do. I hope it will be okay to bring my laptop. I really do have a lot of prep before school starts."

"I understand. And thanks for stepping forward."

"More like I was pushed."

She smiled, squeezed his hand, and turned to leave. He breathed and looked helplessly toward his fellow docents.

"I guess, 'congratulations' is in order?" said Ron.

"No, you guys. I feel terrible for Jerome."

Randi crossed her arms over her chest as the last of the board left. "But Skyler, if Lester didn't want Jerome, there has to be a very good reason."

"Yeah," said Seth. "And I think we all know what that reason is."

It took Skyler a moment to realize what they were saying. "No! No way."

Seth scratched his head. His man bun wobbled. "I don't think it's too far-fetched. He always was a little overbearing to everyone."

"No he wasn't."

"God, Skyler," said Randi, grabbing a chair and folding it up. "He was! Even to you but you're so nice you just never noticed."

"But he wasn't," he said more feebly.

"He was," she insisted. "He totally expected to inherit the job."

Skyler looked to the others and they all nodded in agreement. A soap opera had been going on around him and he never even knew it? He'd have to turn in his gay card. Shaking his head he carried one of the folding chairs back behind the counter. "I can't believe it."

"It's true," said Ron. "But I'm glad you'll be in charge."

"Temporarily. Very temporarily."

"Are you going to tell the board about the missing items?" asked Ron.

"Eventually. But I want to do more research first. Before anyone accuses anyone."

There was more than one eyeroll.

"This is serious. We are talking about thousands of dollars here. An accusation like this could ruin a life. So let's all agree to keep this under our hats, okay. Agreed?"

Reluctant nods all around. Skyler sighed. "I hate to demand and run but I have a class to attend tonight. I'll see you guys tomorrow."

He fled amid a chorus of "Bye, Skylers" and hurried to his car.

Chapter Five

SKYLER STEERED INTO A PARKING SPACE IN FRONT of the community center just as Jamie pulled up in his red Wrangler. "Right on time, Skyboy!" he yelled from his car.

Skyler waited for Jamie on the steps of the old 1930s mission-style building. They marched in together and assembled in the main hall. Looking around, Skyler's heart sank. He and Jamie were the only men there.

But Jamie didn't seem to notice. He was busy chatting up two women in exercise clothes. Skyler was prompted by a woman sitting at a table by the doorway to sign in. He had to pay a fee and then called Jamie over to sign up.

"It's nice to see some men in here," she said.

"Really?" said Jamie, finally looking around. "Looks like we're in the minority."

"It's okay," she said cheerfully. "Everyone *should* come to this. You just never know."

"That's what I was saying to Skyler, here. You just don't know, do you?"

Jamie's strident voice could be heard across the hall. Sure enough, some of the women with gaydar headed over. *Looks like they found their new gay best friend*, he mused. Sidney would be laughing her head off.

"All right everyone!" A beefy man with a shaved head called out to the crowd and everyone quieted. Next to him was a Hispanic man in a thick-padded costume. The bald guy swept everyone with his glance, lingered on Skyler and Jamie with a raised brow. "I'm Steve

Larson, and this is Federico Rojas, your instructors. Thank you all for coming tonight and participating in our six week course. In it, you will learn some of the rudimentary techniques to get yourself out of trouble should the need arise. This is self-*defense*, not *offense*. We aren't going out and looking for trouble from this class."

Everyone laughed nervously.

"As you can see," he said, gesturing, "we have mats set up to do our training."

As instructed, they all made their way toward the mats and took off their shoes. Skyler counted eight others besides him and Jamie. There were the obvious soccer moms, some heftier women, and even some middle-aged women.

"There will be homework assigned tonight. After our session, I'd like you to watch my YouTube instruction videos to get an idea of the sort of thing we'll be working on. You'll get all that after class. I'm sure you're ready to begin, so let's start with getting out of an attacker's grasp. I'll show you some techniques you can use to get away from your attacker. And it is about getting away. You may have to do some damage to him to achieve that, but that's okay. It's important to understand that these are designed for you to escape. Now I'm going to need a volunteer. You there?"

Skyler looked behind him and realized with a sinking heart that Larson was looking at him. Reluctantly, he shuffled forward.

"Go get 'em, Skyler," said Jamie with an encouraging smile.

"Hi there," said Larson.

"Hi."

"And your name is…?"

"Skyler."

"Thanks for coming up, Skyler. Now first, I'll show you the technique in slow motion, and then you'll try to get away from me, okay?"

"Sure."

Larson got in front of Skyler and showed him the proper movements when an attacker grabbed from behind. He repeated them slowly, in slow motion as he said, and then sped it up having Skyler and the others mirror what he was doing.

"Let's show you on Federico." In real time, Federico grabbed Steve from behind, Steve hooked one leg around Federico's. He grabbed his hands, pulled up his thumb, and twisted, jamming his elbow into Federico's protected face in one smooth motion.

"All right then. Are we ready to try it? Are you ready, Skyler?"

"I guess so."

He positioned himself behind Skyler.

"Now in a real situation," he said to the crowd, "it isn't likely you will be expecting a grab from behind but that's precisely what an attacker wants to do; get you off guard. But we're starting slow tonight so we're going to take it easy. In slow motion, Skyler, I'm grabbing you now."

He grabbed Skyler around the waist and Skyler hooked one leg as instructed. He fumbled for the man's hands but managed to grab a digit and pull on it.

"Now elbow me."

Slow motion, Skyler did.

"Good. Now did you see, he couldn't get my thumb but any finger will do. It really hurts to be grabbed like that so it's more than likely your attacker will let you go. Now, once more, Skyler."

Skyler jogged in place, breathing out. His adrenalin was up and when Steve grabbed him, he hooked his leg, grabbed the thumb, and elbowed hard...right in the man's nose. Blood suddenly gushed down his face. A woman screamed.

Skyler whirled, hands to his mouth. "Oh my God! I'm so sorry!"

Federico was there with a towel and Steve blinked a few times, smiling under his towel. "That's all right. It's totally to be expected. Of course, that's why Federico is in padding. Take the next ones, homey."

The padded man took the women one by one.

Skyler cringed and knelt by Steve. "I am sooo sorry."

He laughed. "It's okay, Skyler. Maybe I was a little rough on *you* last time we met. I bet you don't remember me." He said the last softly.

Skyler took a minute before recognition flooded in. "Steve! Oh man. I didn't recognize you without the..." He motioned at his head.

"Yeah, when I started losing my hair I decided to shave it. I haven't been to Trixx in a long, long time. How is it going for you?"

"Well...I've got a boyfriend now."

"Oh really? Well, well. Skyler Foxe got himself a boyfriend at last. Must be someone special to catch *your* eye."

"He is. He's the one who signed me up for this class."

"That's very thoughtful of him. Is that him?" He thumbed toward Jamie.

"Jamie? Oh no! Keith's at home."

"You live together? Wow."

"Yeah...well. Times do change. He is something special."

"That's too bad. I would love to have gotten together with you after class."

"I'm definitely off the market."

"That's too bad. Wanna help me up?"

"I'm sorry I got a little out of hand there."

"You did just what you were supposed to do. Can't fault you there. I should have let Federico handle it but I have to admit...I enjoyed touching you again."

He waggled a finger at him. "Now, now."

He smiled. "All in good fun." He took the towel away and dabbed his nose. "Looks like the blood has stopped."

"I'm so sorry."

"Never mind it, Skyler. Maybe you should help your friend over there. He doesn't seem to have gotten the hang of it."

When Skyler turned, he saw Jamie with his two feet hooked around both Federico's legs and he was grasping both his arms. They were turning and spinning until Jamie fell back on Federico as he slammed down on the mat.

"Round one!" yelled Jamie to the laughter of the class.

"Keith!" Skyler called, slamming the door behind him. "Hey, Keith!"

Keith poked his head out from the bedroom. "What's all the yelling about?"

"Have I got a lot to tell *you*!"

"Well, let me get a drink first." He shuffled into the kitchen and pulled down a bottle of bourbon from a cupboard. He was dressed in sweat shorts and a tight t-shirt. He must have just showered since his black hair sparkled from water droplets.

"Are you cooking? Something smells good."

"I picked up bar-be-que on the way home. It's warming in the oven."

"Oh. So listen." Keith handed Skyler his Grey Goose on the rocks. "Thanks." He slurped a sip. "So, the board came to the museum after hours. Oh wait. Let me back up. Looks like stuff has been missing from the museum for quite some time."

"What do you mean missing?" Keith's highball glass sweated with moisture as he took it to the living room and settled in his recliner.

"I mean," said Skyler, hurrying after him and sitting cross-legged on the sofa, "that things have been disappearing with no good reason. Sometimes historians or students check out books for research or items get sent away for repair. But none of those things had any of those notes attached. They just vanished. Poof!"

"You mean someone's stealing them."

"Yeah." He sat back, took a sip, and sighed. "And I guess the prime suspect is Mr. Huxley."

"Can that be?"

"I don't know. Could be his nephew. I'm more inclined to believe that of him. Oh! And get this. The board wants *me* to take over as temporary director."

"Did you acquaint them with the fact that you are a full time teacher?"

"I did, but they want me until school starts. Just so they have some time to find a replacement."

"I thought Jerome Williams…"

"So did he. And he left in a huge huff when they passed him over. Not just passed him over but told him to his face in no uncertain terms that they didn't think him qualified, that Lester recommended *against* him."

"Ouch. Did they say why?"

"No, but I guess maybe Lester suspected *him* of stealing the exhibits. Maybe that was what he was going to tell me."

"A lot of conjecture."

"But that's how it's done, right? You find your clues, you gather your suspects."

Keith's narrowed eyes gazed at him over the rim of his glass. "Mmm," he said noncommittedly.

"Anyway, I agreed to step in until school starts. I mean, I feel it's the least I can do."

"If you think you can handle the extra work."

"Denise from the board basically gave me permission to do my school prep in the museum office while at work. I guess they're that desperate. It's only through the next week. I wonder who they'll get in that timeframe."

"Maybe they should just close the doors until they can figure out what's happening."

Skyler glared. "Bite your tongue! Lester would have hated that. What about the tourists? What about the students? We can't close up. And the board recognizes that."

"I'm just surprised, is all. I'm sure you'll do fine, Skyler. You know it like the back of your hand, don't you?"

"Yeah, I guess. And the other docents have been there for years. I have no idea if Jerome is coming back or it's a permanent huff."

"Kind of tacky of him."

"He's under a lot of stress right now. And I suppose he was clueless about how his uncle and the board felt about him. Apparently, I was too. The other docents told me what a jerk he's been to them."

Keith said nothing. Just sipped his drink. After a moment he asked, "How was the self-defense class?"

"Oh, that was great! Jamie came—and we were the only men there, thank you very much. Except for the instructors, one of whom I knew."

"Knew. In the biblical sense?"

"Well…it's a small town, you know. Only so many men travel through Trixx."

"Okay."

"Keith. You promised. My past is my past."

"I know, I know," he muttered, swallowing what looked like a big gulp out of his glass before he rose to set the table. Skyler followed him, slurping from his own drink.

"So what about *your* stalker?" Skyler said, quickly changing the subject. "Find out anything about him?" *I'm not the only one with a past, you know.*

"Not yet." Keith placed the dishes on the table and set each place. "But I will. Don't worry about him, Skyler. I'm taking care of it."

"Famous last words."

Keith scowled.

"It is one of the reasons I'm taking this class, right? So anyway, we learned how to get away from an attacker." He set his drink down. "Come back to the living room. I'll show you."

Keith paused. He was bending into the oven, retrieving the cartons and foil packets of bar-be-que. "What? Now?"

"Yes now. Come on."

He set the items on the table, slipped off the oven mitts, and tromped into the living room. "What, Skyler?"

"Okay. You come at me from behind and grab me."

"Hmm. Sounds like a plan." He suddenly grabbed Skyler and began kissing his neck.

"No, stop that. That's not what I meant. Like you're attacking me."

Keith nipped at the tender flesh just under Skyler's ear. "What makes you think I'm not?"

"Keith! I'm trying to show you something."

"Okay, okay." Reluctantly, he let Skyler go. "Just grab you from behind?"

"Yeah. Like you're going to drag me off." Of course, the very idea of Keith doing that was sort of turning him on. He shook it off.

Keith's arms were quickly around him. Skyler hooked a leg around Keith's hard thigh and grabbed at his hands, trying to pry a finger up, but he couldn't get a grip of any of them. He struggled for a few moments before saying, "Wait, wait. Let's start over."

Sighing, Keith let him go and stood back.

"Okay. Try again."

Keith enclosed Skyler's chest with his beefy arms once more, Skyler hooked his leg, and grabbed for Keith's tightly clenched hands. "I can't...I can't..." Skyler grunted, working hard. "Keith, you're doing this wrong..."

"*I'm* doing this wrong?" And seemingly to prove his point he walked around the room carrying Skyler who still had one leg hooked around Keith's.

"Hey! Wait. Stop!" Disentangling himself he stared at the floor, thinking. "This should have worked. It worked in class."

"Maybe you just need more practice. I'd be happy to grab you all night."

Skyler slowly turned and measured Keith's lop-sided smile and sparkle in his eye. "Oh really?"

"Yeah. Maybe…we should try this without any clothes. Maybe that's the problem."

"Maybe it is."

Dinner got cold on the dining room table for a good long time.

Skyler sighed, lying back against the pillow and licking the sauce from a pork rib. "You know, I think I almost got the hang of that release thing from an attacker."

"Yeah. You very nearly got my thumb the last time."

"I don't know what's wrong. You are clearly some super human X-Man or something."

"Clearly." Keith slurped the last of the baked beans from his spoon and set the Styrofoam cup aside on his bedside table. He licked his lips and drank down the dregs from his bottle of beer. "Maybe it's because I know some countermeasures. Ever think of that?"

"What? You cheated?"

"I only did what I was trained to do."

Skyler sat up. His napkin fell away from his naked lap. "You totally cheated. Why didn't you say something?"

He shrugged but he couldn't hide his smile behind that extra slice of cornbread he snagged from its foil wrapper. Their picnic was spread out over the towel-covered bed. "I just wanted to see how far you'd take it."

"Well it's a good thing I didn't take it that far. I'm supposed to elbow you in the face and knee you in the groin."

"And then we wouldn't have just enjoyed this lovely evening."

"No we wouldn't," he said, but he still felt taken advantage of. He folded his arms over his chest. "I thought *I* was doing it wrong."

Keith chuckled and set the cornbread down. He leaned over and kissed the side of Skyler's head. "I'm sorry, sweetheart. As far as I could tell, you were doing it just fine."

"You are a terrible person, Keith Fletcher."

"I know."

Skyler licked his bar-be-que covered fingers before he slid his arms around Keith's neck. "But I'll forgive you just this once."

Skyler's phone buzzed. He saw it was Sidney. He slumped reluctantly away from Keith and grabbed the phone. "Hey, Sid. What's up?"

"Skyler...God, I really hate calling you out of the blue like this."

"You're not cancelling on dinner tomorrow, are you?"

"Oh shit. Yeah, I guess I'm doing that, too. But that's not what I'm calling you about—"

"Dammit, Sidney, that's the third time in so many weeks."

"I know, Skyler, but work is really busy right now and Mike and I...there's stuff I need to talk to you about..."

"Okay. Then come to dinner."

"I can't. Stop interrupting me, this is hard enough."

Skyler didn't like the sound of that. He slid to the edge of the bed and leaned over and spoke quietly. "You and Mike aren't breaking up, are you?"

"What? No! What makes you think that?"

"I don't know. The way you're being all mysterious and—" Skyler gasped. "Is someone hurt? Is it my mom? My dad? Jamie? Philip?"

"Stop, just stop. It is *nothing* like that. Shut up, already. Let me talk. You listen."

"Okay." But now his heart was pounding a million miles an hour. Sometimes he really hated that she was a cop.

"Just as a precaution, the county did a tox screen on Lester Huxley."

"Lester?" He sat upright at the non sequitur. "What do you mean tox screen?"

Keith stirred and moved to sit next to Skyler. He had a concerned look on his face.

"A tox screen," said Sidney from the phone, "because of the circumstances of his death—outside in public like that—they performed an autopsy and there was nothing wrong with his heart. No stroke. No communicable diseases. They were looking for cause of death. And the tox screen…well, found it."

"And?"

She sighed. "So I really hate to tell you this, but it looks like he's been poisoned. It's now a murder investigation."

Chapter Six

"POISON? AS IN SOMEONE *POISONED* HIM?"

"I'm afraid so, Skyler."

He couldn't speak. His throat constricted, aching.

"Skyler," said Keith beside him. "Is that Sidney? Let me talk to her." He didn't wait for Skyler to reply. He simply plucked the phone from his hand and put it to his ear. "Sidney, it's Keith. What have you got?" He nodded. "Yeah. Okay. Hmm. Yeah. Yeah."

Skyler watched Keith listening intently but it was only then that the implication of it all sank in. Someone had *murdered* Lester Huxley! Murdered this man who was a mentor, a father, a friend. The lump in his throat ached deeper, and hot angry tears shimmered in his eyes. How *dare* they? How dare this unknown person take his friend's life? He gritted his teeth. Who could have done it? And why? And in so callous a way.

He was breathing hard by the time he tuned back into Keith and heard him say, "Okay then. Do you want to talk to Skyler again?" Keith handed the phone back to him and Skyler white-knuckled it, pressed it to his ear.

"What have you got, Sidney?" he said sternly.

"Not much. Someone slipped poison into his coffee as far as we can tell."

"Are there any leads?"

"Not as yet. Skyler. Now listen to me. I know this man was important to you but I do not—repeat—do *not* want you meddling. Do you understand me?"

"Gotta go, Sidney. Bye."

He clicked the phone off and sat at the edge of the bed. He felt suddenly cold and realized he was still naked. Phone in hand he rose and grabbed his sweats.

"Skyler?"

"Uh huh?" he said absently, disappearing into the bathroom.

"Skyler." Keith was standing in the doorway, naked, looking down at him with furrowed brows. "What did Sidney say?"

"You talked to her. You should know."

"No, about..." Keith put a hand to his face and smoothed his palm down his stubbled upper lip to stubbled chin. Taking a breath he raised his eyes to Skyler's. "I'm thinking that the last thing she probably said was to tell you not to investigate."

"Uh huh," he said, running the hot water into the sink and dipping a washcloth in.

"I see." Keith turned so that he rested his back against the door jamb, shoulder blades framing the molding. After a long interval where Skyler was able to clean himself up, Keith heaved a sigh. "Okay then. Do you have a key to the museum?"

Skyler turned, warm washcloth dangling from his hand. "Yeah..."

"Then get dressed."

He left the doorway and Skyler trailed after him. "Wh-what...? What are you...?"

"Get dressed. Wear something dark. I'm going with you."

He blinked until the soaking washcloth dribbled cooling water down his leg, snapping him out of it. "Going with me...where?"

Keith had pulled underwear and socks from the dresser drawer and sat on the bed to sort them out. "To the museum. To investigate. I assume you plan on doing so, correct? I'm going with you."

"Going with me...to investigate? Going *with* me? You're...you're not going to scold me and tell me to stay out of it?"

"Nope. This person was important to you. I get it. Hurry up."

"Keith...?" He watched the man dress for a moment more before he couldn't help it. He launched on top of him, knocking Keith backward to the bed. Skyler straddled him and kissed his cheeks, forehead, and finally his mouth where he spent the longest. "Keith." Propping his hands and looking down at the man beneath him he shook his head. "I can't believe...I don't understand...but I love you *so* much, you know that?"

Keith smiled. "Yeah. I do. And I know there is nothing I can say that will deter you and so...as I promised a while ago," he said with a grimace, "I will, um...help you."

"What about Sidney?"

"We report our findings."

"Oh my God, Keith! You don't know what this means to me!" Skyler kissed him again.

Keith sighed and looked up at him with lazy lids. "If you don't get moving and get dressed we will be delayed...for quite a while."

Skyler felt that bulge beneath him growing and he quickly jumped off. Investigate now, sex later.

He ran to the closet and excitedly cast each hanger aside. He couldn't believe it. Keith was going with him. Investigating *with* him. He and Keith, sleuthing! Sherlock Homo and his own sexy Dr. Watson.

He scrambled to find a dark shirt, shoved his head in and pulled it through the neck. He yanked down a pair of black skinny jeans from its hanger and danced inside the closet, pulling each leg through.

Keith was dressed and poking his head through the closet door. "Dressed yet?"

"Almost. Keith, this is so exciting. You honestly don't know what this means to me."

"I think I do. But we don't do anything dangerous or illegal."

"Isn't breaking into the museum kind of illegal?"

"You have a key, don't you? That's not breaking in."

"But I don't have a good reason to be there. It's after hours."

"Weren't you telling me how worried you were with all those missing items? You're just double checking something."

He zipped up and put his hands on his hips. "You know, Special Agent Fletcher, there's just a smidgeon of larceny in you, isn't there?"

It looked to Skyler as if Keith were trying not to smile. "No comment. Are you ready to go?"

Skin tingling from excitement as they left the house, Skyler followed Keith out. They got into Keith's black F-150, and once the engine roared to life, they maneuvered onto Olive Street and drove several blocks into the night, past tall swaying Washingtonia palms, past more rambling Victorian houses in various states of renovation and repair, through pools of street light.

They turned the corner at the back of the museum and Skyler jumped out. The air was still warm and he could easily have stayed in shorts, but then his white legs would have shone like a beacon. "Let's go in through the back door," he whispered. Glancing around, he didn't see anyone on the street and slipped quickly into the shadows behind the building. Keith was right behind him when he clenched the key in his hand. There was a security keypad next to the door and Skyler entered the five digit code before turning the key in the lock. It clicked softly open. He held the door for Keith before closing and locking again.

"We're in!"

"It's not like you picked the lock," Keith said softly.

"I know but it kind of feels like it. Covert and all."

"You really do enjoy this, don't you?" he said, looking around.

Skyler paused. Yes, he supposed he did. But then he felt terrible. The only reason they were here at all was because someone killed Lester Huxley. He said nothing as he moved toward the desk and switched on the desk lamp, an old style library lamp with a green glass shade, the same kind Skyler had at home at his roll top desk.

Keith didn't move. He merely surveyed the office. "What's that door lead to?" He pointed to the only other door.

"It's to the museum."

"Is it armed?"

"No. Only the exterior doors and windows. And I turned that off with the keypad."

"Is there a record of the keypad entries?"

"What do you mean?"

"Well..." Keith leaned back and sat on the edge of Lester's desk and crossed his arms. "Sometimes security locks not only keep a record of when they were entered but by whom."

"No, we don't have anything that sophisticated here. It's just a straight-up alarm system. Open the doors or windows without using the code and an alarm goes off."

"Hmmm." Keith reached into his jeans pocket and pulled out two pairs of purple latex gloves. He shook them out and handed a pair to Skyler and then slipped them on his own hands.

Skyler stared at them. "Just out of curiosity, do you always carry these around?"

He smirked. "You never know."

"Kinky."

"Quiet, you. Put 'em on."

"Why? I work here."

"Just...put 'em on."

"Yes, sir, Special Agent."

Sighing, Keith turned to him. "I know you're enjoying yourself but it is serious business. I could lose my badge for this."

Skyler sobered. "I know. And I really appreciate your, um, helping me. It really means a lot."

Keith nodded and rose. "So who has a key?"

"Well...me, Lester, Jerome, the board. Everyone, really."

"All the docents?"

"Yeah. It just made more sense."

"What about cleaning crew?"

"You're looking at him. And the other docents."

"And the code for the keypad? Everyone has that, too, I suppose?"

"I see where you're going with this. Anyone could have gotten in and stolen that stuff. Dammit. This is so not right."

"And poisoned Lester Huxley."

"Oh my God. And everyone knows he uses a Thermos. Even though we have a perfectly decent coffeemaker, he never uses it. He always brings his coffee from home. So that must mean he was poisoned by someone who works here."

"Not necessarily," said Keith. "It could still be someone out in public. And it wouldn't rouse suspicion out in full view because he knew a lot of people. They could have stopped by quickly, slipped it to him, and left just as quickly. No one would be the wiser. But, uh, you're forgetting a third possibility."

"What's that?"

Keith approached the door and carefully grabbed the doorknob. Turning it slowly he pulled the door open noiselessly and peered into the darkened museum. It was stuffy with the air turned off. And hot.

"Well, Skyler..." Keith began. "It was in his coffee Thermos. There is the distinct possibility...that he did it himself."

"No! No way. He'd never have done that. He was very religious."

"Okay. I was just putting it out there."

He walked into the museum and Skyler followed. Keith got out his phone and switched on the flashlight app, shining it around the display cases, careful to keep the beam away from the windows.

"So the sorts of things that were missing. Very expensive?"

"Oh yeah. Christie's Auction House expensive. Irreplaceable. Someone could get a lot of money for them in the right auction."

"What about provenance? Wouldn't it be known they were stolen from a museum?"

"Not necessarily. I mean, if we hadn't noticed, if someone had written them on the sheet, we wouldn't scour the auctions looking for them. As it is, I guess the first order of business for me is to inform the board of our findings and start getting the word out." Skyler stopped. "Oh for crying out loud!"

"What, Skyler?"

He gestured toward a glass case. "Something else is missing. Goddammit!" He pressed himself against the glass. Mary Lincoln's opera glasses and Tad's spats. Both missing. "Jesus Christ, this happened *today*! These were here this afternoon. What are we gonna do?"

"Well the first thing *I'd* do is install some cameras and keep them hidden. I can help you out with that."

"This really sucks." He turned to Keith. "I guess that leaves Lester off the hook. Oh! Do you think the same person stealing these things killed Lester?"

"I don't know. It's an awfully big coincidence if they didn't."

"It has to be an inside job. But how can it be any of these people I work with? I just can't fathom it. They loved Lester. It's not like he caught them at stealing and they hit him over the head. They planned it. They had to go to the trouble of getting the poison and deliberately put it in his Thermos." He clutched his hair. "I can't wrap my head around something so diabolical. God, Keith. It's just...just...*evil*."

"I know, sweetheart. We're doing something about it."

He looked up at Keith. "Yeah, *we* are. Thank you again."

Keith smiled grimly. "The things you've noticed missing. Can you see who was on the schedule the day before?"

Skyler's heart swelled. Yes! They were doing something, and Keith was offering brilliant ideas. His solid calm presence was giving Skyler confidence. "Let's go look." He retreated to the office and grabbed his notepad of missing items and pulled the clipboard with the schedule off the wall. He sat in Lester's old seat without even thinking about it and laid them side by side. Running a finger down the list of items he compared the docents and dates when the missing exhibits.

Skyler sat back in a slump. "Damn. It's all random. There isn't any one person on all the days when we noticed an exhibit missing the next day. Except for me...and I didn't do it."

"Hmm."

"What are you thinking?"

"I don't know."

"Do you think Sidney will question all the docents...or should we?"

"Well, *I* can't. But *you* could."

"I guess I've got to tell her about the missing exhibits. That's motive, isn't it?"

"Could be."

"Shoot. I thought we could do this."

"We might be able to help in ways Sidney can't, and still keep it more or less legal. I'll help you to make sure you don't taint evidence. I think for now, you can subtly ask the docents about, well, motive. Did they need the money for something? Was there recently a life-changing incident in their lives? That sort of thing. Subtle, Skyler."

"I can be subtle."

"Since when?"

"I *can*. I've just never needed to be subtle with you."

"You can't let a suspect know you're on to them. Just make it everyday conversation."

"Okay. Good note."

"I'll see what I can do on the FBI end of things. I'll have them be on the lookout for the items in auctions. They have a better database for that sort of thing. Get a list to me as soon as you —"

Something slammed against the front door, startling the both of them. Skyler thought something heavy had been thrown against it until he heard, "Police! Open up! Throw down your weapons!"

Chapter Seven

KEITH INSTRUCTED SKYLER TO STRIP OFF THEIR gloves and toss them into the bin.

"Keith!" he whispered desperately, pulling off his gloves with shaky hands. The gloves were suddenly like glue and wouldn't come off. "What do we do?"

"We stay calm, and we put our hands up. No sudden moves. I'll go first."

He pulled out his badge and held it high along with his other hand. Skyler, heart in his throat, held up his hands too.

Keith yelled at the front door. "I'm FBI and I'm going to open the door and do exactly as you say, okay?"

"Open the door," said the cop on the other side.

Keith grabbed the knob and turned one last time to Skyler. "We're gonna be okay," he said quietly. "Follow my lead and don't say anything until I do."

Mutely, Skyler nodded.

Keith pushed open the door slowly. "I'm holding up my badge," he said loudly.

Once the door was open Skyler could see the flashing lights of the squad car. There were two cops, illuminated by the outdoor lights of the museum. Both officers were pointing their guns and flashlights at Keith.

Skyler kept admonishing himself for putting Keith in this situation. What if something happened to him? It would all be Skyler's fault. He was an idiot. He really didn't know what he was doing. Why did he keep doing these things?

Keith blocked the doorway. Skyler realized he was shielding him in case it went south.

One of the officers gestured with his free hand while still training his gun on Keith. "Let's have the badge."

Keith handed over the folded leather with his ID and kept both hands up. He was calm, at least he looked calm on the outside. But Skyler could tell that his breathing had sped up and his jaw muscles had tensed.

The one officer looked at his badge, looked at Keith, then studied the badge again.

"We're friends with homicide detective Sidney Feldman if that helps," said Keith.

The cop's head snapped up. "Detective Feldman?" He read Keith's badge again. "Keith Fletcher. I think I've heard her mention you. Who's with you?"

"S-Skyler Foxe." said Skyler, uncertainly. He nudged Keith aside. Skyler kept his hands up. "I'm Detective Feldman's friend. Skyler Foxe?"

Finally, both officers lowered their weapons. The first one handed back Keith's badge. "What are you two doing here? We got a call that someone was sneaking into the museum."

Damn! Skyler never counted on nosy neighbors.

Keith stuffed his badge away and lowered his arms. "You might have heard that the director of this museum died the other day. It was determined it was a homicide. There have also been some items missing from the museum and the Bureau thought it might be connected."

A little white lie, but Skyler saw the reason in is keeping his mouth shut while Keith wove his tale.

"Skyler here works at the museum. In fact, he's acting director until they can hire a new one. He let me in."

A flashlight was shined in Skyler's face.

"Oh yeah," said the officer. "I recognize you. You guys could have warned us."

"We didn't think it was necessary. We're all done for now. Can we go?"

The guns were holstered and the other officer was radioing in the all clear on his shoulder set.

"I don't see why not. Bureau's investigating the thefts?"

"We're looking into an Interpol connection. These are one-of-a-kind objects. Americana. The Bureau doesn't look too kindly on them leaving the country."

"Hell no. Abraham Lincoln." He stuck his head in and gave a quick look. "I've never been here myself but I suppose I should give it a visit."

"It's free," said Skyler shakily, getting his breath back. "Open from one to five every day."

He smiled and tipped his hand in a salute to Skyler. "I'll do that. Here." He reached into his pocket for a business card and handed it to Skyler. It read Officer Frank Carey and a phone number. "Call me first next time. You gentlemen have a good night."

"You, too, officer," said Keith in his most officious manner. They watched the cops retreat to their squad car. Keith waved, friendly but professional, until the officers got in their car and drove off.

He dropped the façade.

"You told a lot of lies there," said Skyler, relieved.

"Some whoppers. We'd better get out of here. Can we leave by the front?"

"Might as well." Skyler let Keith by him as he pulled the doors closed. He input the number on the keypad.

Keith got in close and examined it. "Can you reset the code?"

"I guess so. I have the instructions in there somewhere."

"Maybe you should do that. But don't give it to anyone else just yet."

"And how do I explain that?"

"Tell them it's protocol. Do you think they'll question you?"

"I don't know. Jerome won't like it. If he ever comes back."

"Then do it now, Skyler. Go back in and get the instructions."

Skyler grumbled as he keyed in the code again. He passed through the darkened museum to the office, switched on the light since it didn't matter anymore, and rummaged through the files until he found the instructions and pulled them out.

He walked slowly back to the front door with his nose in the papers when Keith snatched it out of his hands.

"Hey!"

"Sorry, it's just that I have a lot of experience with these things." Keith zipped through it and nodded his head. "Pretty standard. Here's what you do." He explained it to Skyler and when Skyler picked another code, he entered it and checked that it worked. He then called the alarm company and verified the new code.

"No one gets the new code, Skyler. Got it?"

"Yeah, I got it. I just think everyone is going to be pissed off at me."

"Only the thief will be."

"Oh! Good thinking!"

"Let's get out of here before the nosy neighbors call the cops again."

They got into the truck and headed back home.

❖

Skyler brooded in the living room in the dark.

"Skyler! Come to bed," said Keith from the other room."

"In a minute."

"Skyler, you aren't going to solve this crime having spent two minutes at the museum."

"I know! I just…what did we learn from that little trip anyway?"

There was a rustling from the other room and then Keith appeared in the doorway, hair pleasantly ruffled, bare-chested in wrinkled boxers. He scrubbed at his hair. "You learned that someone was able to steal something right out from under your noses."

"Yeah. About that. I am positive those opera glasses were there when I left. Almost positive. It wasn't written down as missing, anyway. So someone clearly broke in right after we closed."

"But you also learned that it isn't so easy to get in there after hours because of nosey neighbors."

Skyler sat up. "That's right," he said thoughtfully. "They would have been spotted, too. So how *did* they do it?" He snapped his fingers. "I bet they used the cover of the Redlands Bowl! With all these people coming and going across lawns and parking lots, who would notice if someone got into the museum? Oh man. I wonder if these things were stolen on Tuesdays and Fridays. I bet they were. I'll ask at the museum tomorrow. What a scam!"

"I think maybe you're right. That would be the easiest method."

"Will you buy the cameras tomorrow while I'm at the museum? And then we can install them after hours.

Tomorrow's Thursday. We can certainly test my theory on Saturday."

"Great. *Now* can we go to bed?"

Skyler glanced at Keith sidelong. "Why? Is there something in particular you wanted from me?" He batted his lashes.

Keith's features softened. "As a matter of fact, there just might be. How did that attacking thing go again? I'm supposed to grab you from behind..." He lunged for Skyler, and laughing, Skyler ran for the bedroom.

❖

After a morning of workshops Skyler got to the museum half an hour early. That way he figured he wouldn't have to explain about the code yet. In fact, if he put himself on the schedule for the rest of his run he wouldn't have to explain it until school started.

He set up his laptop in the office and set his folders next to it. He had already turned in his lesson plans, but he had some coordination to do. And lots of curriculum tweaking.

But before he did all that, he grabbed the clipboards of the missing exhibits. Randi and Rob had even noted when they noticed them turn up missing, and when Skyler compared the dates to the days of the week...sure enough. They happened Wednesday and Saturday, the days *after* the Redlands Bowl had its concerts. So he must have been mistaken about the opera glasses. "Now we're getting somewhere."

"You certainly are."

Skyler jerked back in his seat, pressing a hand to his racing heart. "Jeez, Jerome. You scared me."

"Yeah, you're getting somewhere. Getting comfortable in my uncle's chair?"

"Look, Jerome." He stood, edging away from the offending desk. "I didn't know any of that was going to happen..."

"Sure you didn't. 'Course not. That's why you flexing there and I'm looking for another job."

"Jerome, you shouldn't..."

"Look, I get it. I know how it is. This is Redlands. Lily-white Redlands."

"Oh, now that's out of line. You know perfectly well..."

"I don't know shit, Skyler. How many board members are black, huh?"

Skyler paused. Jerome had a point as far as that went. And it made him think about the school and how many African American teachers there were. Not many.

"I...I can't speak for the board but everyone here..." Everyone here apparently didn't like Jerome. But that didn't make them racists. He let his sentence drop away. "Look, Jerome. Don't do anything drastic, okay? In a week, I'll be back in school and then things will go back to some kind of normal, I guess."

"For you. But I'm assed out of my job, and on top of that, I'm been told my uncle was murdered."

"I know. I'm sorry."

"You *know*?"

"Um...I was told. Because I found Lester..."

"I see." He stared at the floor.

The silence went on uncomfortably. Skyler reached for the schedule for something to do. "You aren't on the schedule for the day. Did you want to hang around anyway?"

He snorted a humorless laugh. "Why the hell would I do that? Later, Foxe."

He pushed Skyler aside making his way out of the office. Skyler was beginning to see what the others complained about.

Seth walked through the office door. "Just saw Jerome leave. Is he still in a huff?"

"Seems like it. Hey by the way, Seth. When you noticed the stuff missing, what day was that?"

"What do you mean? What day of the week?"

"Yeah. If you can recall."

He scratched his head, bobbing his man bun. "Seems to me it was a Wednesday. Yup. Is that significant?"

"Might be, thanks." *Aha!* Skyler watched the man set his go-cup on the front counter in the rotunda and settle in. Keith had suggested he question the docents. Now was as good a time as any. "So, uh, how's it going, Seth? It seems we don't get to talk much."

He turned a placid expression on Skyler. Seth seemed like a mellow guy. He, too, worked at the museum only in the summer.

"I can't recall what you said you did for a living, Seth."

"Oh, this and that. Whatever will pay the rent. Mostly I work at the medical marijuana clinic."

"Oh. But you're here one to five every other day."

"They have some pretty flexible hours. And I like working here. It's quiet."

"So that works out for you. Moneywise."

"I get by. I don't need much. I got my bike, I got a cool roommate. It's sweet."

"That's...awesome." Skyler smiled.

"How about you, Skyler? You've been into some pretty weird shit."

"Weird...?"

"Murders, dude. That's some scary shit."

"Well… It's not like I mean to get into it. It just sort of happens."

Seth shook his head. "Not me, bruh. Not me. I stay as far away from dead dudes as possible. Oh!" His face crumpled. "Oh shit. I didn't mean about Lester. I mean, I was glad you were there, you know."

"I know. I kind of feel the same way."

Seth grabbed his go-cup and sipped at it, looking away. Skyler took the hint and wandered back into the office.

Seth seemed okay. This was the second summer he'd worked with him and he was as mellow as they came. But he'd seen enough TV to know that it was always the guy you least suspected. It's not as if he would broadcast that he was short of cash. Who really knew what was going on in the secret lives of people he only knew scantly?

He squinted back at Seth over his shoulder, but the man was looking through the paperwork, as he always did.

Skyler shook his head. This being suspicious of his co-workers was not what he had planned. He certainly didn't like the way it made him feel. He slumped back into the office, thinking hard about what he wanted to accomplish and if it was all worth it.

❖

With the museum up and open and the occasional tourist wandering in, Skyler worked a little while on his schoolwork, poking his head out of the office occasionally when he felt guilty that he wasn't doing his fair share out in the rotunda. He finally emerged from the office late in the afternoon just as his favorite former sophomore students entered. First came red-headed Amber Watson. Amber was his star pupil who was also on Student Council. And by the cheerleading outfit she was sporting, it looked as if she was branching out with her school spirit held high.

Her Goth best friend Heather Munson trudged in right after her. Except Heather was looking decidedly *un*-Gothy since she was also in a cheerleading outfit.

Rick Flores came ambling in the rear, one earbud in his ear, the other dangling across his chest.

"Hi guys," he said to them. He couldn't avoid staring at Heather and her unusual garb.

"Hi, Mr. Foxe," said Amber cheerfully.

"What are you guys doing here?"

"We're waiting for Alex," she said, bouncing on her tennis shoe heels.

"And where is he?"

"At the police station," said Rick. Before Skyler could react, Rick continued. "He's taking classes at the Teen Police Academy, remember?"

Skyler breathed again. "Oh that's right! How's that going for him?"

Rick tucked his hands into the back pockets of his low-slung shorts. "He's in his element, that's for sure. Who knew my boyfriend was cop material?"

"It seems really good for him," offered Amber. "He's really serious about it. I think we'll see a whole new Alex when school starts."

"I think that's great." His gaze slid toward Heather again. She seemed fidgety and quiet. "Uh, Heather, I couldn't help but notice that you're, uh…" He gestured toward her. "Dressed as a cheerleader?"

She rolled her eyes, eyes that used to be raccooned in heavy black kohl but were now limned with a delicate hand of eye-liner. "I'm not *dressed* as a cheerleader. I *am* a cheerleader."

"Okaaay. So congratulations...right?"

"I guess." She slumped, toeing the floor with her shoe.

Amber smiled. "She's doing it for Drew."

"I am not!"

"But...he is your boyfriend, isn't he?" asked Skyler. The two seemed to really connect at the GSA summer trip to the beach.

"Yes, but...gah!" She shrugged as if shaking off the weight of the world. "You don't need to make a big deal out of it. Amber talked me into it. I never thought they'd actually put me on the team."

"Oh...um, so..."

"Don't listen to her, Mr. Foxe," said Amber in a stage whisper. "She's really loving it. And so is Drew. He was so busy watching her at cheerleading practice today that a football he was supposed to catch hit him in the head."

Heather turned away but Skyler caught the glimmer of a smile on her face. Ah, the mating rituals of the teen animal.

"Well, feel free to look around. If you have any questions, let me know."

"It's so great that you do this, Mr. Foxe," gushed Amber. She still seemed to have a bit of a crush on him. "Maybe *I* could—"

Oh God, just what he needed. He rushed in with, "You have to be eighteen, Amber. Maybe in a few years." A little white lie.

Reluctantly, she turned away, but Rick startled them all when he cried out, "Whoa!" He yanked out his ear bud and then he pulled the ear jack from the phone.

Suddenly, there was Keith's voice coming out of the speakers. What was he doing on the radio?

"They're interviewing Coach Fletcher," said Rick. He turned up the volume.

Keith was in mid-sentence. "...best choice for the team and we're pretty proud of her."

The female interviewer then asked, "But won't there be all sorts of problems with a girl as part of the football team? I'm not just talking about locker rooms either."

"Yes," Keith admitted. "But I'm sure the same was said when talking about integrating football, too. We have to make these changes if we are to progress. I'm not saying that just any girl can make the team. They have to have certain qualities. Of course, the same can be said of our male team members. It's a skill set not everyone has."

"What about head injuries? There has been so much lately in the news about concussions causing brain damage. Last year Missouri high schools simply cancelled their football programs. Should *any* child be playing the game? Should James Polk High get rid of their football program?"

"I've done some soul-searching on that very matter of late. I'm in talks now with our league coaches. It comes down to either cancelling the program altogether—which kids are reluctant to do—or a fundamental change in the game itself. I'm for changing how the game is played so we can continue to allow our kids to play. But let me make it clear. It's a tough game. But it shouldn't be life-threatening or severely handicap you later in life. It's supposed to be fun, to promote sportsmanship and teamwork. If I didn't think Elei Sapani was up to it, believe me, I wouldn't have put her on the team. She'll be a wonderful asset. And as far as I'm concerned there will be *no* harassment. I'm gonna see to that."

"There you have it. Thank you, Coach Fletcher. The newest up and coming football star, Elei Sapani at James Polk High. This is Sandra Contreras, KAEH, Beaumont."

Keith on the radio. Weird.

"Hey, Coach did aight," said Rick, popping the earbud back in his ear.

"Yeah. He sounded great."

"I am worried she's going to get hurt though," said Amber. "It won't look good for the school if she is."

"Coach says she won't be harassed on his watch," said Heather, "but I just know she's going to get shi — um, crap from the team. Well, if not them, then from the opposing team."

But Amber suddenly brightened. "You know what we should do? We should come up with some cheers just for her!"

Heather wilted. "Oh, I don't know, Amber…"

"I bet the squad will love the idea. We should go work on something —"

Heather hesitated. "I thought you wanted to check out the museum."

"Yeah," said Rick. "And it's nice and cool in here." He grabbed the front of his buff tank top and flapped it. Skyler didn't think Rick would be interested in the Civil War but the teen often surprised him. "Besides, I gotta wait around for my homey. But you don't have to stay."

"No," said Amber primly. "We agreed we would. And yes, I do want to look around."

Skyler gave them a little wave. "We close at five, guys, in about twenty minutes. I have to get back to work."

"Thanks, Mr. Foxe," said Amber. "That was awesome about Mr. Fletcher on the radio, wasn't it?"

"Yeah. Awesome."

Keith sounded good. So professional. Like those sports guys on TV. He was proud of his man. But he worried, too, about any possible repercussions should she get hurt...or hazed. Although if he knew Keith — and he did — he'd make sure the team was too scared of *him* to do anything to *her*.

Skyler spent some time in the office on his laptop, checking some auction sites and their catalogues before he thought to check eBay. But even as he clicked along, he was pretty sure anyone who stole from the museum wouldn't be stupid enough to...

"Oh my God!" And there it was. On eBay of all places. One of the missing exhibits. Mary Todd's gloves. "Who is this son-of-a-bitch?" But as he suspected, there was a company name, not an individual. Could he report it to eBay? But he didn't want to scare the suspect off. Call Sidney? She'd be proud of him for once. He got on the phone but of course it went to voice mail.

"Sid, you're never around, you know that? You always say you want to talk to me about something but then when I call you... Never mind. Look, remember about the stolen stuff at the museum I left a message for you about? Well I found a piece on eBay. What should I do? It's a fake company name, no person. Should I contact eBay or...? You know what? I did my job and reported it to you, so I'm going to contact eBay. Bye. Try to find time to call me."

He clicked her off. She was really beginning to annoy him. Cancelling on him and Keith for dinner, she never answered her phone. And she kept saying she needed to talk to him. "So talk!" he admonished to the ether.

He found the contact email and fired off a sternly worded message, putting the contact info for the museum at the bottom, including the museum's phone number. But then he deleted that and put his personal phone number instead. No need to tip off the staff that he'd found it.

The last twenty minutes breezed by. He got up to drag in the open sign. Rick and Heather were already outside, but Amber was talking intently to Seth about a display. Heather rolled her eyes and stuck her head back in the door. "Am-ber! These people would like to close up."

"Oh! Sorry." She thanked Seth and he followed her out, unchaining his bike from the outside bike rack. He waved to Skyler as he stood outside, just as Alex came trotting up. He offered a big smile to Rick, a smaller one to the girls, and then widened his eyes at Skyler.

"Mr. Foxe. What are you doing here?"

"I work here." He gestured toward the museum.

"You work here? You aren't giving up being a teacher are you?"

"No, Alex. I have to have a summer job when I'm off work. They don't pay me through the summer, you know."

"They don't? That sucks."

"Yeah. So I hear you're doing well at the Teen Police Academy."

He couldn't seem to stop the smile from spreading across his face. "Yeah. The officer in charge, Officer Hitchens, said that I was really far ahead of the others. She said she'd write a recommendation for me to the real police academy."

"Wow, Alex. That's wonderful."

"I know. I'm pretty stoked."

"Hey guys, while I've got you here." They gathered around him. "I'm going to be having a sixth period this year. You probably know that since most of you have signed up for it; English Comp? So that means two things for the GSA. Number one, it's going to have to be *after* sixth period on Fridays—so let me know if that might interfere with any of your afterschool activities, like football or cheerleading. And because of the change in time, it will be in my classroom instead of Mr. Fontana's."

"That might interfere with football," said Alex.

"Well, I have an alternative. We could meet on Fridays in my class during lunch period. How does that sound?"

"I think that might work out better for most people," said Amber. "Especially the drama kids."

"That's what I thought. Well then, spread the word, would you? We'll need flyers."

"I'm on it!" said Amber with a salute. They turned and walked together down the path, the girls leaning in toward Alex as he talked about his day at the teen academy, while Rick looked on, beaming.

He was so darned proud of his kids!

All the docents had gone and Skyler slapped off the lights as he retreated into the office. He turned off his laptop and stuffed it into his satchel. As he rose and turned to leave, two people stood in the doorway.

Jerome stepped into the light of the office and for the first time, Skyler was a little leery of him. "Hey Jerome. What's up?"

"I wanted to get some of my things. Who knows when I'll be back here?"

"Jerome," he began wearily.

"Just being realistic, Skyler." He moved in and grabbed a leather case from the top of the file cabinet.

The step in the doorway reminded Skyler that Jerome hadn't come alone, but the other figure still stood in the shadows. Jerome noticed Skyler looking as he grabbed his mug from the coffee area. "That's my boyfriend. I don't think you ever knew I was bi. Not that you bothered to find out."

No, he hadn't known. He could kick himself for not knowing.

"Why didn't you ever tell me?"

He shrugged. "Didn't seem important. Ethan Cooper, meet Skyler Foxe."

"We've met," said that voice that Skyler couldn't seem to get out of his mind.

He turned. The man stepped out of the shadows. The blond head, the snarky curve of his lips. He smiled at Skyler, waited for Jerome to pass him in the doorway, and then aimed a finger at Skyler like a gun, pretending to shoot.

Chapter Eight

SKYLER SCRAMBLED FOR HIS PHONE BUT HE couldn't get a hold of Keith. Throwing his satchel into the car he slammed himself against the car seat. Voicemail. "Goddammit! Why is every one of my calls going to voicemail these days? So guess what, Keith? Your stalkery ex is boyfriends with Jerome Williams. Did any of your crack FBI friends discover *that*? Or did you just not tell me. Call me!"

He tried Sidney again and miraculously got her.

"Sidney! Jesus, you are hard to get a hold of."

"I'm sorry. I have something called a *job*."

"So do I. *Two* of them. Look. Do you have any time now? I know you've wanted to talk to me. Wanna meet at the Shakespearean for a pint? I really need someone to talk to right now."

"That sounds like a great idea. Meet you there in twenty."

She clicked off and Skyler buckled his seat belt and started the car.

He was there in six minutes, parked, and found a table inside by the window. Service was slow, and he hadn't even put in his drink order when Sidney swept through. She was wearing a silk short-sleeved T with skinny jeans, looking great as usual. She sat in the chair opposite and immediately motioned to the waiter, whistling for him.

"I wish you wouldn't do that," said Skyler shrinking slightly in his seat.

"We'd never get served if I didn't."

The waiter came over with a world-weary expression and asked for their orders. Skyler ordered a Boddington's while Sidney went for a Shock Top.

"So. What's going on with eBay and these thefts?"

"No," said Skyler, trying to calm himself. He itched to talk. Had sooo much to tell her but she'd also been trying to talk to him for ages. "You go first. I feel bad that we haven't talked...and that you've cancelled dinner *three* times."

"I'm sorry. I said I was sorry."

"I know. It's just that the guilt works so well on you."

"What are you, my mother's emissary?"

The beers arrived and as Skyler sipped, Sidney sat back in her chair and sighed. "It's just...stuff between Mike and me. I think the schedule is getting to him. We see a lot of shit all day. I mean a *lot* of shit. And then he comes home and there's no relief from it. I mean...I'm there, too. I know it has to remind him of it. It's like we're on the job all the time."

"Oh. You don't think he's...he's..."

"No, he doesn't want to break up. I out-and-out asked him."

"That must have been a fun conversation."

"Oh, it was. But it was good to get it out in the open. The job is hella stressful...*and* he's also getting pressure from his family."

"About what?"

She took a long swig from the bottle and then set it down. "It seems that some are not so hot about him having a white girlfriend, and being a Jewish girl and all. Plus his family is staunch Catholics, remember?"

"Uh oh." He leaned in and touched her hand. "Is he caving?"

"No. And he won't. At least I don't think so. But it's hard, you know?"

"Yeah. Maybe you guys need some time away from it all. You should take a weekend and go out of town."

"You think so?"

"Of course. You just need some you and him time. Reconnect. Time to remember why you got together in the first place. You still love him, don't you?"

"Like my heart-ripped-out love him."

Slowly he grinned. "That sounds like a lot."

She slapped his hand, took up her beer, and took another swallow. "Like you and Keith."

Skyler smiled dreamily, thinking of Keith. He knew he did that a lot when thinking of his boyfriend—Sidney called him on it more than once, even took a picture of him and taunted him with it, making embarrassing memes—but then his dreamy expression soon faded. "I have to tell you something."

She signaled to the waiter to bring another round. Skyler had barely touched his but Sidney had nearly downed her own beer. "What?"

"Remember when I told you about Keith's creepy ex at the Bowl?"

"Yeah. Has the FBI gotten any farther in tracking him down?"

"They don't have to. Apparently, Jerome is bi—something I never knew. Some gaydar *I* have. But get this. He walks in tonight with his boyfriend, one *Ethan* Cooper."

"Not the same guy?"

"Oh yes. Very much the same guy, with the same creepy leer. First off, is he boyfriends with Jerome just to get to me? What's his endgame?"

"Skyler, that's gotta be a coincidence."

"I don't think so."

"We're not doing some wacky conspiracy theory thing. He moves to Redlands, never even knowing Keith is here, he runs into Jerome, they hit it off, and then he hears about Jerome's co-worker Skyler Foxe and the Big Scandal at the school with the football coach who is his boyfriend. Keith Fletcher. Ever hear of him?" She grabbed her pint and took another long slug. Lowering the glass, she belched.

"Excuse you," he said absently. "That's quite a scenario you just wove."

"And it's probably close to the truth. Now that he's here, he's just going to mess with you. Because he's an asshole."

"That's what Keith said."

"I wouldn't worry about it. But if it will make you feel better, I'll track him down."

"Would you? That would be great."

"So what is Jerome's problem? Do you think he's stealing priceless artifacts?"

"He might be. I don't know. I don't want to accuse anyone without some proof. But I did find out that most of them were noticed missing the day *after* the Redlands Bowl concerts, on Wednesdays and Saturdays. And he was on the schedule on Redlands Bowl days."

"Using the hubbub of the Bowl as cover?"

"That's what I think. Because the other night when Keith and I broke into the museum…"

"You *what*?"

"Well, we didn't exactly break in, I *do* have a key."

"Keith is now an accomplice? How did you talk him into that?"

"He promised he would help me the next time I went sleuthing. Because he knew he couldn't stop me."

"Oy. You and your tricks. They just follow you around anywhere, no matter what stupid thing you get up to."

"He's not a trick. And anyway, he loves me and doesn't want me to get hurt."

"You love saying that, don't you? So are you now over your commitment issues? When are wedding bells gonna chime?"

Skyler drew back. "No one said anything about wedding bells."

"Aaaand they're back."

"Just…chill, will you? I've come a long way. I think I'm doing just fine."

"For you? I gotta admit."

"*So*," he said loudly and snapping his fingers in her face to get her attention. "You really think this Ethan guy isn't dangerous?"

"Yeah. He's just a dickwad. But I'll check it out. Feel better?"

"Much. How about you?"

She rocked her head. "Yeah. I guess. I'll talk to Mike tonight about a getaway. We haven't had any real time off in a long time. Maybe this weekend. You have no idea what sort of shenanigans our fellow citizens get into."

"Do I want to know?"

"Definitely no." She finished her beer and started on the second one.

❖

When he left Sidney he felt better that she was on the case and it wasn't until he pulled up along the curb in front of his apartment that Keith called him back.

"Skyler, what were you going on about?"

He glanced along the street for Keith's truck but didn't see it. "Where are you? Why aren't you home yet?"

"I was having a meeting with Wesley Sherman about our newest football recruit."

"You mean Elei? What did he have to say? Didn't you consult him first?" Skyler grabbed his satchel and made his way to the steps and began to climb.

"I mentioned it to him but I'm supposed to have autonomy as head coach. Apparently, 'autonomy' is in the eye of the beholder."

Skyler reached the front door and unlocked it. "Uh oh. Are you in trouble?"

"Not in so many words."

Closing the door behind him Skyler locked it and strode across the room to his desk in the bay window, laying his satchel inside the roll top.

"But I am supposed to consult the administration before I do media interviews if at all possible," Keith went on. "I don't recall reading that in the handbook but I suppose it's getting an overhaul."

"Whoops. I heard that today on the radio, by the way. You sounded very professional to me. You represented well."

"I thought I had. Mr. Sherman was less than pleased. I think he's nervous about the reaction to Elei's presence on the team and how the boys will treat her."

"If you put the fear of God in them…"

"Oh I have. Believe me."

Skyler leaned against the desk and stared out the window toward the miniature orange trees in the front yard. "So when are you coming home?"

"In a few. Then we'll talk about our Ethan problem."

"Yes, let's." He didn't like the sarcastic tone coming into his voice, but hell. He had been a little freaked today. "Don't forget the cameras for the museum."

"Oh yeah. Then it will be a little more than a few minutes."

Skyler clicked off, poured himself a Grey Goose, and commenced preparing the ahi he had marinating in the fridge. Some basmati rice with a side of spicy string beans, along with a Thai red curry sauce for the fish fleshed out the meal.

His phone rang and he looked at the screen. He paused, took a breath. "Hi, Mom."

"Hello, sweetie. Do you think you can drop over tomorrow afternoon to pick up that garden statuary?"

"Uh…which one was that again?"

"The little bird feeder. It would be adorable on your balcony."

"I don't have a lot of room out there…"

"I know, but it's so small and delicate. And I have so many. I'm always winning these things from my garden club."

"Then stop buying raffle tickets."

"I have to support our causes. I can't help it if I keep winning."

"How about investing in a lottery ticket instead?"

"I don't like those things. You know that."

He rolled his eyes. "Well, it will have to be around noon. Will you be home? Because then I have to rush off to the Lincoln Shrine."

"I heard about Mr. Huxley. How are you holding up, dear?"

"It was a shock, that's for sure. I don't know whether you heard the latest…but it turns out it was…foul play."

"Oh no! Poor Mr. Huxley." There was a pause. "Skyler, I want you to promise me something. I don't want you to investigate it."

"Mom, I…I'm already sort of…"

"No, Skyler! I forbid it. You got into so much danger last time."

"I'll be fine. Keith's helping me."

There was a gasp and he immediately wanted to take back his words.

She took a deep breath and in her sternest voice said, "Is Keith there?"

"No, he isn't."

"When he gets there you have him call me."

"No, I won't. I won't have you berating him."

"Then I'll just call back later."

"Mom…I appreciate your concern, but I'll be fine. I'm, uh, taking a self-defense class."

"Oh! Finally, something intelligent."

"Hey!"

"Well, if you don't want to use your own common sense that the good Lord gave you, at least be prepared for all eventualities."

"Look, Mom…uh, by the way, how's Dad?" He was a bit miffed that his mother and father seemed to be dating again, and Dale hadn't even bothered to call him lately. Typical.

"He's just fine, Skyler. Didn't he call you?"

"No, he didn't."

"That man. I'll let him know. You two should really get together for a father/son date."

His dad had finally made contact with Skyler again after a thirteen year silence. Though he'd been over for dinner and Skyler had had one drink out with him, Skyler still wasn't entirely comfortable with the whole father/son dynamic. He sighed into the phone. "I guess. I have to attend my sauce, Mom. I'll be by tomorrow."

"All right, dear. Love to Keith. No, I take that back. Tell him I am very displeased with him. Good-bye, sweetheart."

He stuffed the phone in his pocket. Poor Keith was in for it.

❖

He was stirring the sauce in the pan when Keith finally arrived. He dropped his gym bag full of game binders and a plastic bag from Best Buy by the hall tree—something Skyler told him countless times *not* to do—and proceeded to the kitchen cupboard where they kept their bottles of liquor. "This is a *four* fingers of bourbon kind of day," he muttered.

Keith looked a bit beaten down and Skyler felt badly about his earlier voicemail message but every time he thought of Ethan—and those fingers firing imaginary bullets at him—he shivered.

"I'm sorry you had a shitty day."

Keith looked up from his glass, licking his lips from the bourbon. "Sounds like yours wasn't much better."

Before Skyler could speak, Keith leaned in and planted a bourbony peck on the lips. "I'm glad to be home."

Skyler melted a little. "Yeah. Me, too." They both drank quietly for a moment before Keith heaved a sigh and stretched, cracking his back in little pops.

"So tell me, Skyler. What happened? And how is it that you never knew Jerome was bi?"

"Believe me," he said, turning the fire down under the saucepan, "I am trying to figure that out myself. It's not like he couldn't have mentioned it. No one did. I don't think anyone knows. He couldn't have failed to hear about the shitstorm I went through when I was outed…"

Oops. A sore point between them since it was Keith's fault. He glanced at Keith, but the man was deep into his glass.

"So anyway, there he was when I was trying to close up all alone. Jerome, I mean. And he says he's picking up his stuff like he's quitting—and to tell you the truth, it might be the best for everyone—and then Miss Thing walks in and grins at me. Points a finger like this right at me." He mimed the gun.

"He is *such* an asshole," Keith muttered into his glass, shaking his head.

"Yeah, well. It kind of freaked me out. It was very Glenn Close/Fatal Attraction and I didn't appreciate it."

"He's not violent. He's just a jerk."

"How do you know? It's been years. He might have a rap sheet by now."

He snorted into his drink. "I don't think so."

"Well, you misjudged his character before. Maybe he had a hidden side."

"Skyler, I would have known."

"You didn't know he was cheating on you." Shit. He hadn't meant to invoke that, and by Keith's stiffening shoulders it had definitely been the wrong thing to say. "I'm sorry. I shouldn't have said that…"

"But it's true. Maybe I should have known that. We can't know everything about our partners… In so short a time."

He moved into the living room and Skyler clenched his eyes closed. Shit, shit, shit.

"Keith, I'm really sorry. That was truly out of line. I have no excuse except that I'm a little...concerned." He almost said "scared" but he refused the notion. He was *not* scared. Especially not with Sidney on it.

"I saw Sidney today. We finally had our talk. She said she'd look into Ethan."

Keith whipped his head around. "I told you I'd handle it."

"So what's the big deal? Now *she* can look into it, too. Anyway, she was worried about Mike—"

"Skyler, I don't like that you can't trust me on this."

The interruption threw him. "What? I didn't know this was exclusive to you and your investigation. More eyes on it. Doesn't that make sense?"

"It's...an embarrassing part of my past. I'd rather handle it myself."

"Well...okay. I'll just tell Sid not to bother."

"Good. I'd appreciate it."

"Okay." Skyler stirred the sauce and looked over his shoulder at his boyfriend, drinking thoughtfully in the living room. He made his silent apologies to Keith. Because now he *definitely* wanted Sidney to look into it.

They returned to the museum after dinner. Skyler flourished his hands over the keyboard, trying to look to the nosey neighbors that he belonged, that he wasn't hiding anything. Keith chuckled. This time Skyler turned on the lights. Since he was on the call list to the alarm company he hoped he would be the one called if someone alerted the cops again.

Keith had procured nine cameras. He set one high in the office first and then placed them in various spots in the rest of the place, two in the rotunda, and three each in both the east and west wings.

It took several hours and a downloaded app to Skyler's phone but Keith got them working and they were barely noticeable. "That's perfect," said Skyler, watching on his phone as one camera after another scanned the room and fed it back to him.

"I hope that helps," said Keith, scrunching up the bag and stuffing it in his pocket.

"It should stop the thievery. And maybe catch a murderer."

"Well, you never know. They might have been spooked."

"But greed has no bounds."

"You got that from TV, didn't you?"

"Maybe. But it's a well-known fact. I feel better that these cameras are here. Anyway, in another week, it won't be my problem anymore."

They shut off the lights, Skyler locked it up, and they returned home in Keith's truck. He kept checking the app, looking at each camera view, and was happy to see nothing out of the ordinary.

Checking the app again before brushing his teeth, Skyler thought about his mom and dad, about Sidney and her problems with Mike...and about Keith and his ex. Relationships were hard work. When he rinsed and spit, he paused, listening to the sounds of Keith getting into the bed they shared. Switching off the light, he grabbed his phone and left the bathroom, shed his sweats, and got into bed naked. "You know, we're pretty lucky."

"I think that every day," came that rumbling voice in the dark.

"No, I mean we don't have family problems like Mike and Sidney. I hope they stay together. Family can be a bitch on relationships."

"Yes. I'm still smarting from your mother's words."

"She didn't even talk to you yet."

"But I can hear them nonetheless."

He settled down on his back, head sinking into the pillow. "She means well."

"I know."

"I'm kind of worried about her and my dad."

Keith turned over to face him. Skyler's eyes had adjusted to the dark and he could now see some of his features from the light of the moon seeping through the drapes. His eyes were bright and the edge of his chin stubble caught the silver light in a faint glow. "Why? Aren't they getting along now?"

"Too well. I worry that he'll end up hurting her again. And I don't think I could stand for that to happen."

"What can you do, Skyler? She's a grown woman."

"I think it's time for my dad and me to have a heart to heart."

Keith rustled under the sheets. "You could do that. He'd have every right to tell you to mind your own business."

He squinted at Keith's shadowed features. "Whose side are you on?"

"Yours. But he *could* tell you that."

"And I could tell him a few things."

Keith slid over and scooped Skyler in his arms. His kissed the top of his head. "You're a good son to your mom. But just don't get too confrontational. You and your dad are just beginning to know each other again. I'd hate for that tenuous relationship to falter."

"I know. It's just...weird, mostly."

"Yeah." He kissed Skyler's temple. "Let's go to sleep, huh? I've got to get up early again."

"God, when does that end?"

"When it gets a bit cooler. End of September, maybe."

"Can't they practice inside the gym?"

"No. Go to sleep, Skyler. Love you."

"Love you, too."

But Skyler lay awake a long time, worrying about his mother.

In the morning, he dug his face into the pillow as Keith left before sunrise. But it wasn't long until Skyler dragged himself out of bed to the siren call of the coffee that Keith had left brewing for him.

It was Friday. Last Redlands Bowl concert of the season. It was going to be a long day and a long night ahead.

Chapter Nine

WHEN SKYLER GOT TO HIS CLASSROOM HE TURNED on the fan on his desk. It seemed they barely turned on the air conditioner for these prep days. "Cheap bastards," he muttered, blaming the district for putting such restrictions on the budget. Despite that, Skyler readied his room for the coming school year. He returned his framed posters to the walls and added flourishes of borders near the ceiling with quotations from classical authors swashed upon them. Jane Austen, Shakespeare, and even Nathanial Hawthorne leant their wisdom in a fancy script. He had borrowed a ladder from the janitor and was just admiring his handiwork before he folded it and leaned it against the window wall. He'd have to return it to the janitor's closet as soon as he rearranged his bookshelf.

The room was looking bright and colorful. "And ready for kids to learn!" he said. He was overjoyed to get his district paperwork after Mr. Sherman had handed him a pink slip at the end of last term. Even though he had reassured Skyler that it was something that happened to most new teachers, he hadn't felt better until that paperwork had arrived a month ago. Tricia Hornbeck got the pink, too, but was also returning. He was glad of it. He had gotten to know and become friends with the bird-like calculus teacher last year when all the troubles began.

His second year. It was hard to believe. Hard to believe all that had happened in his first year. Murders, Keith, coming out. He vowed that this second year would be free of drama...but who was he kidding? This was *him* he was talking about. And he was already knee-deep investigating another murder. Well, not really. He was trying not to. But every time he thought about poor Lester dying like that at the Bowl, it made him incredibly angry. Who would do such a thing and in so public a setting? Someone who really had it in for him, that's for sure. And he really didn't want it to be Jerome, though wasn't he the most likely candidate? Murder was usually committed by a relative. But Jerome had expected to inherit the job at the museum and he didn't have to murder to get it. Lester was going to retire. So if he *did* murder him, it was for some other reason. And the only other reason he could think of was the thefts. This was turning into a pretty horrible case.

"Hi, Mr. Foxe!"

He whipped his head around. Amber was wearing her cheerleading outfit. Heather stood right behind her, looking self-conscious in her own cheerleading garb. "The classroom looks wonderful," said Amber.

He glanced around with her. "Thanks. I'm rather proud of it."

"Can't wait for school to start!"

"I think you're the only student to ever say that."

"No, I've met at least one other student."

"She means Ravi Chaudhri," said Heather, enjoying just a little too much her friend's sudden squirming. "He's just as nerdy as Amb."

"I think I have him in my class." He came around to the front of the desk and clicked on the computer. "Yup. He's in our Junior Comp class. Looks like he might give you a run for your money, Amber. He's a pretty smart cookie."

"Oh, I don't mind," she said dreamily.

Oh ho! Maybe her crush on Skyler was about to be...crushed.

"Just starting cheerleader practice or just ending it?" he asked.

"Just ended. I've been checking to see what my teachers are doing in their classrooms."

"Oh." He was pretty sure *he* was never that enthusiastic. "Well, do we pass muster?"

"The math teachers don't seem to change much in their rooms, though Ms. Hornbeck has a very colorful wall about calculus."

"She's letting her creative side out. That's good. Well, ladies, I'd love to chat but I was just about to wrap things up..."

"You go ahead, Amber. I wanted to ask Mr. Foxe a question. I'll catch up to you. Are we still going to Sprouts?"

"Yeah. I'll meet you there."

Amber bounded out, her ponytails flopping.

Skyler turned to Heather apprehensively. "So..." she began. "Amber really likes that guy, Ravi Chaudhri. Not that she's said anything to him yet, but I've seen him look at her, too. It's only a matter of time. But I'm afraid what her parents might say."

He sat back against his desk. "They really have a problem with that kind of thing, huh?"

She shook her head. "With *everything*. Homophobic, xenophobic. You name it, just add a 'phobic'."

"Well, the only advice I can give is to be a friend to her, Heather. She's going to need one."

She blew out a breath and glanced aside. "Yeah. I thought as much."

"Heather, I can't really talk to her parents, especially since nothing has happened yet. And I might be the last person they *want* to talk to."

"I know. I just thought I'd let you know. She would just die if this emotional crap affected her grades."

"I'll keep an eye on her. Thanks for letting me know."

"You cool, that's why, Mr. F." She raised her fist for a bump and Skyler complied. "Laters."

He watched her go and heaved a sigh. Such fear and hate out there. Was it so hard just letting your kids be kids?

He tried to imagine kids of his own. Would he be overprotective of them? Would he let them be kids to make their own mistakes, to get emotionally hurt? He supposed there were just some things you couldn't prevent, but being a bigot was certainly one of them. No doubt any kid of *his* wouldn't—whoa! Where had that come from?

He glanced around, as if searching for the mischievous angel that had planted that thought into his mind.

"No kids," he muttered to himself. He had plenty at school, thank you very much. He happened to notice the clock. "And speaking of kids getting hurt…if I don't get to my mom's right now…"

He packed up his things, locked his door, and trotted down the stairs.

❖

His mother's house was only a few blocks away. Ordinarily he'd pull into the driveway of the single car garage, but her car was already there. Cynthia Foxe seemed to be taking another "staycation," though sometimes she went on trips with her girlfriends. She used this time to get her garden in order, to spruce up the house, and to simply putter. The gardener, Mr. Munoz, had parked his truck directly in front of the house, so Skyler maneuvered his Bug in front of that and parked in the shade of an elm. The sounds of lawnmowers and leaf blowers rang in the air. Skyler inhaled the scent of newly cut grass, remembering his long summers of mowing lawns in the neighborhood to earn money before he got his job at the museum. That seemed like a long time ago, but it was really only thirteen years.

It's strange to even think of something as ten years ago, he mused. *I'm getting old. Ripe old age of twenty-six!*

He walked up the flagstone walkway and knocked.

His mother in a fresh, lavender linen top and white linen shorts, opened the door immediately. "Why don't you just use your key?" She leaned in and kissed his cheek. "Go on in, sweetheart. I have to talk to Mr. Munoz for a second. He keeps treating my seedlings like weeds." She strode briskly across the lawn in her Tory Burch sandals and headed for the man in the khaki uniform and wide-brimmed straw hat. He watched her go and stand before the man. Mr. Munoz nodded, listening. He'd probably heard it before. And there was his mom. Still trim. Looking pretty good for her age, really. Her legs still looked shapely and unmarred.

Skyler stepped inside to the cool air conditioning and closed the door after him. Same old house. The very same he grew up in. His mother had refreshed the design with new paint and new knickknacks, of course. Even changed out the furniture, but it was essentially the same. Except...there were odd things here and there.

A few items he didn't recognize and were definitely not his mother's style. Maybe they were gifts.

He went into the kitchen to get a glass of iced tea and upon opening the fridge, he saw more things that seemed out of place for her style. Food she would never buy for herself. Bottles of beer? What was going on?

He stood for a moment with the pitcher of iced tea in hand, staring into the fridge, when it occurred to him. He set the pitcher down, and with a glance back at the front door, he stalked toward his mother's bedroom.

He didn't even need to cast open the closet. He saw the men's slippers on the floor, the large bathrobe strewn across the bed. And then there it was in the closet. Proof positive.

He stomped out of the bedroom just as his mother walked in through the front door. "Mom! Does Dad *live* here now?"

She stopped dead, her hand to her throat. She released her frozen face in an exhale of exasperation. "Hasn't that man talked to you yet?"

"How long has *this* been going on? When were you going to tell me?"

She crossed her arms and raised her chin. "Don't take that tone with me. I'm still your mother."

He took a calming breath. "Okay. Sorry, but seriously? No one thought to tell me? Your only son?"

"We...we planned to. And then...well. He...he moved in about a month ago. We were dating and we were hitting it off. He was spending a lot of nights here and it seemed silly to..."

"God, don't tell me that! Gah!" He walked across the room and then crossed back to face her. "So he's living here now. Like permanently? Are you two...getting married again?"

"We discussed it and then we decided against it. Too much work combining resources. All that paperwork. So I guess…we'll just be living in sin." She gave a weird little smile. It was an expression he had never seen her wear before.

"Mom!"

"Look who's talking? You're living with Keith."

"Yeah, but…"

"Oh, double standard. I see."

"That's not exactly…I mean it's not really the same…hey! Don't try to turn it around on me. This is about you and Dad."

"Well it really isn't any of your business. It's not like I have to ask your permission."

"We could have discussed it. Like how bad an idea it was. Have you forgotten how he left us high and dry?"

"No, I haven't forgotten and I made sure he didn't either. Skyler, don't you think we've talked about things? It's not *all* about sex."

"MOM!"

She had that smug look again. She was enjoying this! He clenched his fists and stood his ground. "Okay. Okay, fine. It's not like I didn't pick up the pieces the last time. But when he walks out on you again—"

"Skyler Leslie Foxe, I am *this* close to smacking you."

He pulled up short, eyes wide, mouth hanging open.

"Now you settle down, mister. Sit over there." She pointed toward the couch with an imperious hand. Feeling ten years old, Skyler shuffled across the carpet, shoulders slumped, and sat hard onto the couch. Cynthia moved to sit beside him. She took his hand and rubbed it gently between her own. "I…appreciate your concern. I know you are only looking out for me. You're a good son, Skyler. I have always depended on you as the man of the house. But. I've done a lot of growing up in the last few years. There's my career at the department store. I enjoy working in the buying department and it looks like they appreciate me. I've gotten a raise this year."

"Oh, Mom, that's great."

"Yes. Yes it is. And yet I've been thinking about my retirement. I'm sixty, you know. In five years I'll qualify for social security. With my 401Ks in good shape and the house paid off—all thanks to your help, honey—I know I'll be all right. I have my friends. And I never really expected to date again or have a man in my life. I just…it was never something I was looking for. I was in love with your father. He's the only man I ever felt that way about. When he left, it was as if that part of my life was just…gone. Never to be rekindled."

She looked at his hand as she rubbed it.

His chest hurt. His mother's pain, mingled with his own confusion, brought back a lot of unpleasant memories. He had spent a decade angry at his father and then—he thought—he'd grown indifferent. But when Dale Foxe had returned a few months ago all those years of pain had come rushing back. It took Skyler a while to notice that Dale really had seemed like a changed man.

She looked up into his eyes and Skyler gazed back. He had his father's eyes, those gray ones. His mother's were blue. "But when he came back," she went on, "well…it wasn't exactly where we left off since that was a rather low point in my life. But he's matured, too. He's had his ups and downs as well. We came to an understanding. And then those old feelings crept back. For the both of us. Oh, I know what you're going to say. It's the familiar. It's safe. As soon as he got what he wanted he'd leave again. I told myself that, too. But he hasn't. We have a new honesty between us. I have told him straight out he had better tell me what's on his mind or it's out the door he goes. He talks to me now, sweetie. And I...I...talk to him."

Skyler swallowed. He hadn't realized how tensed his muscles were until he tried to loosen his shoulders. "Wow, Mom," he said quietly. "I guess...things *are* different."

"You'd better believe it. Do you think *I* want to get hurt again? But Skyler, it's nice having your father around. He's different...but also the same. The good things about him that attracted me in the first place are still there. The bad things have fallen away and have been replaced by maturity. I've given him a chance. Won't you? Won't you trust me?"

He squeezed her hand and held it tight for a long while. "I just don't want a repeat," he said feebly.

"I know, sweetheart. Believe me, neither do I."

He leaned over and kissed her cheek. "Well. If you believe in him, who am I to say? But I will call him and set up an evening out. I'll let him talk."

"Good. I think you should. Now. About you and your Keith investigating..."

"Heh, look at the time! I have to scoot." He released her hand and rose, making for the door.

"Skyler! I mean it. I don't want you to put yourself into danger."

"You asked me to trust *you*. Now I'm asking *you* to trust *me*."

She pursed her mouth and narrowed her eyes.

"Shouldn't we...you know...get that bird feeder?" he mumbled.

Without another word she gave him a scathing look and turned. She retrieved it from the back porch laundry room and held it aloft. It was made of iron, painted in such a way as to look old but it had long elegant lines and a diminutive dish for bird seed. He immediately took to it.

She handed it over and Skyler grasped it. "Thanks, Mom."

"You're welcome," she said coolly.

Dammit. He hated when she did that. He sighed. "Mom. Please?"

She gave the same exasperated sigh as he did and opened her arms. Skyler slipped into them and embraced her with his free hand. "I love you, Mom," he mumbled into her shoulder.

"I love you, too, Skyler. You take care of yourself."

"I will. And, uh, love to Dad."

"I'll tell him." That smirk again. Skyler shook his head, clutched the birdfeeder, and left out the front door. He waved to Mr. Munoz, got into his car, and drove to The Bean.

When he walked in Rodolfo and Philip were in full argument mode. He pivoted on his heel to leave when they spotted him.

"Here is *amante*!" said Rodolfo. "He'll decide."

Still backing toward the door, Skyler said, "Boy, I really don't want to be put in the middle..."

"Don't be ridiculous, Skyler," said Philip. "We're just having a disagreement about the front counter."

"*I* think it should be stretched," said Rodolfo, gesturing expansively. "And turn the corner here."

"And *I* think it's already big enough. What do *you* think?"

Skyler smiled in relief. He was glad it wasn't one of their blowouts. "So that's what this is about? Redecorating? Why do you think Philip should have a bigger counter?"

Rodolfo grinned and slipped his arm into Philip's. "Because *minino* and I are going into business together. Isn't that wonderful?"

"You are? You guys!" He grabbed them both into a hug. "Congratulations!"

"And we are moving in together, too," said Rodolfo quietly. He kissed Philip's cheek and Philip turned away, reddening.

"Yes, well…"

"Wow." Skyler expected it but it was still a little bit of a shock. His friends were all pairing up. And that was great. Even moving in together. Then why did he suddenly feel weird about it, as if things were changing too rapidly.

Philip had a concerned tone to his voice. "What's wrong, Skyler?"

"Um…nothing. It's great. I'm happy for you guys. But is there room back there for Rodolfo to bake?"

"Well that's the bigger news," said Philip. "We're going to have to expand. We're buying the shop next door. You know it's been empty for ages so we made an offer and got a real deal. He'll have his bakery there and we'll sell some here, hence more display cases."

"Whoa. That's even better news. Boy, everyone's… growing up."

"Isn't that what we're supposed to do? Besides, you're the youngest among us. I'm nearly thirty and Rodolfo is —"

"Never mind what Rodolfo is," Rodolfo cut in. He smoothed down his shiny tank top. "The important thing is we are moving forward. This is what I dreamed about when I left Ecuador. My own pastry shop."

"You deserve it, sweetheart," said Philip in that syrupy tone he reserved only for Rodolfo.

"That's amazing," agreed Skyler. "So when does it open?"

"Eight weeks if we're lucky," said Philip, ticking it off. "The place needs to be gutted. And lots of permits are needed. Inspections, design…"

Rodolfo smiled and leaned into Skyler. "Philip is in his element, no?"

"What's that, Rodolfo?"

"Nothing, *minino*. But what is Skyler doing here in the middle of the day?"

"Just came in to grab a quick bite before I head to the museum."

"What's going on with that, Skyler?" asked Philip, making his way behind the counter. He began fixing Skyler's favorite sandwich without being asked. Philip added quietly, "About the murder."

Sidling up to the counter, Skyler leaned in and spoke just as quietly. "Keith and I haven't gotten very far with that."

Philip stopped, one hand holding half a roll, the other brandishing a butter knife. "Surely you mean *Sidney* hasn't gotten far with it."

He waggled his eyebrows. "Well…*you* know. *Keith* and I."

Philip slammed down the knife and nearly leapt over the counter, leaning in so far his chest lay on it. "What is the matter with you?" he stage whispered. "Haven't you learned *anything*?"

"I've been busy. I know I haven't gotten very far investigating…"

"That's not what I meant. Oh for the love of God. You can't keep doing this, Skyler. You'll get yourself hurt."

"I'm fine. And I'm taking those self-defense classes."

Exasperated, he looked to his boyfriend. "Can't you talk some sense into him?"

But Rodolfo seemed to have that gleam in his eye, the same he had whenever he joined Skyler in his sleuthing. Philip noticed it too late. "Oh no! No, no, no, no. We are *not* going to help this idiot."

"But Philip," purred Rodolfo, his accent thickening. His body language morphed into something feline, and he was practically making love to the counter. "We cannot let Skyler do this on his own. He needs our help."

"Do you not remember, Rodolfo, when you nearly got killed?"

"And Skyler rescued me, didn't you, *amante*?"

"I mean it, Skyler. Do *not* call us asking to help you."

"Oh Philip," said Rodolfo, "lighten up. We always have a good time helping Skyler. You just call me direct, okay *amante*?"

"No, he won't!" Philp tried to swat Rodolfo from over the counter but couldn't reach him. "We nearly got arrested one time. Got tangled in a dangerous plot in another. Just what is so fun about that?"

"The thrill of it all!" he said, gesturing dramatically.

The time was ticking, and that sandwich wasn't going to make itself. "Uh…Philip," urged Skyler. "I only have so much time…"

"Oh sure." He flourished the knife, swiping it in the aioli, and slapping it over the buns. He tossed on the sprouts and flapped down the turkey slices. "Must get your lunch ready. God knows it's more important than my boyfriend's life."

"Nobody's risking anyone's life," said Skyler. "Look, Philip, if you really feel that way about it…"

Philip stopped again and pointedly glared at Skyler.

"*And*...I can see that you do...I just won't call you for help. Even if I need your specialized assistance and my life hangs in the balance. I just won't phone. Feel better?"

"Much," he muttered, still slapping ingredients together and flopping the completed sandwich on a plate. "Chips or carrots?" he bit out.

"Carrots, please."

Philip scooped up a healthy helping of the crinkle cut carrots and dumped them on the plate. "Chai?"

"Yes, please."

He shoved the plate across the counter and turned to get Skyler's tea.

"Your customer service leaves much to be desired!" Skyler called after him.

He got another over-the-shoulder glare for his trouble.

Rodolfo walked with Skyler to a little table and sat with him. "Don't mind Philip. He's a cuddly tiger, really. But he is very protective of me."

"I know. I don't mean to get into danger. It just...happens. I won't call you if it will cause trouble between you two." He picked up his sandwich and bit into it.

"You'd better! I don't want to be left out."

"Are you sure? He looks pretty mad."

Philip slammed down Skyler's chai and stood over him, arms folded. "Have a good lunch." He gave a grimace of a smile before turning on his heel.

"That," said Skyler gesturing after him. "That is what you can expect if I call you."

Rodolfo waved his hand in dismissal. "Oh I know how to handle that." The purr was back in his voice. Skyler recalled their own time together when they had hooked up and remembered Rodolfo's particular talents. He adjusted himself in his seat.

"I'll bet," he murmured and dug into his sandwich again.

Philip was still frosty when Skyler said his farewells, but he knew he would thaw eventually. He'd have to call him later. Maybe he could convince him to come to the last concert of the season.

On the way to the museum, he knew it would feel weird at the Bowl, thinking about what happened to Lester on Tuesday. The police tape had been there on the benches for days. It was only finally taken down this morning. And once everyone got to the museum, they seemed to feel it, too. Everyone dragged. Usually lively conversation was stunted. Fortunately, the busy tourists kept their minds occupied.

Skyler was working the gift counter with Randi. She was shoving plastic bags on a shelf under the register. As casually as he could, he asked, "So, uh, how's school going, Randi?"

Her pony tail bobbed as she turned her head. "Fine. Looking forward to starting the year. Fall semester starts at the beginning of September. So only a few weeks away."

"You're on a scholarship, aren't you?"

"Yeah. But it barely covers anything. If it weren't for this job, I'd be on the streets. My parents just don't make enough money to help out."

"Are they local?"

"Bakersfield."

"So no. What brought you out here to Redlands, then?"

"I wanted to get out of Bakersfield." She smiled. "Mom and Dad weren't thrilled but Redlands is in an area they approved of — sort of half ag, half city — and I really like it. Plus there's the Baptist connection to the school. You went to UR, didn't you, Skyler?"

"Go, Bulldogs," he said, fist raised.

"Did you know H.R. Haldeman went there, too? The Watergate guy?"

He nodded. "Yeah. Weird, huh?"

"I like the school. If only I can figure out what I want to do."

"You will."

"Did you know when you went there, Skyler?"

"Oh yeah. I always wanted to teach. I knew that in high school."

"You're lucky. Not everyone is."

"I know. I went there on a scholarship, too. Paid for everything. Well, most things. I worked here putting myself through. Mr. Huxley actually helped me out with extra cash. Students are always in need. How, uh, how do *you* manage?"

She shrugged. "I don't eat."

"That's not good for you," he said in his teacher voice.

Sighing, she leaned back against the counter. "You sound like my dad. I'm fine. Besides, I hear Top Ramen builds bones twelve ways."

Skyler shuddered. "I lived off that stuff a bit, too. Except that my mom lives here and more often than not, I had food waiting for me back at my dorm room. Come to think of it, I don't know how she got in there." Randi chuckled. He moved closer and spoke quietly, "But if you ever find yourself in a serious bind, don't hesitate to call. I mean it. You can't starve yourself and expect to do all your schoolwork."

Her cheeks reddened and her gaze slid away. "Thanks, Skyler. But I'm fine. I've...worked it out." She wouldn't look at him as she straightened and brushed at her short skirt. "Mind if I leave early? I have some reading I should really do."

"Sure. No problem."

Without looking at him, she hurried away. Skyler frowned. It seemed Randi *was* in need of funds. And for all he knew, so was Seth. This wasn't looking very good for at least three current docents. Well, who knew exactly what Jerome's problem was?

Ron was doing his usual job of spot polishing the floor, rag in one hand, spray bottle hanging out of his back pants pocket. His white running shoes were spotless as always. Skyler knew he worked at an auto parts place three days a week. Ron was Skyler's age and trying to get a full time gig at a bigger museum or gallery, but those jobs were few and far between.

"How's the job hunt going, Ron?" he asked.

Ron pulled his gaze away from the floor and looked up at Skyler. "Slow. There's a gallery in Palm Springs but I don't know if I'm more qualified than any of the other applicants. It's a jungle out there."

"I hear ya."

"Say Skyler." He sidled closer. "You know me. I've worked here for three years now. Do you think I have a shot at the director's job?"

Skyler hadn't thought of it before, but if Jerome was effectively out of the running, Ron would certainly qualify. "I don't know if I have a say or not, or whether they'd rather hire outside of us, but I'd be happy to recommend you. I didn't know that you wanted to stay in this little ole museum."

"You gotta start someplace. And anyway, Lester taught us all so much. It was like a master class."

"Yeah." Mr. Huxley's murder stung Skyler afresh. "It just won't be the same without him."

"But I'd carry on his traditions. The Lincoln Shrine wouldn't be the shrine without Lester's touches."

Skyler smiled. It was Lester who put in the TV screens and procured the videos that ran all day. School children were transfixed as always to a video screen, but the displays made it the place to come. And all those missing museum exhibits...Skyler was determined to get them back and make the scoundrel pay!

Thinking about the empty displays, he couldn't put it off any longer. He had to call Denise Suzuki and tell her the news that irreplaceable items have been stolen.

He retreated into the office and closed the door. Picking up the office phone he dialed her. She picked up after the third ring.

"Denise Suzuki," came her clipped, professional voice on the line.

"Hi, Denise, it's Skyler Foxe."

"Hi, Skyler," she said warily. "What can I do for you?"

"Well...with all the bad news lately, I really hate to add to it. But the thing of it is, there have been some things gone missing from the museum."

Silence. And then, "Things missing. What do you mean?"

"I mean...just what it sounds like. Someone has been stealing display pieces from the shrine."

"Oh my God. Is it bad?"

"Pretty bad. The stove pipe is gone. Some of Mary Todd's items. Quite a haul, actually."

"How is this possible?"

"I don't know. But I started noticing it the day…the day Lester died. For a while there I actually suspected him."

"And now you don't."

"Not when things continue to be stolen."

"Have you called the police?"

"It's obviously an inside job."

"Skyler, have you called the police?"

He slumped back in his chair. Yes, any responsible citizen would have done so right away. "The thing of it is, Denise, if it's someone here, someone I know, I'd rather just talk to them to get it all back."

Another silence. "The amount of money involved amounts to a felony, Skyler."

"I know. But my friend the police detective has been informed, and my boyfriend who has connections with the FBI is checking on it, too."

She sighed heavily. "Well… You're right, of course. It would be best to keep it in-house. I don't think the museum could take another hit to its reputation."

"That's what I was thinking."

"Skyler, you're a good man. I truly wish you could take over duties permanently."

"And if I didn't have another career I'd jump on it. But as it is…"

"You've only got one more week."

"Yes. I'm afraid so. I'm truly sorry."

"We all are, believe me. Well, do what you can. The board appreciates your dedication."

"Thanks, Denise."

"Oh, and Skyler, will you be at the Bowl tonight?"

"Yeah. Volunteering. The last night of the season."

"Yes. The board was coming tonight to do a little dedication to Lester. I wanted you and the docents to be there, if they can."

"I'll let them know. Thanks for understanding, Denise."

"Yes. These are very troubling times."

She signed off and Skyler sat, looking at the phone for a while, before he picked up the receiver again and dialed Keith. "Hey, I wonder if you wanted to come to the last Bowl night. They're doing a dedication for Lester."

"Sure, babe. Our usual spot?"

"Yeah. Thanks. I know you must be tired."

"It will be nice to unwind. Should I pick up some cheese and stuff from Gerrards?"

Skyler smiled. Keith knew he liked the food from the high-end market. "Yeah. That would be great."

"I'll get the wine and everything. Don't worry about any of it. See you later."

"Thanks, Keith. I love you."

"Love you, too, babe."

He had to get out his own phone to call Jamie and Philip, and he felt better that the whole SFC agreed to be there. Lester needed a good send off.

And tomorrow was his funeral. Jeez. What a week!

Before closing, Skyler gathered Seth, Randi, and Ron and told them about tonight. They agreed to attend. When he called Jerome he didn't pick up so he left a voicemail.

Once Skyler locked up, Seth was at the keypad punching in numbers but the green light wouldn't change to red. Randi pushed him aside. "Let me try." She got the same result and it was only then Skyler realized he should have taken over. Now it was too late.

"Oh, uh…" He gently nudged her aside and punched in the new code. "I, um, changed the code the other day."

"Thanks for telling us," said Ron. He said it sarcastically but also good-naturedly. "So what's the new code?"

Everyone was staring at him. It was hot outside as they stood under the museum's eaves, but that's not what made the sweat trickle down his back. "Um…actually, I'm not allowed to say." *Good one, Skyler. Blame it on the board. It won't matter in a week anyway*, he kept telling himself.

Ron exchanged glances with the other docents. "Wait. Are you saying we don't get to know the code?"

"Not until a new director is chosen. Then he or she can decide. What with the stuff being stolen and all…"

"Bruh," said Seth. "Are you saying that *we're* suspects?"

"Uh, not exactly…"

Randi dropped her head in her hands. "That *is* exactly what you're saying. Wow."

"Guys, I'm sorry. You know I am."

"Well," said Ron, not so good-naturedly now, "I'm glad at least one of us is above reproach. I see *you* got the new code."

"Guys…"

"Oh leave Skyler alone," said Randi. "You know he *is* above reproach. The man is squeaky clean."

"And the rest of us?" Ron shook his head. "That's pretty rude."

Seth looked down at his key and twisted it back and forth. "Should we turn in our keys? They aren't much good if we don't know the codes? So are you gonna come down on the weekend and open up for us?"

Oh. Skyler hadn't thought about that. This was stupid. Should he run back and forth here all weekend? He *had* to trust somebody. "You're right. Here's the code—"

Ron threw up his hands. "Are you sure? I mean, we could be criminals, fencing the stuff. Are you sure you want to give us free rein here?"

"Dude," said Seth, "give the man a break. He's in a tough spot."

"You know I didn't ask for this," said Skyler quietly.

"Wait," said Randi. "What if you just give the code to one person who'll be here on the weekend?"

"No way," said Ron. "And then something is stolen and that person gets blamed? No! Either we all get it or none of us."

Skyler was getting a headache. Could be from all the clenching his jaw was doing? "Then what do you guys want? Should I just open up on the weekend or give everyone the code?" Was that the Keith voice in the back of his head saying, "*Don't* give them the code"? But it suddenly felt wrong not to. His brilliant plan wasn't turning out to be so brilliant when faced with the people he was hurting.

Everyone was staring at their feet. Finally Seth said, "Either you trust us or you don't. Up to you, man."

Skyler looked at each in turn. With a sigh he said, "Here's the code."

Everyone looked relieved. They waved as they left, promising to come tonight for Lester's dedication. Skyler felt better, too, though he couldn't help but feel a tiny bit stupid for caving so quickly. Maybe it was the exact wrong thing to do. Too late now. But he wasn't about to tell Keith.

Chapter Ten

KEITH HAD ARRIVED EARLY TO SET UP THEIR blanket and chairs, but when Skyler approached their picnic, Keith was frowning at his phone.

"Problem?" asked Skyler.

Keith looked startled and quickly shut it off and stuffed it away. "No. I'm fine."

"You don't look fine."

"I said I was fine."

"And now you're testy."

"Skyler, no I'm not. Just...sit down or something."

Widening his eyes but holding his tongue Skyler looked down into the picnic basket Keith had packed. He couldn't stay annoyed when he saw all his favorite things from Gerrards. All kinds of cheeses, pate, grapes, the cold curried cous cous salad from the deli and some sliced cold meats. There was wine in a cooler as well. "Thanks for getting this. I still have volunteering to do before I can sit with you."

"Okay," he said in a clipped tone.

"You sure you don't want to tell me what's bothering you? I *am* your partner, you know."

Keith looked abashed at that. "I'm sorry. It's...it's just a text from Ethan."

"Oh?" Just the merest stab of jealousy speared Skyler's chest. "What does he have to say for himself?"

"Nothing worth sharing."

Skyler waited but Keith was close-lipped and wasn't looking at him.

Super. "Okay," replied Skyler coolly. If Keith didn't want to share, he didn't want to share. Skyler turned on his heel and retreated toward the volunteer tent. He looked back once at Keith with his face buried in his phone again. "Nothing worth sharing my ass!"

Skyler helped the other volunteers by walking through the picnickers and handing out programs. He went from one side of the bowl to the other, out into the lawn areas and in through the bench seating.

The sun was finally going down creating a pink glow behind the bowl. The first stars winked down out of a cerulean sky. And then he spotted his fellow docents. He made his way over to them on the benches. "Hey, guys."

"Is there nothing you don't do in this town?" asked Randi. She wore a halter top and shorts. Ron seemed to be appreciating her outfit, and was slow to look up at Skyler. Seth was playing some game on his phone and just nodded toward Skyler without looking from his screen.

"I haven't run for city manager yet," he quipped.

"That's only a matter of time," said Ron. The man seemed to like his polo shirts, but he was also wearing shorts and white running shoes. Skyler noticed he had nice legs fuzzed with light hair, but steered his gaze away.

Seth grunted his agreement.

Randi sipped at her Redlands Bulldog tumbler. "So when do they plan to do the dedication? I'd like to stay for the whole concert but I do have other stuff to catch up on."

"Yeah," said Seth, putting down his phone at last. "Are they gonna do it right away or…?"

"Not really sure. They usually do that kind of stuff right away, though."

"Good," said Ron. "I've got stuff to do, too."

Skyler looked back at Keith, still frowning at his phone and furiously texting. "Are you guys going to the funeral tomorrow?"

Solemnly they nodded. "Bruh," said Seth. "It's the least we can do."

"Has anyone seen Jerome lately?" asked Ron. "Is he coming back to work, or what? He's on for Saturday…but, uh, under the circumstances…"

"I guess we shouldn't expect him on Saturday. Maybe we should just close Saturday. Seems pointless to be open. We'll all be at the funeral. But now that you mention him, do you really have a hard time working with him?"

"It's his sense of entitlement, you know?" said Randi. "I mean, I guess he's an okay guy. It's just sometimes it was all, 'My uncle told me this,' and 'he said I'd be doing that.' It was annoying."

"But just annoying, right? You didn't get any other kind of other vibe from him?"

Ron leaned forward. "Do you mean a *thief* kind of vibe? Maybe."

Seth shook his head. "You're projecting. Jerome couldn't steal from the museum any more than the rest of us. Oh…well." He seemed to remember they were all suspects. "Any more than *Skyler*, then."

"I don't know," said Randi, thoughtfully. "He's also kind of secretive. He never talks about his days off, what he does. And I did catch him a couple of times, like, fondling the exhibits."

"'Fondling'?" asked Skyler.

"Yeah. You know. Lovingly touching the things. He was really absorbed in it. He didn't even notice me and was a total asshole when I kind of made fun of him for it."

"He's a serious dude," said Seth. "He's not a prankster. He hates being made fun of."

But Skyler couldn't get that image out of his head. "He was fondling the exhibits?"

"Probably figuring out the eBay price for it," said Ron.

Randi ticked a finger at him. "That isn't nice, Ron. You don't know for sure."

"I know he hasn't been around and that I've had to cover the time for him. I know stuff has turned up missing the days after he worked."

"The same could be said for a lot of us," she countered.

They all suddenly looked at Skyler. "Is that right?" asked Seth, looking worried.

"Well...yeah. There hasn't been any one person working on those days."

They all fell silent. Until Seth yawned wide. "I hope this doesn't run late. I have to get up early tomorrow. Going on a ride with some friends."

"Okay. I have to get back to it. I'll see you guys later." Skyler walked away, looking back at his docents. He always thought everyone got along. But he had been blind to their little quirks and discrepancies. And speaking of quirks. Keith was still hunched over his phone. What the hell was Ethan texting him about? Threats?

He wanted to know. Was there a way of finding out without Keith knowing?

"Hi, Sky!" Jamie popped up seemingly out of nowhere and waved jazz hands at him. Dave strode up sedately behind him, carrying a cooler.

"I've lived in Redlands a couple of years now," said Dave, "and I don't think I've been to the Bowl in all that time as much as I have this year."

Skyler smiled. "Due to me, no doubt. Bringing culture to yet another sad Redlandsian."

Dave chuckled. "I don't know about that."

"Is Keith here?" said Jamie, looking around.

"Yeah, in our usual spot."

They both turned and Dave headed in that direction. Skyler grabbed Jamie's arm and pulled him back. Dave didn't seem to notice as he hailed Keith, who finally looked up and set his phone aside.

"What's up, Skyboy?"

"Listen, Jamie. Can you…hack into phones?"

"Better than a group of FBI agents around a confiscated iPhone. Why?"

"Well…" He glanced at Keith from over Jamie's shoulder. "Keith is being weird about Ethan again. I guess the jerk is texting him. For all I know, he's here, watching us right now."

Jamie swiveled his head. "That's kind of a creepy thought."

"Yeah. So I wondered. Could you—"

"You want me to hack into *Keith's* phone? No way!"

"Just a little bit. So I could see those texts."

"Skyler! You should be ashamed of yourself. You should trust your partner."

"But he's not sharing with me. What could it be that he's not sharing?"

"Uh *personal* things, maybe? Things he doesn't want you to know about? We all have those things. If he hasn't given you his password then I guess it's none of your business."

Skyler pulled back and stared. "This, coming from *you*? The biggest gossip I know?"

"Hey! I only share things that would be of mutual interest. And usually it's about people we don't personally know. Sometimes. This is a huge invasion of privacy."

"But Jamie, what if it's more than that? What if he's threatening us? This guy is getting pretty stalkery. What if something happens to Keith and you could have helped prevent it?"

He put his hands on his hips and stared down his nose at Skyler. "That's not playing fair."

"I know, but shit seems to happen to us all the time. Please, Jamie. Won't you try?"

"Dammit." Jamie glanced over his shoulder. Dave and Keith were talking amiably enough, but Skyler saw the shadow in Keith's eyes. Something big was bothering him. And there was his phone, sitting there on the blanket between them.

"Could you do it right here, right now without him noticing?"

"I don't know." Jamie gnawed on a fingernail. "I guess…if I could get it long enough."

"It's there on the blanket. If you could sneak it away and then, say, go to the bathroom, could you do it?"

"Yessss," he hissed with an exasperated tone. "I could get in, email the texts to my phone, and then send them to you later. Will that make you happy?"

"Extraordinarily happy."

"You will owe me *so* much for this!"

"I know. Thanks, Jamie."

Jamie made a distressed noise and then stomped over to the blanket. Skyler watched them for a while, hoping to see Jamie steal the phone, but he glared at

Skyler instead until it was time for him to go off to his volunteer duties again.

Philip and Rodolfo were late and hadn't yet arrived when his phone buzzed. He thought it might be them, but the screenname said "Dale Foxe." "Shit." He answered with a, "Hi, Dad."

"Hi, son. Your, uh, mother made me call. Seems you were over at her place today—"

"Don't you mean *your* place?"

He clucked his tongue. "Well, uh, yeah."

"How long has this been going on?"

"Couple of months. I thought you'd be a little happier that your parents got back together."

"Well I'm not. You aren't a very reliable husband... Boyfriend... Husband. Shit, what the hell do I call you?"

"You call me 'father'. And you should have a little more respect about it, ideally."

"I don't see why."

"Look, I thought we were getting along pretty well a few months ago."

"I...ugh! Dad, this is hard for me. It's been...a really long time since you were in our lives. I just worry about Mom, you know?"

"I know, son." His voice was softer, placating. It gave Skyler pause. Maybe...maybe his dad did love her...again...still. Skyler was too new to relationships himself to be able to tell.

He scouted around to make sure he wasn't immediately needed and walked along the pathway, avoiding a rollerblader and countless moms with strollers. "Do you want to meet? Have coffee?"

"I was thinking more like brunch. Tomorrow. That sound okay to you?"

"I have a funeral at two."

"A funeral?"

"My boss here at the museum. He was...he died." No need to tell him the gory details, but then, of course, his mom probably already told him, their living together and all.

"That's right. I heard about that. You aren't...your mother mentioned that you might be investigating that."

"I'm *fine*," he insisted.

"I know. You're a grown man, Skyler. I admire you for stepping up to the plate. Keith is there to back you up, right?"

"Yeah."

"So just take his advice, okay? He's the expert."

Wait. Was his dad *approving* of this? Skyler straightened. "Okay."

"Want to meet me at McDuff's?"

"Sure, Dad. Ten?"

"Okay. It's a date! Ha! I bet that's easy for you with a dude."

"Dad!"

"I'm just poking at you. See you tomorrow at ten."

He stared at his phone. His dad making bad jokes about being gay? His life had really gone surreal.

Skyler returned to passing out programs, directing people to where the bathrooms were, and generally answering questions. Then the lights flickered and dimmed. A jazz band was scheduled to play tonight and the stage was set with chairs, a piano, with a magenta light splashed up into the curve of the bowl's back wall.

The president of the Redlands Community Music Association came out to the downstage mic to the audience's applause. He made some announcements, thanked everyone for the wonderful job they did putting on the performances for the season, and took a moment to thank the volunteers. A few audience members sitting near Skyler turned to him and clapped purposefully toward him. With a smile he took a bow.

Tucking the programs under his arm he returned to their picnic blanket, nestling in his beach chair with Keith on one side and Jamie on the other. He gave Jamie a significant look, but the man shook his head. Then the president introduced Denise Suzuki and Skyler sat at attention.

She clacked on her heels up to the mic and looked over the audience. He always thought of her as petite, but looking at her up there on the stage, he realized she wasn't really. She had a presence about her that seemed to take charge. She'd run the museum board almost as long as Lester had held the reins. She was smart in a light-colored blouse and matching skirt that reached to just above the knee. It was hard to tell how old she was but he knew she was in her early sixties.

Her bracelet flashed in the stage lighting as she raised her notes on their 3 x 5 cards. "Thank you, Mr. President, thank you Bowl volunteers and programmers, and our wonderful audience members. I'll only take a few moments of your time. I'm Denise Suzuki, president of the Lincoln Museum Board of Directors. Across the park, behind the A.K. Smiley Library, is a little museum some of you may not have been aware of. We call it the Lincoln Shrine. In it is housed some truly remarkable artifacts from the American Civil War, and of Abraham Lincoln and his family. Its renown is recognized far and wide, all across the world. And it's one of the many treasures here in Redlands, just like our own Redlands Bowl. There has been one man who had it running smoothly and efficiently with a smile and a friendly word for the last thirty years. I wish I was standing here announcing his retirement, which he did have planned for later this year. Instead, sadly, Lester Huxley died earlier this week." There were sounds of surprise from the crowd. Denise went on. "Those of us who worked closely with him wanted to pay him tribute. So tonight, the Redlands Community Music Association have dedicated this our last night of the summer music festival to our friend and colleague Mr. Lester Huxley."

A projection of Lester's smiling face suddenly came up on the back of the bowl's wall. It was odd mixed with the magenta color of the lights and the curve of the plaster, but it was nice to see nonetheless. Skyler wiped away a tear.

Polite applause followed, swelling slightly, until they died down again as Denise left the stage. The picture remained for a moment more, before it, too, faded.

Skyler turned to Keith who gave him a comforting look. And as he settled back in his seat, Skyler noticed the phone on the blanket between them. While Keith was looking in the other direction, he leaned over just enough to reach it and carefully held it against his stomach. He put it in his other hand and quickly slapped it to Jamie's chest. Jamie squeaked and grabbed it, looking down in horror when it was in his hand. He fumbled it up under his shirt and looked around red-faced and guilty as hell.

Jamie leaned over to Dave to excuse himself and rose, glaring at Skyler as he retreated to the bathrooms only a few yards away, a rectangular shape bulging under his tank top.

Skyler tried to settle back and listen to the jazz music as it started. The *tish* of the cymbals and the soft scrape of the brushes over the drums would otherwise have kept his full attention, but he couldn't help but imagine what Jamie might be doing and what he might be discovering.

Fifteen minutes later Jamie returned and shoved the phone at Skyler. It was at that moment that Philip and Rodolfo arrived. Chairs shuffled and it was the perfect cover to drop the phone back where Keith had left it. And no sooner had he done so than Keith scooped it up and stuffed it in his shorts pocket.

They all reassembled themselves with the minimum of fuss. But all through the first part of the concert, Jamie wouldn't look at Skyler.

Intermission came and Skyler had to do his duty. As he roamed around offering the red bowl for people to drop their donations into, he spotted Jerome on the pathway under the street light. He was simply standing there, staring at the stage. Wondering if he should go over to talk to him, Skyler got distracted by a red-headed child running full bore into him, catching him in the solar plexus and knocking the wind out of him. He steadied the kid just as his mother ran up. "I'm so sorry," she said.

Skyler winced his reply. "It's fine," he managed to say and the harried mother took the perhaps three-year-old by the hand and dragged him away.

By the time Skyler looked for Jerome, he was gone.

He glanced over toward the benches where the docents had been and found that all of them had left as well.

Skyler suddenly remembered the camera app on his phone and called it up. The dark museum was visible in a green wash under its night vision lens. But no one disturbed the stillness of any of the rooms.

When the intermission was over, Skyler returned to their picnic. Rodolfo was feeding Philip a grape, Dave lay back his head in Jamie's lap, eyes closed, and Jamie still aimed a narrow-eyed glare at Skyler. And Keith... He was staring at his phone again.

With a world-weary sigh, Skyler flopped into his chair.

"What's the matter, Sky?" asked Philip, rolling over to look at him.

"Nothing. I'm fine. Funeral tomorrow for Lester."

"Oh." He gave him an apologetic expression before he turned around toward Rodolfo. Dave began to snore before Jamie lightly flicked him in the forehead.

"Keith," said Skyler softly. "If you could put that 'nothing worth sharing' away for half a second..."

"What? Oh, sorry, babe." He clicked it off and set it down. "I don't want you to worry about it. I've got it handled."

Skyler sat back against his chair and stared up into the stars. *I've got it handled, too*, he thought, wondering what Jamie would come up with.

When the final concert drew to a close to thundering applause, some even giving it a standing ovation, if not for the jazz band then for the whole summer music series, Skyler shot up to do more of his volunteering routine.

"I'll meet you back at the car," Keith said distractedly. The damn phone was in his hand again.

Skyler was on the other side of the bowl after helping an old lady into her car when he thought to check the museum app again.

He gasped. A hooded figure moved stealthily through the dark rotunda. "Son of a bitch!"

He dialed 9-1-1 as he ran. The alarm company hadn't called him. That meant that the alarm wasn't triggered and *that* must have meant that someone entered the code. "There's been a break-in to the Lincoln Shrine, 125 West Vine Street. It's happening right now! Send a squad car."

He didn't bother to acknowledge the operator when he stuffed the phone back in his pocket. He looked around for Keith or any of the SFC but no one was anywhere to be found. "Shit!" He took a deep breath and tore across the street toward the lawn in front of the building.

He skidded to a stop on the deep thatch and stared at the supposedly quiet museum. "Go in from the back," he told himself and made his way to the office door.

When he turned the corner he saw it was ajar. He crept closer. His phone chimed and he covered his pocket with his hand. Trotting back to the sidewalk he looked at the screen. An email. Could be from Jamie. He opened his phone and called it up. Yup. Jamie left a terse message but there was the conversation with Ethan and Keith, and it said —

A noise in the museum captured his attention again and he stuffed the phone away, making his way stealthily toward the door. Gently he grabbed the edge of it and pulled it open, wondering if it would creak. He breathed again when it didn't and poked his head inside. No one in the office, but he definitely heard footsteps inside. Good thing he never told anyone about the cameras!

Tip-toeing through the office he saw that the door to the museum was open and a shadow passed by it. All he needed was to take a quick look and then go wait outside for the cops. After all, they were just up the street. They'd be there any second.

He managed to get to the door and peer out.

No one. At least not in the rotunda. He heard a shuffling in the west wing and he crept to the archway. There was a dark figure in a hoodie moving along the exhibits near the gift shop counter.

The whoop of a police car sounded outside and he turned his head for only a moment.

A trash bag slammed down over him. Shoved against a wall where he hit his temple and saw bright stars against the blackness, Skyler staggered and struggled with the sack as footsteps ran by him.

When he finally pulled the bag free, he faced the glare of flashlights and police officers shouting, "Hold it right there!"

❖

"I'm Skyler Foxe! Acting museum director. I'm Skyler Foxe!" he kept saying, as they cuffed him and led him outside. By that time a crowd had gathered, no doubt drawn by the police car's flashing lights. Skyler saw the silhouette of a large man push his way through, followed by several others.

"Skyler! Officers, I'm special agent Keith Fletcher." There was that FBI badge again. "This is Skyler Foxe, acting director of the Lincoln Shrine."

The cop holding Skyler's arm at the elbow stopped. "We got a 9-1-1 call."

"That was me!" said Skyler, voice more shrill than he would have liked it to be. "I saw someone breaking in and I came over to see…"

The cop looked him over more critically. "You're the guy from the other night."

"Yes! A friend of Detective Feldman and Detective de Guzman? I'm Skyler Foxe. Remember? And you're Officer Carey."

Carey glanced toward his partner, who seemed to be distancing himself from it all. "Christ," he muttered and uncuffed Skyler. "I thought I told you to call me."

"What's going on?" asked Dave. Jamie had dropped his glare and was now looking concerned. Rodolfo kept what looked like a tight grasp of Philip's arm, but none of them said anything.

Skyler stepped back and rubbed his wrists. "I saw someone in there."

"Do you have a description?" said Carey.

He shook his head. "It was too dark and they were wearing a hoodie. He must have run right past you."

The officers exchanged glances. "We didn't see anyone run out."

"They could have hidden in the office and waited for you to come through."

The officers looked decidedly unhappy with that bit of news. "So it was a man?" asked Carey, all business again.

"I...I don't know. I couldn't honestly say. It was pretty dark in there."

They talked briefly with Skyler for a few more minutes before closing their notebooks and leaving in their squad car.

"They aren't gonna dust the place?" said Skyler, watching them drive away. His adrenalin bubbled up and down his body. He felt too jittery to stand in one spot and tried to pace, until Keith grabbed him by the shoulders and hugged him close.

"Calm down, Skyler. What the hell were you doing going in there by yourself? Why didn't you get me or Dave?"

"I couldn't find any of you! Where were you?"

Keith looked sheepishly toward Dave. "We were looking at Dave's new car. I'm sorry, babe, but that doesn't excuse your going it alone."

"I called 9-1-1," he said softly. The adrenalin was wearing off. And the message in Keith's texts was coming back to the fore. He'd read it right before going into the museum:

If you think you're done with me K, you have another thing coming.

I am more than done with you, Ethan. I'm warning you. Don't bother us again.

Or what? I have some info that might amuse your little boyfriend. How much is it worth to you to keep it quiet?

Are you fucking BLACKMAILING me???

Call it what you like. Do you remember Laurie Henderson? Remember *that night*? Well, my dear Keith, it resulted in a beautiful 7lb 6oz boy named Joshua. He's ten now. Wanna know who he looks like?

Chapter Eleven

SKYLER WANTED TO SAY SOMETHING BUT THIS was hardly the place. Besides, what *could* he say? Keith hadn't yet told him. Maybe he had no intention of telling him. Skyler did glance once at Jamie, who looked back at him worriedly, biting his lip. Of course he'd read it, too. Not the best person in the world to keep a secret.

The police had said that there was nothing they could do, especially since Skyler had found nothing missing. Keith locked up the museum. He ushered Skyler back to the car and they took their leave silently from the SFC.

Skyler said nothing on the ride home, staring out the window at the passing shadows of trees and bright glow of vintage street lamps. He still didn't say anything as they climbed the apartment stairs. Once inside, he absently pet the cat and sat in the wing chair.

Keith knelt in front of him, hands gently grasping his thighs. "You look shaken. Want a drink?"

Skyler nodded. He was shaken, all right, but not from the break-in. How the hell was he going to broach the subject with Keith without letting him know that he hacked his phone? That Keith might...have a child! A ten-year-old boy! Keith would probably sue for custody rights. Skyler would have to be a...a *dad*! And he'd be barely sixteen years older than the kid. What if he was a brat? What if he was already troubled? What if he hated Keith? That would be terrible. But worse. What if he hated Skyler?

Keith was back, offering a Grey Goose in an ice-filled glass. Skyler took it and drank, letting the alcohol burn his throat just a touch before it warmed his belly.

"You shouldn't have gone in," Keith said gently, kneeling again. A warm hand was on Skyler's thigh once more; that hand...the same hand that had, apparently, touched a girl. And *more*. That was something Keith had never told him before. And Skyler was pretty sure he had asked that question once upon a time.

"I would have gone in with you," Keith continued.

Skyler looked up. He was always bowled over at how blue and clear those eyes were, like a glacier. But never cold like one. More like the blue on the horizon on a cold, crisp day. "Thanks. I know. You promised to help me. I looked for you."

"Why didn't you call me?"

"I was calling 9-1-1."

Keith nodded. "For once, something smart."

When Skyler glared, Keith raised a hand in apology. "Sorry. You're right. You did call. That was good. And you're not hurt? Sure?"

Keith reached up and ran his fingers through Skyler's hair. Skyler didn't wince at the touch. There were no bumps. So he guessed he hadn't hit his head *that* hard. Keith's fingers felt good.

"I'm fine," he answered.

"Good. I don't want you hurt."

There's more than one way to hurt me, he thought but didn't say it aloud. *Why aren't you telling me? Why aren't you sharing this?* Skyler waited. They stared into each other's eyes; Keith calmly, Skyler expectantly. But nothing was passing between them. Finally Skyler sighed and looked away. He lifted his glass to his lips.

Keith rose. "So the docents still don't know about the cameras."

"Nope. I purposely didn't tell them."

"What I can't understand, then, is how they got in without tripping the alarm."

"Oh…" Skyler took another swig. The ice shifted and hit him in the nose. He rubbed at it and lowered the glass to his thigh. "About that… They sort of cornered me and I had to confess that we changed it."

"And what did they say?"

"They were pissed. Like they were suspects."

"And they are."

"But I didn't want to be the one to tell them that."

"So what did you do? Skyler, you didn't cave did you? I thought we agreed that you wouldn't give them the code."

He squirmed. "I couldn't help it. They were all so indignant, like I didn't trust them. And you weren't there! You would have given in, too… Maybe. The thing of it is I've worked with some of these guys for years, and I do trust them. Except…that they all seem in need of money in one way or another."

"You trusted them…and look what happened."

"It still might be someone else."

Keith crossed him arms over his chest and slapped on a dubious expression.

"It might," Skyler said in a small voice.

Keith lowered his arms and retreated into the kitchen to get his own drink from the bar cupboard. "Cat's out of the bag. Nothing you can do about it now, I suppose. At least they don't know about the cameras."

"Yeah. There's that." Skyler watched him pour bourbon into his glass. "So…what about Ethan? What was he texting you about?"

Keith's expression shuttered. His jaw tensed, even after he took a swig from his glass before leaving the kitchen. "Nothing you need to worry about. He won't be bothering us again anytime soon. By the way." He sat on the couch and wore a casual air about him. Skyler suspected it was all an act. "I'll be late the next few nights. I have some stuff to catch up on."

Stuff to catch up on? I'll just bet. Like meeting your kid. Talk to me, dammit!

"Sure. I won't wait dinner for you then."

"I'll call you if there's a change in plans."

"Fine."

They sat in silence with just the sound of ice clinking in their drinks. Skyler couldn't stand it. "Are you *sure* there isn't anything you want to tell me?"

"If there was, I'd tell you," he said coolly.

Skyler narrowed his eyes and Keith narrowed his over the rim of his glass.

"Okay," Skyler muttered. Keith closed his eyes and laid his head back.

How was this supposed to work? He thought you didn't keep things from the other person in a relationship. Because it only created misunderstandings. How were they to resolve their problems if they didn't talk?

"So...I'm meeting my dad for brunch tomorrow morning. I hope that's okay."

Keith sat up. "No, that's fine. I should probably get an early start anyway."

"On your *stuff.*"

"Yeah." Either Keith didn't catch the sarcastic tone or he was ignoring it.

"And then I have Lester's funeral."

"I know. Did you want me to go with you?"

"No. I can go on my own. I just hope *Ethan* won't be there."

Keith stiffened at the name. "I doubt it."

"Paid him off to leave, did you?"

He snapped his gaze toward Skyler. "What do you mean?"

"Nothing, nothing. Maybe I should just turn in."

"I'll be there in a minute."

Skyler took the last dregs of his drink with him into the bedroom and stared at the neatly made bed. It was all well and good to know the contents of Keith's text, but another thing to figure out how to talk to him about it. Would Skyler find out only once the kid was moving in? He almost turned around to confront Keith right then and there, but stopped. He didn't relish the part of the conversation that involved stealing his phone and having Jamie hack it. "Shit. How do I get myself into these messes?"

Jamie texted him three times Saturday morning, always asking the same thing: "What did Keith say?"

Since Keith didn't say anything there was very little point in replying. Instead, Skyler got showered and dressed and ready to meet his dad. Keith worked with his biology class folders and football binders, but Skyler also caught him frowning over his phone and tapping out messages.

Hope the custody battle goes okay, he thought with a sneer, but aloud he said, "I'm going. I guess I'll see you later."

Keith got up, still texting.

Skyler lifted his face and puckered his lips for a kiss, but Keith walked by him into the kitchen without even noticing.

Ooo-KAY.

Skyler let the door slam and trotted down the stairs. Certainly not in the best of moods to meet his dad, but when he pulled into the restaurant's parking lot, he put on a game face.

Dale Foxe — blond-haired with a touch of gray, a straight, sharp nose that Skyler also had — was already at a table, waiting for him. As was his custom upon meeting Skyler these days, he rose and gave him a hug. Blushing, Skyler sat opposite him and asked the waitress for coffee.

"Well," said Dale, setting his menu aside. "Here we are."

"Yeah. Here we are. So I guess — "

"If you could — "

They spoke at the same time and both demurred to the other. Dale took the lead.

"I was going to say, that I hoped you could accept the fact that your mother and I have gotten back together."

Skyler picked up his napkin and dropped it into his lap. "It's not a matter of acceptance, it's a matter of...whether it should *be* at all."

Dale sat back. "That's a pretty defeatist attitude. Most children would love to see their parents get back together."

"Most children heard from their estranged father in the thirteen years since he left."

"I thought we were past that. I explained..."

Skyler waved his hand. "I know. I know. I'm sorry. Forget I said that. I am trying to move forward."

"But it's hard. I get it, Skyler. It was unforgiveable and I'll apologize as many times as it will take."

The waitress arrived and they asked for more time.

"Let's, uh, order our brunch first, huh, son? We can argue better on a full stomach."

Skyler ordered his go-to, Eggs Benedict, and Dale took the French toast. Once Skyler got some gulps of his hot coffee he settled in, forearms on the table. "Okay, Dad. So what brought all this on?"

"What do you mean? Your mother is still a very lovely and vibrant woman. I was attracted to her the moment I met her."

"Yes, but…there were other women, too."

To Dale's credit, his cheeks reddened. "I do regret my foolishness of the past. I was young and stupid, son. There's no other explanation that will suffice. I suppose it was also an ego thing. Maybe I had something to prove to myself. But I've grown out of it."

"*Can* you, Dad? Is that really something someone can grow out of?"

"All right, let me ask *you* something. Did you have a lot of…conquests?"

"What does that have to do with —?"

"Just answer the question."

Skyler looked around and scooted closer. Quietly, he said, "Well. Yes. Quite a few, if you must know. But I don't —"

Dale's brows rose. "Okay. And how about now?"

"Now? There's only Keith."

"There you go."

"Wait. When I had my 'conquests' —" and he added air quotes " —I didn't have a regular boyfriend. It's not the same thing."

"Isn't it? Didn't you have something to prove to yourself?"

It smacked him right between the eyes. *Did* Skyler have something to prove to himself? Keeping in the closet for so long he was glad to be able to cast open those doors in college. And after. Staying in the closet at work, he let his freak flag fly on the weekends and week nights at Trixx. And hooked up a *lot*. But it had seemed like simply a release valve for all those years he hid himself. When he had the chance, away from his mother, away from that life, he could finally be his whole self. He had thought he'd never settle down or even settle for one man. It certainly wasn't on his radar. And then Keith had come along.

"All right." He nodded. "I can *sort* of see where you're coming from. But weren't you supposed to sow those oats *before* settling down?"

Before he could answer, the waitress was back with their food. They both picked up forks and dug in. Skyler sighed at the buttery, lemony flavor of the hollandaise and scooped another generous portion of it on his egg and took another bite.

"That's how people are supposed to do it," said Dale, pouring syrup on his French toast slices. "But again. Young, stupid, and full of myself. Unable to realize—or maybe I talked myself out of—the hurt I was causing. Fooling myself, I guess. If she never found out, who was I hurting? It turned out a lot of people. And, of course, your mother isn't stupid. She did find out. And then there was leaving you out of my life." He cut the bread with sharp crossover slices with fork and knife.

"Which is why I'm concerned with this new development," said Skyler, setting down his knife. "I don't want Mom to get hurt. It took her a *long* time to recover."

Dale stopped slicing. His throat rolled from a hard swallow. "I know." His voice was harsh, pained. It almost made Skyler feel guilty. Almost.

Dale looked up. "I love her, son. I don't think I've ever stopped loving her. And I never imagined in a million years she'd give me another chance. But she did. Oh, she read me the riot act."

Good one, Mom.

"But I sure don't plan to step out of line. I know what I've been missing now. And believe me when I say, I don't want to screw it up."

"She said she didn't want to get married."

"Yeah, that kind of threw me. I asked her, you know."

Skyler's silverware clattered to the plate. "You what?"

"I asked her to marry me. What can I say? I'm an old-fashioned guy. She said she'd have none of it. Doesn't want it complicated if I...well, you know. Told me to move in. It wasn't my idea."

"Seriously?"

"Swear to God."

Skyler grabbed his mug and drank the hot coffee, letting it burn down his throat. Shit. His mother, so upright, so prudish. At least she used to be. Maybe she *could* take care of herself. He set the mug down. "I'm...wow."

"Me, too," muttered Dale, taking a bite of French toast dripping with syrup. "Your mother is quite a woman."

They ate in silence. Every time Skyler surreptitiously glanced at his father, Dale seemed to be glancing back at him.

Skyler licked the last of the hollandaise off the tines of his fork and set it down. He stared at his empty plate and took a deep breath. "Dad, can I talk to you about something kind of personal?"

"Anything." Dale dabbed at his lips with his napkin and picked up his mug the same way Skyler did his; hand wrapped around the hot ceramic instead of in the handle.

"I just found out... Well, it looks like Keith might...have a kid."

"Whoa. How did that...I mean is that even possible? He's..."

"I don't know the details. As a matter of fact, he doesn't know that I know. Yet."

"Oh."

"How do I handle this? I mean, I'm not ready to be a father let alone to a ten-year-old."

"So wait, wait. You know for a fact that Keith is the father?"

"Um...not really. But it's probably true."

"First, I would let Keith tell you all the pertinent information. And then I'd take a breath and think. For one, you're effectively the parent to — what? Something like two hundred kids a day?"

One side of his mouth hitched up in a smile. "It's not quite the same the thing."

"The hell it isn't. I know you aren't there 24/7, but then again, some parents aren't either, am I right? And I know you care about them. Weren't you always collecting the waifs in the neighborhood, those kids that never could seem to make friends?"

"I guess."

"Sure you were. I do remember that. You were so sweet. There's no other word for it. I used to call you Mother Hen. Do you remember that?"

"Oh yeah. I do remember that."

"So should this turn out to be true, I don't see you being anything less than up for the task. I mean Jesus, Skyler, you wrangle high school kids all day. What's harder than that?"

"Middle School kids." He shrugged. "But like you said, I don't know anything yet."

"When are you going to know? When are you going to ask him?"

"The thing of it is, I found out under...dubious circumstances."

"What does that mean?"

"I had a friend hack into his phone." Skyler winced before his dad exploded.

"Are you out of your mind?" Other diners turned to look and Dale lowered his voice. "That's an incredible breach of Keith's privacy."

"I know! Why do you think I've put off asking him?"

"Skyler! I thought better of you." He ticked his head.

Skyler shrank in his seat. "I had to do it. He wouldn't tell me what was bothering him. He kept saying he'd handle it."

"So now what? What if he never brings it up? Are you going to break into his private correspondence again?"

"No! I just..." He dropped his chin to his hand. "I already feel terrible for what I did. But this is something that affects me, too."

"Does it?"

"It can. What if he ends up paying child support? Or gets into a custody battle?"

"I'm sure he'd tell you then."

"I wouldn't be too sure. You don't know him. He can be real secretive when he wants to be."

"Then give it time, Skyler. He'll tell you when he's good and ready."

"But what if I — ?"

"Skyler, don't push him. He'll tell you when *he's* ready."

"This sucks."

"There's a lot about relationships that suck. There's a whole lot more that's good, though. Don't spoil what you have. Take it from me."

Skyler nodded. They argued over the bill. Dale finally wrenched it from Skyler's hand and they both walked to the cashier so that Dale could pay. Walking out together to the parking lot Dale grasped him in a hug again.

"Dad, you don't have to do that every time."

"I want to. And I owe you a lot of those."

Skyler chuckled. "Okay."

"Listen." He rested his hand on Skyler's shoulder. "Let Keith tell you. It's gotta be hard for him. It sounds like something he didn't expect, am I right?"

"Yeah. A complete surprise."

"Then let him tell you in his own way. He might be embarrassed, scared, confused."

"That's why I want to help him."

"And that's a wonderful thing. But sometimes the best help is to let him decide on his own what he's going to do."

"Sounds sensible."

"See? Your old man can come up with a few sensible things now and then."

"Right. I still don't think it's a good idea for you two to live together."

"Well…the thing of it is. It really isn't any of your business."

And suddenly, the mellow feelings he was getting from interacting with his father, from getting his sage advice, melted away. He tensed. "But that's just it. It *is* my business. Do you want to know what happens if you walk away again? *I* pick up the pieces. *I* take care of Mom, just as I always had, just as I had to when you left the *first* time."

"You are a piece of work. You catted around yourself. You just told me that. You know, there's nothing worse than a hypocrite."

"*I'm* not the hypocrite. I *know* what I was. And I wasn't married or with a boyfriend. There's a huge difference, you know. Or don't you?"

"Look, Skyler. I don't like that tone."

"You mean the truth hurts, doesn't it?"

Dale clamped his jaw and nodded. "Okay," he said tightly. "Baby steps. Thanks for going to brunch with me." He turned on his heel and headed for his car.

"That's it?" called Skyler after him.

Dale stopped and turned. "You aren't in the mood to listen to me. You're stuck in the past right now. And in the past is where you were hurt. I get it. But I don't have to stand here and take it. And by the way, I don't suppose it's occurred to you that there might be an Oedipal thing going on with you as well." Skyler snorted indignantly. "When you're willing to be civilized we'll talk again."

"Oh really?" he said in his bitchiest tone.

But his dad was already unlocking the car door and getting inside.

A car backing out honked and startled Skyler out of the way. He watched that car slide past him and then looked over the hood to where his dad was backing out of his parking space. He threw his hands up in surrender and retreated to the Bug.

When he got back to his apartment to change, Keith wasn't there, which was just as well. He wanted to complain about his father to someone but then he kept dwelling on Keith's possible fatherhood and decided he didn't want to get into it at all right now.

Instead, he looked over his notes for school, checked on the museum through the phone app (he forgot they had all decided to close it for the funeral so all was dark and undisturbed), got cleaned up and dressed in a charcoal gray suit, and headed over to Hillside Memorial Park on Alessandro.

He pulled into the main building with the other cars and walked to the front entrance. Lester's extended family was there, including Jerome...*and* that asshat Ethan. Why couldn't the man leave him at home? Skyler ignored the blond and moved into the crowd where he was met by Randi and Ron. He suddenly remembered that one of them had attacked him the other night. He tensed as they approached.

"Sucks, doesn't it?" said Ron quietly.

Skyler nodded, thrusting his hands into his trouser pockets, brooding about more than Lester. "Yeah."

"There's Jerome," said Randi. "For a minute there I thought that was you with him."

"No, that's his boyfriend."

Both docents stared at Skyler. "Boyfriend?" Randi whispered. "Since when is Jerome gay?"

"Bi. Since forever, I guess. But if it's any consolation, I didn't know either."

"Who's the dude with Jerome?" said Seth, coming up behind Skyler. "I thought it was Skyler for a minute."

"We were just talking about that," said Ron. "It's Jerome's *boyfriend*."

"Boyfriend? Dude's gay? Why didn't it ever come up?"

Randi snorted. "He's bi, apparently. And who knows with that guy? Oh." She chastened. "This is not the day for grousing. We're here for Lester."

Seth and Ron drifted off, speaking quietly together. Randi watched them go and then sidled closer to Skyler. "Skyler, I was thinking. I didn't want to say anything, but I feel that I should. The other day, I saw Seth spending a lot of time at the gift shop register. So later, I snuck over there and did a recount. It was more than twenty dollars off. But when I looked at the accounting at the end of the day, there was no discrepancy."

"Maybe you miscounted."

She shook her head. "I counted it the next day, and it was still off by twenty-five dollars."

Skyler sighed. Shoot. He didn't want it to be one of them. "Thanks, Randi," was all he said. She gave him a serious expression, nodded, and wandered away.

A hefty African American woman in her middle years approached, heading directly toward Skyler. "Are you Skyler Foxe?"

"Uh...yes."

"I'm Lila Williams, Lester's sister."

"Oh Ms. Williams." He took her hands and she squeezed his back. "I'm so sorry for your loss."

"Thank you. Mr. Foxe, Lester talked about you all the time. He loved his nieces and nephews dearly, but you were like the son he never had. He was so proud you were a teacher, you see, even at the same school he taught at for twenty years. Every time we had family gatherings we were always wondering who this white boy was he was always talking about." She laughed a deep chuckle. Skyler returned a bittersweet smile. "He told us you were over there for meals when Claudine was alive."

"They were so hospitable, so warm to me. And Lester helped me out financially with school."

"My brother was a good man."

"He certainly was."

"And I think the family would very much like for you to speak about Lester at the services. Oh, I know we didn't prepare you. Someone should have tried to contact you — Jerome at the very least." She turned her head and narrowed her eyes at him across the portico. "But my son is..." She shook her head. "The boy is a handful at times."

"Jerome's just very passionate."

She smiled bitterly. "Passionate. That's one word for it. Will you speak?"

"I'd be honored to."

Now Skyler was nervous. He didn't quite know what to say but he supposed a eulogy was about speaking from the heart. He could do that.

The funeral director gathered everyone inside where it was decidedly cooler. Skyler wasn't used to wearing a suit. He usually didn't for school, preferring something more casual, though he sometimes wore a tie.

The casket was at the front, laden with flowers all around it. It was made of polished wood so fine it could have been furniture. Skyler shuddered at the thought of such a thing being put into the ground.

Lester was laid out, head resting on the white pillow within. Skyler swallowed hard and made his way to the front, paying his respects with the others. It didn't quite look like Lester anymore. His skin was stretched unnaturally, but the mortuary techs did a decent job of repair and disguise. After all, he had had an autopsy.

Skyler stood over him and looked down sadly. *I'm so sorry this happened to you, Mr. Huxley. I won't let them get away with it.*

Once everyone had walked passed the casket and found their seats the funeral director introduced a pastor who made a beautiful speech about Lester. Everyone was crying. Skyler glanced surreptitiously at the docents. Did any of them look suspicious? Jerome was seated ahead of him. He seemed stoic but he was also wiping away a tear or two. If he was a murderer would he be so cool at such a place? It seemed cold-blooded indeed to sit at your own victim's funeral and shed crocodile tears for your own amusement.

Who had been in the museum? Who had attacked him? He couldn't be sure. It could have been any one of them, including Randi...and he felt disgusted that it could be any of them, but there was no other explanation.

Others stepped forward to speak. One of Lester's sisters was so overcome that she couldn't get out any words and was gently steered away from the podium, wailing and clutching her chest.

Then it was Jerome's turn. He looked a bit like a funeral director himself in his Sunday best, with a dark suit and tight tie. He walked up to the podium stiffly, his face bitter in its intensity.

"My uncle was murdered," he said in opening. People gasped. It wasn't that they didn't know, but for Jerome to say it so starkly and at such an occasion...

Skyler slid a glance toward the docents and Randi was shaking her head. She looked angry.

"It's true," Jerome went on. "But even though that is the cold hand on our hearts, today we are only speaking of the warmth that was Lester Huxley." The audience visibly relaxed. "I was close to my uncle. We worked together for many years at his beloved museum. But more than that, he spent a lot of time with me when I was growing up. When my own father died, he stepped in and was more than my uncle. We've heard stories today, funny stories, of my uncle's life. And that's what we celebrate today. We won't remember these darkest of days, but on the light, the joy he brought to us all." As with the other speakers, there was a murmur in the crowd when they agreed. To Skyler, it was similar to the call and response in a black church service.

Jerome concluded, and despite Skyler's misgivings, he thought he had done well in the end.

Lila Williams got up and talked about her brother in a fairly calm and florid manner. And when she stepped away, she pointedly looked at Skyler. He guessed he was up.

He rose. So far, he was the only white person to speak, besides the funeral director. And all eyes were definitely on him as he walked to the podium.

He cleared his throat. "Hello. Um, you don't know me, but I'm Skyler Foxe. I know Mr. Huxley told some of you about me..." He could feel the mourners' sigh of recognition. Some nodded encouragingly, smiling at him. He glanced at Jerome. He looked furious.

"And here I'm the only one calling him '*Mister* Huxley.'" He shook his head. "I've known him since I was thirteen and he gave me my first job, and to me he'll always be 'Mr. Huxley.' I don't know what he saw in me all those years ago. But he took me under his wing and nurtured me, taught me, even helped me through school. Maybe he saw a kindred spirit. I know I did. He knew I wanted to be a teacher and he used to tell me the funniest stories of when he taught at James Polk High. I'm sure you know the one about the school alarm." He didn't even have to tell the story. Everyone laughed. They all knew it well. Skyler smiled. "He was full of stories. Full of stories of history, which he loved. And you know, there was always a kind word for everyone. I don't think there was a soul Mr. Huxley didn't like."

His gaze drifted over the audience and fell on the docents. Randi's face was a mess of tears. Did that mean her guilt of regret? Or was it simply a sign of how much she cared about Lester?

Ron, too, frowned, wiping at his face. Was he capable of murder and had the nerve to sit there?

Seth's face was calm with tear streaks streaming down. He didn't even wipe at them. Mellow even in mourning, Seth didn't seem the type, but one never knew. Especially after what Randi said.

Skyler thought of the attack on him in the museum...and it suddenly gave him pause. They hadn't hit him or stabbed him or any other kind of violence. They could have easily killed him and left him there. But it was as if they had deliberately gone out of their way *not* to do him any harm. Was that the action of a murderer?

He swept his gaze over the docents again.

They hadn't hurt him! They hadn't tried to kill him! Maybe they *weren't* murderers.

His eyes searched for Jerome and found him.

Jerome, on the other hand, sat with his arms crossed tightly over his chest. His frown was deeply etched onto his features and his accusing eyes bore into Skyler's. He was angry. Was it because Skyler was speaking at his uncle's funeral? Did he think Skyler was supplanting him at the museum? But Lester himself had told the board that he didn't think Jerome was suited to replacing him...and that really didn't make sense. Unless he *was* the one stealing.

Next to him sat Ethan. He wasn't even looking at Skyler. He looked bored. *What an asshole!*

When Skyler looked up to the rest of the people in the pews, he suddenly realized he hadn't spoken in a while. "Well," he said, clearing his throat again, "I guess I can conclude with my gratitude for Mr. Huxley taking me in, for being the kind of mentor I needed. He will be sorely missed."

Skyler stepped down and the funeral director asked if anyone wanted to visit the deceased one more time before the graveside service.

Row by row, people rose again to pay their respects.

Skyler followed suit and then trailed outside with the rest of them. He stood off by himself, gathering his thoughts, not only about Lester and what he meant to Skyler, but about the docents...and Jerome. When he rose from his thoughts, Seth was standing before him.

"Skyler, what you said was real nice. So I hope you don't mind..." He looked around and got in close, whispering. "Dude, something's got to be done. I know it's not going to be your problem soon, but that only means we'll be especially fucked." He gave another look around. "It's Randi, dude. I just don't think she can be trusted."

You've got to be kidding me, he thought, sagging. "What do you mean?"

"Dude's in need of money bad. I didn't want to say anything, but we've been twenty dollars short at the gift shop register every time she worked it. I keep covering for her but I can't afford it anymore. I spent a hundred bucks of my own money last week. I can't keep doing it, man."

"You shouldn't have to. Did you talk to her?"

"I mentioned that maybe she needs to count more carefully and she got all cranky at me about it. You gonna take care of things, Sky?"

Seth seemed sincere...but then again, so had Randi. He shrugged. "I'll do my best."

Seth gave him a nod and hurried away to meet up with Ron again.

Great. Two inconsistent stories, implicating each other. Who was he to believe?

"Well that was a load."

Skyler jerked. He hadn't been paying attention to the people around him and Ethan had swooped in and cornered him.

"That speech you gave, I mean. Just full of sugar."

"I really don't want to talk to you."

"Yeah, I know." But the man stubbornly stood his ground.

"Look. Lester was a pretty well-loved man. Can you just forget you know me for the next hour and be a human being?"

"Who's not being a human being? I'm not the one keeping secrets from my boyfriend. Oops." He put his hand coyly to his mouth. "I wasn't supposed to say anything. Keith didn't want me to."

Skyler got into his face. "Did he pay you off? Are you going to stop bothering us? Did your blackmail work?"

"Oh. I see he told you."

"Yeah, I know about it," he lied. But this guy didn't deserve the truth. "And it doesn't bother me one bit. Keith and I love each other."

"How disgustingly sweet. And no he didn't pay me. But he needs to. Or the school principal and the school district will hear about his indiscretion. And then maybe the local news will be interested, too. I can see the headline: *Gay Man Knocks Up Girl, Abandons Both.*"

Skyler balled his fist and lifted it. "You little shit! If you think you can ruin his life you've got another thing coming."

Ethan stared at Skyler's fist. "You gonna use that? Come on, pretty boy. I can take you." Ethan leapt back, throwing off his jacket.

Skyler saw red. He was about to tear his own off when Jerome jumped in between them.

"What the hell is this?" But his anger was mostly directed toward Skyler.

Skyler gestured toward Ethan who was smirking at him on the other side of Jerome. "This guy is a…a…" he choked out.

"I don't care what this is about. This is my uncle's goddammed funeral. I want you to leave, Skyler."

That brought him up short. "What? It's not my fault, it's his!"

"I don't care. Leave!"

"But the graveside…"

"Do I have to throw you out?"

Jerome's eyes were wild. They glistened with raw emotion and tears. Skyler blinked at him and realized that this was a fight not worth waging. Whether he was faking it or not, they were making a scene and it didn't belong here.

He looked around and people were staring disapprovingly. He lowered his head in shame. Without another word, Skyler stomped away and headed toward his Bug. He slapped himself into the seat, started the car with shaking fingers, and pulled away down the curving road toward home.

Chapter Twelve

DURING THE BRIEF RIDE HOME SKYLER COULD barely contain his anger. He gripped the steering wheel so tightly he was afraid to crack it and eased off.

But when he parked in front of the old Victorian he called home, he simply sat there. He hadn't even been allowed to be at the graveside. He felt humiliated at the scene he had made, and for what? He had fallen right into Ethan's hands, letting him escalate the situation until Jerome had had no choice. But now Ethan was threatening Keith's very livelihood. What the hell was he going to do?

He got out his phone and dialed Sidney but he got her voicemail. She was probably out of town with Mike. He didn't want to bother her and so he didn't leave a message. Should he call Jamie? Rodolfo? Jamie at least knew the situation but he didn't feel like talking to him about it.

He stared out his windshield a few moments more before he unbuckled the seatbelt and slithered out of the car.

He had barely gotten to the sidewalk when another car pulled up. Great. His mom *and* his dad.

He took off his jacket as they parked and got out.

"Skyler, I want to talk to you." His mother marched up to him and crossed her arms over her chest. She was in that immovable posture he knew all too well and he sighed wearily. This was going to take a while.

"Yes, Mother."

"Your father just told me what you said to him. Honestly! You are just going to have to get over it."

"Mom, do we have to have this discussion right now…"

"Yes. Your father is now back in my life. I know that this may be difficult for you. You spent most of your childhood and adulthood taking care of me, seeing that I had enough money and love, and you did a splendid job. Maybe I let you do too much, and that's *my* fault. But I *can* do this on my own."

"But you're not. You're leaning on Dad again."

"I'm not leaning on anyone. Dammit, Skyler!"

"Mom!" His mother *never* swore. He looked around. "Can't we take this inside instead of airing our dirty laundry on the street?"

"No we will not. I don't care who knows." She turned to face different directions and announced, "I'm shacking up with my ex-husband! And we aren't even married! Did you all hear that?"

Skyler froze, shocked.

Dale was blushing and he gently laid his hands on Cynthia's shoulders. "Cyn, maybe we should take it inside."

"Is every family member a wimp? The two of you! Look, I'm together. I've got this. I'm free as a bird and I choose to live with your father. And I don't want you bad-mouthing him anymore or trying to talk me out of it, is that clear, mister?"

Skyler nodded, feeling properly disciplined. "Yes, Mom."

"Good! That's all we came to say." She turned but then came back. "You look very nice in that suit. I take it you just came from poor Mr. Huxley's funeral."

"Yes."

"Well…" She patted his chest before taking him into a hug. It felt good. He hadn't realized under all the rage how forlorn he had been under the skin. He inhaled her perfume, felt her strong arms around him, and sank into it. She pulled back, kissed his cheek, and nodded. "Come on, Dale."

"Yes, ma'am," he answered. He gave Skyler a look that seemed to say, "You don't have to worry about your mother." And for once, Skyler agreed.

She was as good as her word and got back into the driver seat of the car. Maybe his mom *was* the driver now. He had a whole new admiration for her.

He watched them drive off, flung the suit jacket over his shoulder, and trudged up the stairs.

Keith was there, and he turned when Skyler opened the door.

"I didn't expect you back for a while." He was switching off his phone. No doubt the asshat *Ethan* had given him an update.

"My visit there was cut unexpectedly short. *Ethan* was there."

Keith rose. "What did he say to you?"

"He riled me up. I was kicked out."

"Skyler…"

"I'm all right. Just… And then my mom and dad confronted me outside."

Keith looked toward the door. "Are they coming in?"

"No. They just came over to tell me to get over myself. And I think…I have. My mom can take care of things."

"Oh." Keith stood uncomfortably. "Want to talk about it?"

"No." He plopped down to the sofa, slapping his jacket over the back. "Why is it all so hard? No one tells you it's going to be so hard."

"What is, sweetheart?" Keith sank to the sofa beside him.

"Life! Relationships. Someone needs to offer a class."

"No kidding. But if it's any consolation, we're all in the same boat. No one's mastered it yet."

"I'm not even close to mastering it."

He leaned in to Skyler and kissed his head. "All I know is that I love you and I'd do anything for you."

Skyler looked up. Keith wore a tender expression, and despite the secrets they still kept hidden from one another, Skyler was never in doubt of those sentiments. "Me, too," he said softly.

They sat quietly for some time. Amazingly, Skyler felt more relaxed in Keith's presence. The man did that to him. Made him feel…at home.

Keith smiled. "Looks like your folks are making a fresh start. What about you? Where do you want to be in five years?"

Skyler chuckled. "What is this, an interview?"

"No. But like them, we're still learning about one another and I wondered…"

"Well okay." Skyler laid his head back against the sofa's warm leather. "In five years, I expect to be Teacher of the Year — several years running and oh-so-very-tenured that I won't have to worry about those damned pink slips. They can't get rid of me until they pry my Folger's edition of the Complete Works of William Shakespeare from my cold dead hands."

Keith chuckled. "Well…actually, I was thinking more about…us."

"What do you mean? Where do *you* expect to be in five years…except *five* times CIF champions?"

"That, too. But, well, for one, I expect to be…married."

Skyler shot upright. "*Married*? To whom?"

"To you, you little idiot."

Skyler stopped thinking altogether. And, apparently, breathing.

"Breathe, Skyler," said Keith. He lost that tender expression, replaced by one of hurt. "It's not an unreasonable expectation, you know. I mean, I know that we sort of rushed things in the beginning. That's on me, I'm afraid. I just…get attached very quickly. We haven't been together quite a year yet and now we live together. That's a little accelerated even for me. But I would hope…" He looked at Skyler and took his hand. Skyler knew that his hand was clammy and hoped Keith didn't notice. "I would hope," Keith went on, "that after five years together you might think you can spend the rest of your life…with me."

Was Keith proposing? Skyler tried to slow his breathing, his heartbeat. No, no. He thought back over Keith's words. He seemed to be just speculating. But it also seemed as if he was giving Skyler the heads up…or was it more of an ultimatum?

Skyler slowly took back his hand. "It's…it's not that. I just…I don't know that I even want to get married. I know I said I wasn't against it but I just don't think it's for me. I mean look at my parents. They tried it once. It didn't work. Now they're back together and my mother doesn't want anything to do with it. Some people aren't designed for that kind of emotional commitment. And then finances get tangled together and people argue over money and how it should be spent and then they get hurt."

"Like your folks," said Keith.

Skyler brooded for a moment before he blurted, "My dad told me I have an Oedipus complex. You don't think that's it, do you?"

"Well…"

"Oh my God, you do!"

"I don't know if you do or you don't. But it was just you and your mom for a long time and you did take care of her and here is your dad suddenly showing up supplanting you… It could be something like that."

"Oh Jesus. I do, don't I? Isn't that just another swell thing in the Life of Skyler Foxe."

"Skyler, it's a good thing that you care about your mother. You should. But it's also a good thing to maybe give your dad a break. Let them work it out. See what happens. It doesn't have to end in disaster." His eyes darted earnestly back and forth across Skyler's face. "I know when *you* think of marriage you envision your parents. But when *I* think of marriage, I see *mine*. Happy together for over forty years. I want that. It took a while for your dad to come around. Maybe they'll have that. And I'm hoping that with time, you'll change your mind and we can, too."

"And…if I don't?"

"Well…we'll play it by ear. Things, circumstances change. You never thought you'd have a boyfriend, after all. But I will always love you…even if your love fades."

He scooted to the edge of the sofa. "It won't fade! I never meant *that*. Keith, I love you. I really do. I never said that to any man before and I can't see saying it to any other man ever. I love *you*. I promise I do."

"'I promise I do.' And *that's* what a wedding is, my friend." He touched Skyler on the tip of his nose to punctuate it. He started walking toward the kitchen when Skyler called after him.

"Keith, can't we just go on like this? What's wrong with what we've got now?"

Keith stopped and took a deep breath. Without turning, he replied, "Nothing. Nothing at all, Skyler."

Skyler watched him go with trepidation. What was all this out of the blue? Oh God, did Keith want to propose because he *did* have a kid?

It seemed like a very long weekend. Keith acted perfectly normal…on the outside, but there was still some kind of shadow on the inside. Was it because of the child issue or because of the marrying issue? Skyler didn't know and now he didn't want to ask. Why was he so squeamish about getting married? He approved of it in general. Especially for his parents. And why was he being such a prude about that? They were married once. But now they weren't. It just didn't seem right when it was his own parents. His dad was right, though. He *was* a hypocrite. Yet it seemed different for him, "catting" around as his father put it. *He* wasn't married… And then it all rolled around back to Keith again.

Skyler was twenty-six years old. He was too young for such a thing. Of course, Keith was now thirty-six. Maybe he was feeling that time was a-wastin'.

He wanted to put it out of his mind. He tried to concentrate on his lesson plans, adding Post-It Notes to flag some rough patches. He even sat on the floor, surrounded by the books he was going to teach from this year. He picked up one paperback after the other, going over the Post-Its colorfully arrayed in his copies. He thought he was finally making some headway when Keith appeared in front of him.

"Feel like breaking for dinner? I was going to ask an hour ago but you looked so deeply into it."

"Oh." Skyler glanced at the clock. Eight o'clock on a Sunday night. It was one more week before school. One more week of the museum. One more week to find a killer. "I guess this is as good a time as any."

Keith offered him a hand to help him up. He took it and stood next to him. There was nothing wrong with Keith. He was everything Skyler thought of as the ideal man; strong, sophisticated, a fantastic lover...though maybe a wee bit needy emotionally.

Skyler smiled. "What did you have in mind for dinner?"

A knock on the door, followed by someone jabbing the doorbell. He exchanged glances with Keith and went to the door. Looking through the keyhole he smiled and threw it open. "Hey Sidney, Mike."

Sidney bounded in. He'd never seen her so energetic before. She was clutching Mike's hand and he was grinning from ear to ear.

"I couldn't wait to come over. I didn't want to call," she said. She was actually bubbly. Was she high?

"Okay," he said with a laugh, her good spirits infectious. "What's up, you guys?"

She thrust out her hand and wiggled her fingers. Skyler didn't know what he was supposed to see for a full three seconds until...there it was. A ring. On her left ring finger.

"We went to Vegas!" she cried. "And we *got married*!"

Chapter Thirteen

KEITH MOVED IN FIRST, SHAKING MIKE'S HAND and then hugging Sidney.

But Skyler couldn't move. He knew his jaw was hanging open but he was helpless to do anything about it.

Sidney faced him with a grin and held out her arms. But instead of hugging her, he blinked. He should have been overjoyed for her but he felt instead a pang of betrayal. "You didn't tell me. You...you always said...and I wasn't there..."

"Oh, come here, Skyboy." She closed him in a hug and Skyler felt her arms around him, her long hair tangling in his face. "I would have. But it was such a sudden thing," she said in his ear. "Mike and I went off to Vegas for a weekend getaway, and then we got to talking about his family and what we wanted, and we just...decided! You know I always wanted you to be a part of it and you still can be. We're going to throw a big party for the guys at the station and the SFC." She drew back and looked him in the eye. "Will you throw me my party? You're my best man, after all? *And* my maid of honor."

"You got married," he said.

"I think he's in shock. Skyler? Are you in there?" She knocked on his forehead.

He grabbed her hand and pulled it away. "I *am* in shock. I'm...really surprised."

"So were we. We had a really nice little ceremony. It wasn't an Elvis one or anything. Small and tasteful. Well, as tasteful as you can get for Vegas."

"We even won at the slots," said Mike. "It paid for everything."

Skyler looked from one to the other. He suddenly realized what a jerk he was being and pulled Sidney in again. "You got married. I'm so happy for you. You are happy, aren't you?"

"Deliriously."

He turned to Mike and grabbed him into a hug. "My brother-in-law!"

Mike laughed. "Thanks, Skyler."

He held them each by the arm. "You guys! I'm really, really happy for you. Mike, is this going to be all right with your folks?"

"My folks will be pissed we didn't have a big Catholic wedding but they'll be fine about it. I'll have some aunts and uncles who won't be thrilled—"

"But fuck 'em!" said Sidney with a flick of her hand.

"Have you guys eaten? Keith and I were about to do something about dinner. We should go out!"

They all agreed on a slightly upscale restaurant. Skyler changed his clothes, thinking to himself that he was happy for Sidney. He'd never seen her as happy as she was right now. Even with the specter of marriage hanging over his own head, he was glad it worked out for his friend. What a turn of events! He never would have guessed they'd go away for a heart to heart talk and come back husband and wife.

He emerged from the bedroom, cologned and changed. Sidney was hugging Fishbreath. After all, it had been her cat. If Mike hadn't been so allergic to him, they'd still be cat owners. "How's my sweetie?" she said in a baby voice. "Mommy's got a new Daddy. Wave to Daddy." She waved the cat's paw to Mike. But he was beginning to look like he had reached his limit of cat hair, and she put the fat tabby down. "Let's go," she said, shaking out her clothes and leading the way out the door.

"Should we call the SFC?" asked Skyler, following her down the stairs.

"Naw. Tonight it's just you and me."

Warmth radiated throughout his chest. After all, it had been him and Sidney from the very first.

They got to the restaurant, waited only a few minutes, and were seated.

Sidney regaled them on stories of the strip and their gambling attempts at poker and craps.

"Turns out I'm a slots guy," said Mike.

Skyler burst out laughing, followed by Sidney. Keith laughed into his hand.

"Oh, shit. I didn't mean it like that. You guys all have filthy minds."

They ate, drank two bottles of wine, and stayed long after the staff wanted to close their doors. It wasn't until someone from the restaurant brought out a vacuum and began on the carpets that they decided they should probably leave.

In the parking lot, Skyler hugged Sidney tightly again. "You did it, bitch."

"I know. I'm a lawfully married woman. How the fuck did that happen?"

"Are you Sidney de Guzman now?"

"Hell no!"

Mike looked at her askance.

"That is to say," she amended, blowing him a kiss. "I don't wish to change my name. Hey, I worked hard to make detective, the first woman in the department, and I'd like to keep that name. We'll see what the future holds. And for you, too, Skyboy."

Skyler's smile faded. "What does that mean?"

She glanced once at Keith. "It means maybe I'll be tossing *you* the bouquet next."

Keith took Skyler's shoulders and steered him toward the truck. "I don't think Skyler's quite ready for that."

He couldn't disagree. But he didn't want to reinforce the strained look on Keith's face when it had been so carefree before. So he said nothing. He waved to Sidney and Mike, got into the truck, and sat next to Keith silently as they headed home.

Sidney called the next morning as he was getting ready to shower. "Aren't you supposed to be on your honeymoon?" he asked.

"In a few months. We have to put in for the time off."

"How did everyone at work take the news?"

"Are you kidding? It's suddenly like a frat party here. Even the captain smuggled in some beer. And it's only nine o'clock. I hope the criminals take it easy today because none of us want to chase them down right now."

"Oh, so noted. Today is a good day to rob a bank."

"But seriously, Skyler. I know we took you by surprise. You were a deer in the headlights for sure. And it sort of looked like you and Keith…well, like you were having a similar discussion? Just by the looks on your faces."

Skyler settled into his wing chair, stroking the cat with his bare foot. Fishbreath rolled over, offering his tummy for a rub. "I don't know what you mean."

"Skyler, Skyler, Skyler. You're a terrible liar."

"I'm not lying about anything. But just say, hypothetically…"

"Yeah, hypothetically…"

"What would have happened if *you* wanted to get married and Mike hadn't?"

"Well, if you want the truth, I couldn't see us staying together."

Skyler's breath hitched. "Why not? You love each other, right? Isn't *that* what it's all about?"

She sighed. "No, it's more than that. If you had told me this a few years ago, I wouldn't have believed it. I always thought living together was just as good as being married. But once you marry, you make that commitment—I mean *really* commit, with paperwork and everything. It *is* different. I *feel* different. That we've crossed some sort of threshold. Skyler, there's nothing like this feeling. Mike and I are looking down a long road of our lives together and there's a future there."

He'd been listening intently and spoke in the same soft tone. "Wow. I never heard you wax poetic like that before."

"I never felt poetic like that before."

"But…you love him. Are you saying that you'd fall *out* of love with him if he didn't want to get married?"

She paused. "It means we don't want the same things. It means we're on different paths. How could we stay together after that?"

"Oh God."

"What? What have you done, Skyler?"

"I didn't do anything," he said petulantly. "Why am I always the bad guy?"

"Skyler?"

"So okay. Keith mentioned that—down the road, mind you—he might want to, you know, get married."

"And you fucked it up and said you didn't."

"Yeah, but we…we love each other…"

"Maybe for some that's good enough. But you said he wants kids."

He might have them already, he thought bitterly.

"He wants the life his parents had," she went on.

"But we're gay! We don't have to have that life."

"But now you can. Not all gay men are alike. Some don't want that hetero lifestyle with marriage and kids and a white picket fence. But some do. Some heteros don't want it and it's perfectly fine. But you both have to be on the same page for it to last."

Skyler chewed on a nail. His eyes scanned the room of football trophies mixed with framed prints of Black Motown musicians, wingchair and recliner, weight set and china set. He and Keith already blended. It wasn't even a year and they seemed to mesh. "Sid," he said in a small voice, "what am I gonna do?"

"You don't have to decide right now."

"I guess."

"Do the Dear Abby test if you're worried about it."

"What's that?"

"It's normally about women divorcing their spouses but the test is this: Are you better off *with* him or *without* him?"

"With him," he answered without thinking. "But I'm with him now and we aren't m-married."

She sighed. "My fucked-up little friend. You're going to have to think about this, and when I say 'think' I don't mean 'obsess'."

"Too late," he said, before hanging up.

The week cranked on. Skyler worried over Seth's story and Randi's assertions. Who was right? He kept an eagle eye on them both, particularly when they were near the cash register. Wednesday, Skyler and Jamie returned to the self-defense class and learned new escape techniques, which Skyler promptly urged Keith to try. How was it he had success in class but with Keith it was impossible?

And he would have liked those techniques to work if only to wrench a discussion out of him. He still refused to say anything and Skyler was left dangling, wondering what the hell was going on. Jamie's persistent questions on the subject were certainly wearing Skyler down. How did Keith do it, hold out on him like that?

Every night, Skyler watched the museum app relentlessly, obsessively, but nothing else happened. No midnight visitors when he looked later at the recorded video. Had the thief stopped now that the jig was up? And he hadn't heard back from his eBay message either. In fact, the page was deleted and the name on it couldn't be found anywhere on the site.

On Thursday, Ron entered the museum office where Skyler was multi-tasking between museum business and school prep. "I have some receipts. Can I get a reimbursement check?"

Skyler opened the drawer and reached for the checkbook folder before he realized that Lester had said they were out of checks and Skyler hadn't ordered any. "Shoot, Ron. There aren't any more checks…" But as he opened the cover, the spiral-bound checkbook was full of them. "Oh," he said. Since Skyler's name was also on the account, he took the receipt, wrote out a check, marked it in the ledger, and handed Ron the paper. "Here you go."

Ron hesitated. "It's just not gonna be the same without Lester."

"Yeah, I know."

"Listen, Skyler. With all that's going on, I didn't want to say anything…"

Oh Jesus, now what?

"…but just the other day," Ron continued, "I noticed Seth kind of standing near the exhibits and messing on his phone. He's a mellow guy, so I didn't bother him about it. Whatever floats his boat, right? But he kept on doing it. You know, looking at the exhibits and checking his phone. So I walked over casually and glanced over his shoulder, and he had an eBay page up and was checking Civil War stuff. I don't want to accuse anyone, but with the thefts…I thought you should know."

"It could be perfectly innocent."

"Oh, yeah, totally. But…I thought you should know."

"Thanks."

That was two against Seth. Dammit. He didn't want it to be him. He didn't want it to be any of them.

Skyler slowly closed the checkbook when remembered he had his own reimbursements to receive. He dug out the receipts from the drawer where Lester had put them. It was a decent amount this time. Usually they were small amounts for and often he had told Lester to forget about it. But Lester was always insistent that the museum should pay the docents back. He opened the checkbook, marked it in the ledger, and wrote himself a check. He tucked it away into his wallet and slid the checkbook back into the drawer.

He stared at the far wall of the office, hung with old black and white pictures of the construction of the shrine. Men in shirtsleeves, suspenders, and soft hats, stood looking at the camera, leaning on shovels and picks. Mustachioed gentlemen from days gone by. And now Lester was one of them, men to be remembered only in old photographs. Except that Skyler would always remember and honor him. And one of the concrete ways he could honor his memory was to find out who killed him. He had been certain that his last week at the museum would not only turn up a thief but also a murderer. It baffled him that it hadn't been so simple, but even with Ron and Randi's accusations, the trail was grower colder by the day.

"Sidney," he asked her later at home over the phone, "have there been any more leads on Lester's death?"

"I wish I could tell you there were. But we just can't find any direction to go in."

"This sucks, Sid. We can't let his murderer go free!" And then he asked what he hadn't wanted to. "Did you talk to Jerome?"

"Let's just call him a hostile witness for now."

"No help there? Was he at the Bowl that night?"

"Yup, but so were all our suspects."

"You gotta be kidding me."

"Nope. I never thought I'd be saying this, but if you've got any ideas I'd like to hear them."

"What about Ethan?"

"As a murderer?"

Hmm. Skyler only meant about why Ethan was here at all. He hadn't thought of that possibility before. What would be the motivation and in such a deliberate and premeditated way? "I wasn't thinking of that but…yeah, what about him?"

"He's living in Redlands, all innocently as far as I can tell. He has a job and probably just found out about you and Keith accidentally like I said."

"Where does he live?"

"Uh-uh. Nothing doing."

"Come on, Sidney!"

"No! I will not be responsible for you committing a felony. Just leave the guy alone."

"But he's a blackmailer!"

He slapped his hand over his mouth. He really hadn't meant to say that.

"Say what?"

"Um…nothing?"

"Skyler. What. Did. You. Say?"

He paused for an entire three seconds before it all came tumbling out. "He threatened Keith, tried to blackmail him. He was going to tell the school district that Keith had a kid out of wedlock and abandoned it."

"*What*? Wait a second. Keith has a kid?"

"Possibly."

"Well, what did he say about it?"

"He…hasn't said anything about it. Yet. He, uh, doesn't know that I know."

"And just how is it that *you* know without *his* knowing you know?"

"I had Jamie swipe his phone and hack into his texts."

He held the phone away from his ear as the tirade spilled out. He heard choice phrases like "fucking ridiculous" and "what the cunt?" and "shitting privacy". The highlights.

Finally, he brought the phone gingerly back to his ear and yelled, "Sid! Stop talking a minute. Jeez, the phone is gonna melt."

"I cannot believe you, Skyler."

"Yeah, well, it's probably a new low for me. But he was looking pretty stressed and I'd never seen him like that. And he wouldn't talk to me about it, Sidney."

"What's he gonna say when he finds out?"

"I…don't know. I don't want to think about that. But we are all missing the bigger picture here. A kid. Keith. This Ethan Crapfest."

"I don't know what to tell you, Skyboy. I guess you're gonna be a daddy before you're a bride."

"It's not funny. This is a huge upheaval in our lives. I'm not ready for it, Sidney."

"Not ready for what?" said Keith, walking through the bedroom.

Skyler startled and tried to recover. "Not ready for…Sidney…and…her shenanigans. Heh. So good-bye, Sidney."

"Chickenshit!" she called before he clicked off.

"That was Sidney," said Skyler, thumbing toward his phone.

"Yeah, I gathered that. I'm an FBI agent, remember?" He winked.

"We were talking about her party. The one I'm throwing them next Saturday. So…so, Keith!" He followed him into the closet. Keith was shedding his coach clothes and getting into tank top and shorts.

"Yeah?"

"Is there any more news about Ethan? About what he wants?"

Keith frowned. He yanked his shorts up and zipped. "I told you if I found out anything I'd let you know."

"I know but it's almost been two weeks…"

He turned to Skyler with a closed expression. "I said I'd tell you."

Drooping, Skyler nodded. "Yeah. You said that."

But as the days went on, Keith didn't say anything. And no murderers were discovered. But there were also no new thefts. The only good thing to come out of it — he supposed it was good — was that Jerome had returned to work. No fanfare, no apologies. He just dug into work and never mentioned the upheaval.

On Friday, Skyler's last day, Denise Suzuki arrived near five o'clock. The docents shut the door and stood around her in the rotunda. All of them were there. Randi had brought a little cake from the local bakery to wish Skyler well in his new school year.

"I see there's a celebration going on," said Denise.

Randi grabbed a small plate and offered Denise a slice, which she declined. "We thought we all needed something to cheer about," said Randi.

"I see. Well, here's one more thing. After some consideration, the board has chosen a replacement for Lester Huxley. Congratulations…Ron Harper."

Everyone gasped. But instead of congratulating Ron, they all glanced toward Jerome.

"I see," said Jerome and a visibly abashed Ron. "I can't believe you'd do this."

"Mr. Williams," Denise began.

He shook his head and backed toward the door. "I don't know what's going on, but I'm going to get to the bottom of it."

They watched him slam the doors open and stomp out. That was a strange exit line, considering, thought Skyler, but he figured that this time, it was the last time Jerome would be back.

Chapter Fourteen

THE FIRST DAY OF SCHOOL WAS AS CHAOTIC AS last year, and Skyler was knee-deep in confused students, a down computer network, and general turmoil. He had no time to think about the museum, thieves or murderers, and had to place it on the backburner in favor of his current situation at school. Skyler was so busy, in fact, that he skipped lunch and wolfed down a Powerbar instead as he worked on his files manually.

When sixth period finally rolled around and his new juniors trudged in, he smiled. His favorite class of students. He felt he could finally relax a little.

All the usual suspects were there: Amber and Heather, of course; and Alex and his boyfriend Rick; Heather's boyfriend and football player Drew; Stewart, whose scraggly blond hair was even more scraggly and his scrappy goatee was trying to flourish. He'd had a rough patch when his mom came out unexpectedly about six months ago, but he seemed to be doing better.

And even über-Christian Becky had signed up for his class. Maybe she couldn't get into another comp class, or maybe she really did like Skyler despite his sin of Sodom.

And finally, in came the newest football star. Elei Sapani was a big girl; broad shouldered, big arms and thighs, a wide flat face with a shower of dark, kinked hair spilling down past her shoulders.

Despite her status as new school celebrity, she seemed shy, almost embarrassed by the figure she cut, and she sidled into the aisles, head down, books clutched hard to her side like a football in play.

"Welcome everyone to the new school year! Some of you know me but I do see quite a few new faces. I'm Mr. Foxe and I am proud and pleased to be your comp teacher. I know it doesn't feel like it now. It only feels like one more class you have to take to get through high school, but I can assure you that in *my* class, we are going to do far more than that!"

"That's for sure," quipped Rick from his usual spot in the front and center of the classroom. The others laughed.

"I'm not certain I want to know what you mean by that, Mr. Flores, but we will have a good time and learn something, too. It's about communicating. And to that end, I think we should all introduce ourselves."

The class moaned.

"I know it sounds lame, but we're all going to get to know each other well in this class. It isn't just a heads-down-let-me-do-my-work-and-please-god-don't-let-him-call-on-me sort of class. My by-word is 'class participation', even as we write our compositions. And a composition is all about clearly communicating your ideas. So let us begin. Amber, will you start us off?"

Amber, only too happy to in a preppy skirt and blouse ensemble, jumped to her feet and faced the class, her red hair in pony tails bobbing. "I'm Amber Watson, and I'm running for Student Council again—"

"Hey, Watson," said Rick, "no political speeches, eh?"

The class laughed, settling in.

She blushed and frowned at Rick. "I wasn't doing that. I was just telling about myself. I was sophomore secretary last year, and I was on the dance committee, and now I'm running for Junior Secretary, and this year's dance committee, and I'm also on the cheerleading squad." She sat, satisfied.

Stewart was behind her and looked up awkwardly. "I don't have to stand, do I?"

"No, Mr. Richardson," said Skyler. "Whatever feels comfortable."

"Um, okay. I'm Stewart. Hi." He waved. "I'm a shredder when it comes to skating and I'm a BAMF when it comes to gaming." He bowed when some applauded.

It went around the room and landed on a new student. Skyler couldn't help but shoot a glance toward Amber.

The boy with the tan skin tones and dark hair rose. He was lank, like most of his fellow teens, but he seemed poised in his stylishly threadbare t-shirt, skinny jeans, and Muk Luk Cade sneakers. He adjusted his glasses. "I'm Ravi Chaudhri," he said, with just the slightest of an Indian accent. "I'm an English major and I like to write. So though this isn't a creative writing class, I've heard about Mr. Foxe and the fun kids have had in his classes, so I'm looking forward to it." He sat. Several boys exchanged looks and rolled-eyes.

Amber seemed enchanted and Heather had to poke her in the shoulder to stop staring. Skyler noted that Ravi viewed *her* out of the corner of his own eye.

More students introduced themselves, some sullenly, some with a certain level of enthusiasm until it eventually moseyed to Drew. He never moved from his slouched position in his desk but to raise his hand straight up above his head and give a shaka gesture. "Drew O'Connor, wide receiver, number nineteen on the football team. Go Panthers!"

Students whooped and pounded their desks.

Alex sighed when it came to him in the back of the room. "Uh, Alex Ryan. Number forty-nine on the Panther's team."

He received a subdued response but Amber clapped loudly.

And finally it came to Elei. She seemed hesitant until Skyler gave her an encouraging smile. She stood and seemed to keep on climbing higher. Yup, she was taller than Skyler.

"Hey. I'm Elei Sapani. I'm new to this school. My family moved here from Hawaii…"

"Dude," said Rick. "Why'd you leave Hawaii to come to the crappy Inland Empire?"

She shrugged. "I don't know. They wouldn't let me play on the team in Hawaii, but I'm on the team now. Football. Um, number fifteen, wide receiver." She waved to Drew, who gave her the thumbs up. "Me and Drew and Alex are all on the same team and I'm happy to be able to play." She looked around sheepishly. "That's it, I guess."

"Are you Hawaiian?" asked Stewart.

"No. I'm Samoan. That's like twenty-five hundred miles from Hawaii to American Samoa."

"Whoa," said Rick. "That's like a whole United States away."

"Very good, Mr. Flores," said Skyler.

Alex made a muttered comment from the back of the room and Skyler raised his chin. "What was that, Alex?"

"Nothing, Mr. Foxe."

"He said, that she should have stayed in Hawaii," said Tyler, a boy with long brown hair and a smug expression.

Everyone turned toward Alex.

He seemed as if he had been simmering...and then finally exploded. "Well she should've. Girls don't belong on a football team!"

"Alex!" said Skyler.

The room erupted in shouts and put downs. Some were on Alex's side, but most were on Elei's.

Elei shrunk down in her seat, arms tight over her chest, shaking her head. She wouldn't look back at Alex.

Skyler tried to quiet everyone. "Anyone has the right to be on the team, Alex, as long as they can fulfill their roles. It doesn't matter who they are."

"That's not true, Mr. Foxe," he said. His face was reddening. "She can play okay but she wasn't the best. I think Coach just picked her cause he wants all this equality crap."

Skyler was speechless, but not so much for the students.

"Alex Ryan, you sexist fucktard," said Heather.

Skyler nearly choked. "Ms. Munson! We don't call people names in here...and we especially use a better choice of vocabulary."

"Sorry, Mr. Foxe. But I call 'em like I see 'em."

"Alex, dude," said Drew, twisting in his seat to stare back at the angry teen. "You gotta get over it. Elei is great. She's dope on the field. Even you could see that."

"All I see is we gotta be careful around her. 'Elei can't get hurt,'" he said in a mock "adult" voice. "'Elei doesn't ask for special favors'... but she gets them."

"Like not changing in the same locker room?" asked Heather, the same sneer on her face from her first remark. "Where's she supposed to change? In a bathroom stall in the *boy's* locker room?"

"That makes her not part of the team."

"Just 'cause she can't shoot a jock strap at you?" asked Stewart. "Dude, that's hella false."

Elei jolted from her seat and spun toward Alex. "You've been an asshole to me since day one."

Rick had turned all the way round in his desk and was shaking his head at Alex. "Homey," he whispered.

Alex stumbled out of his seat and stomped toward her.

Skyler moved to get between them. "Sit down! Both of you."

Elei, bristling with emotion, jutted a finger at Alex. "All I hear out you, Ryan, is bitching, and I don't see a lot of playing."

Alex pushed against Skyler. "Coach is crazy. And *you're* the bitch!"

Drew rose and stepped toward them. "You're out of line, Ryan. She plays just as good as you!"

"Fuck you, O'Connor!"

Skyler grabbed Alex's shoulder. "Sit DOWN, Mr. Ryan! That's enough out of you. And you sit down, too, Drew."

"Girls don't belong on the team. What happens when she goes all PMS?"

It happened so fast Skyler could barely tell what happened. The class went ballistic after Alex's remark. Some of the boys were giggling into their hands, but all of the girls began yelling, some rose to their feet, an arm shot past Skyler and suddenly Alex was down.

Skyler looked back at Elei who was rubbing her knuckles and not looking contrite in the least. And Alex was sitting on the floor, looking up at her and clutching his jaw. He sprang to his feet and postured, fists flexing until he seemed to realize he couldn't hit back.

But now all the jeering was aimed at Alex. Catcalls of "pussy!" and "Ryan got knocked out by a girl!" filled the rafters.

Rick was at Alex's side. Red-faced and tight-lipped he held on to his boyfriend's arm.

But Skyler snatched that same arm and gripped it. He yanked Alex and Elei out to the hallway.

Over his shoulder he called back to the room, "Everyone better be sitting down and quiet by the time I get back or everyone's getting detention!"

He marched them to the hall and down the corridor. He stopped on the landing, away from the prying eyes of the other classrooms and let them go.

Breathing hard he calmed himself before he spoke. "Mr. Ryan, I don't know what the heck's gotten into you but I hope you know that this outburst jeopardizes your place on the football team."

"But she —"

"Not one more word, Alex! Of all the people... Don't you know that *everything* you just said, has been said, *is* being said about gay people?"

Alex, still red-faced, still tensed with arms bowed and ready to strike out... sagged against the wall. "It is?" he asked, panting.

"Of course it is! Don't you think Coach makes sure no one says that or thinks that about *you*?"

With the contortions of his brows Alex seemed to be processing that information. Disgusted, Skyler turned toward Elei. "And what was all that about, Ms. Sapani? I will not have violence in my class. You just might have lost your chance to stay on the team."

"He's always baiting me!" she shouted, eyes shimmering with tears.

"Keep your voice down," Skyler hissed. He stared his harshest teacher glare at them. "You should both be sent to the office."

Alex, looking sheepish, had completely recovered from his rage and had apparently figured out the error of his ways. "Mr. Foxe…"

"Don't, Alex. What have you got to say for yourself?"

"I'm…I'm sorry…for disrupting your class."

"And?"

Reluctantly he turned toward Elei but he looked at the floor and not at her face. "I'm sorry for what I said. I'm just not used to girls on the team. I still don't think…"

"Alex," Skyler warned.

"I'm sorry," he concluded.

"I didn't know you were queer," she said. She looked up suddenly at Skyler. "Oh. Is that okay to say? Everyone says that you and Coach are…together…"

"I don't mind the term as long as you don't use it in the pejorative sense." She clearly didn't know what he was talking about. "But never mind that. You simply cannot settle your differences by resorting to violence. You cannot hit people, Elei."

"He's been on me since I got on the team."

"I don't care what he says or how he says it, you *cannot* hit people. It's assault and you could be arrested."

"What? People get into fights all the time at school and don't get arrested."

"Well, this is another day and another school. We have zero tolerance for fighting nowadays. Not only can you get kicked off the team—something you've worked very hard to achieve—but also kicked out of James Polk High."

She rubbed at her face, her eyes shining.

"Is there something you need to say to Alex?"

She looked at him. He was still flushed, still breathing hard. They both suddenly realized how much trouble they were in. "I'm sorry, Alex. I didn't mean to hit you."

"You didn't hurt me," he was quick to say.

"I know."

Skyler was certain of one thing: she did know how to handle boys. Granted, it was after the fact, but still...

"But can't you accept that I got on the team fair and square? In our scrimmages, I catch the ball. I do my job. I run and do push-ups with the rest of you. Coach isn't any easier on me. I run just as many laps as you do. You're being a jerk, Alex, and it's not fair."

Alex shoved his hands into his shorts pockets and turned his face away.

"Well, Alex?" asked Skyler. "Is this true?"

He shrugged, still looking away.

"Alex, answer me."

He sighed and rolled his eyes toward the ceiling. "Yes! Okay, yes. He works her just like he works us."

"Then what is all this? If you've seen that, if you've played with her, then why all the anger?"

He aimed a finger at her and spoke loudly until Skyler shushed him. "Cause she comes along and suddenly there are reporters and all sorts of shit on the news and they never did that for us before. But now with a chick on the team suddenly we're not losers."

Oh Alex. You're envious. But how to handle that without saying it outright?

"Attention on just one player can be hard for the whole team to accept. After all, you're supposed to be together, work as a team."

"Yeah," he grumbled.

"But doesn't the quarterback get most of the attention anyway? In high school and pro ball? He's not the only team member but because he's in the center of it all, he gets more attention, right?" He hoped he was getting that correct.

"Yeah," Alex conceded.

"And you don't begrudge *him*, do you?"

"But this is different, Mr. Foxe. And it will always be different."

"That's true. Elei is...the exception. Just like an openly gay player is the exception."

Alex said nothing. He stared at the floor again.

"And though you haven't had press conferences and people taking *your* picture for the newspapers..."

"I don't want that!" he cried. "Not just because I'm...I'm gay." He said the last quietly.

"And I don't want it just because I'm a girl." Elei tossed her head. She'd obviously been to this rodeo before. "And no, I am not trans. I *am* a girl. I was born a girl and I don't want to be anything else *but* a girl. And I am not a dyke, either. I just like football, okay. I'm big. I can do sports. My whole family can do sports. It's the twenty-first century, Ryan. What's wrong with a girl playing sports?"

He said nothing, but at least this time he was looking at her.

Skyler sighed and breathed easier. "Okay. I don't want to turn you guys in because I know how important football is to the two of you. But there are consequences to our actions. You will both do detention with me for a week after school for one hour."

"But we have practice!" they said at the same time.

"I know. You'll come back to my class *after* practice. And you have no idea how lenient I'm being with you two. I'm taking time out of *my* day to stick around here just to discipline you. Do you realize how much trouble you are now causing *me*?"

"I'm sorry, Mr. Foxe."

"Maybe you'll learn not to open your mouth next time, Alex. I'm sure they talked about controlling your temper in the Teen Police Academy, didn't they? Don't you watch TV? Haven't you seen cops get in trouble because they couldn't control themselves or their bigotry?"

"God," he whispered.

"And Elei, surely you realize that violence isn't the answer. I know you must have heard it all, been made fun of. But that's not how you settle it."

"My dad says it is."

"Well your dad is wrong. That is not what people do in a civilized society. And although sometimes it doesn't look as if we live in one, I think it best that we all treat it as if it were. It starts with you. One person."

She bit her lip. "You shouldn't have to stay all that time after school just for us, Mr. Foxe. What if we…what if Ryan and I come and do detention in your class at lunchtime?"

"But that's when I'm with Rick!"

She gave Alex a disgusted look. "We're supposed to be punished, Ryan. That means we give up something. It's only for a week. It's better than getting kicked off the team, isn't it?"

He laid his head back against the wall. "Shit. Okay. If that's okay with Mr. Foxe."

"All right. That's a good compromise. I appreciate the suggestion, Ms. Sapani. So. Agreed? Starting tomorrow, the two of you will bring your lunch to my classroom. And I want you there promptly. No excuses. You'll do extra work I assign you as well."

"Yes, Mr. Foxe," they said together.

"Good."

"Mr. Foxe?" asked Alex. "Do we have to tell Coach Fletcher about this?"

Skyler ran the possibilities through his head. No scenario looked good. Eventually, he said, "Uh, I wouldn't."

"Dude," he muttered, brows raised.

Yeah, he just admitted he lied to Keith. *Way to mentor, Skyler!* He looked at his watch. "Well, class is just about over now anyway. Thanks for that. Go back and collect your stuff."

They climbed the stairs and he walked behind them as they shuffled slowly forward. When they opened the door and sat at their respective desks, Skyler could have heard a pin drop.

"Elei, Alex, do you have something to say to the class?"

Elei stood and faced them. "I'm sorry for interrupting the class."

Alex stood and tugged at his tank top. "Yeah. I'm sorry, too."

They both sat and everyone stared at them.

"I think that we'd all appreciate it," said Skyler, knowing it might be a useless exercise, "if you didn't mention this incident outside of class. After all, what happens in Mr. Foxe's class stays in Mr. Foxe's class. Or something like that. It's our problem to work out, okay?"

"But there's a zero tolerance policy in this school," piped up Becky.

Right on cue, he thought.

"I realize that, Becky, but every rule deserves a gray area. That's what teachers are for, to discern the situation and coordinate the proper response."

"But isn't the very nature of a zero tolerance policy..."

"Becky, it's handled, okay? Punishment is meted out. End of discussion."

The bell rang, and not a moment too soon. "You're homework assignment is on the board. It's due tomorrow. Class is dismissed."

In dead silence, they all stayed to write it down. Then, one by one, they gathered their backpacks and edged their way out. Amber hovered in the doorway, but Heather and Drew shooed her down the corridor. And Skyler could just hear Heather's rushed, "He doesn't want to talk right now," as it dissipated down the hall.

Once the class was empty Skyler sat at his desk and toyed with his pen. Had he just made a strategic error? He knew he should have marched them both to the principal's office and be done with it. But he had so much invested in Alex. Was it only because he was gay? Or was it because he'd been troubled? Of course, those two things were intimately intertwined.

And Elei. Was he treating her with kid gloves because she was a girl on the football team and he wanted her to have that chance? What would Keith have done? He'd been a teacher a lot longer than Skyler had been. He suddenly felt stupid and wishy-washy, and now he was second-guessing himself. Would *he* be in trouble if the administration heard about it? Who was he kidding? Of course they'd hear about it. How was he going to explain his actions?

"I looked on them as individuals, not a zero tolerance policy." And that was certainly true. He hated the inflexibility of "zero tolerance" anyway. He understood why it was there—fear had put it in place, both the fear of parents and of teachers who didn't want the responsibility for possibly getting sued for making the wrong choice…

Come to think of it, he could see the wisdom of it.

No! He *had* made the right decision. He knew he did.

Skyler's classroom phone buzzed. He reached for it. "Yes?"

"Mr. Foxe," said an unusually formal Pauline Hingle, office manager. "Mr. Sherman would like to speak to you. Immediately."

"I'll be right there, Pauline." He hung up, resting his hand on the phone. "Well, that didn't take long."

Chapter Fifteen

SKYLER TRUDGED WITH HIS SCHOOL SATCHEL IN hand to the office. Pauline looked up to acknowledge him. Usually they shared a little light-hearted repartee but not today. She looked away quickly toward her computer screen and simply said, "Mr. Sherman is waiting for you. You can go right in."

"Thanks."

Skyler felt as if he were walking to his doom. And he very well might be.

He stood before Mr. Sherman's door and took a deep breath. Mr. Wesley Sherman had always been fair to him, since his first instances at the school. Their bond might have been forged when Skyler solved his son's murder, or because his son was also gay. Whatever it was, he had afforded Skyler unusual leeway where his teaching style was concerned. But he had the feeling that his luck was about to run out.

He raised his hand and rapped lightly on the door.

"Come in."

Skyler opened the door and peered inside.

Mr. Sherman was sitting at his desk with a pile of paperwork in front of him. The computers had finally gone back online once the bell had rung at the end of the day, and he looked as harried as Skyler suddenly felt. He usually wore short-sleeved dress shirts and today was no exception. His tie hung flaccidly from his collar and his short brown hair lay just as disinterested on his head.

He glanced up from his papers only momentarily and gestured to the chair in front of the desk. "Have a seat, Mr. Foxe."

Skyler set his satchel down and sat gingerly.

Mr. Sherman made him wait—a long-standing principal tactic. *Now you just sit there and think about what you've done.* Skyler squirmed miserably. He was ready to confess anything and everything.

Finally, Mr. Sherman set his papers aside and folded his hands on the desk's top. "Now. A little bird told me a tale about your sixth period class, Mr. Foxe. Care to tell me the details?"

"W-what have you heard?"

"Don't be coy. We don't need to play games. There was a fight in your class and you failed to report it."

"Oh, no. It wasn't a fight."

He sighed and sat back in his chair, regarding Skyler with a skeptical expression.

"Well...it was almost a fight. I mean..." Skyler sank down. "A punch was thrown, apologies were made. It won't happen again. I didn't feel that the zero tolerance rule would be fair to these students..."

"The zero tolerance policy is there so that the teachers don't have to make that judgment."

"And what kind of screwed-up rule is that? Isn't that the nature of what we're supposed to be doing as teachers? I make judgment calls all day! Just like I can't fail a kid strictly on tests. I measure each student and their efforts and give them the benefit of the doubt."

"Mr. Foxe..."

"No, I mean it, Mr. Sherman. We can't be doing that to these kids. Okay, a gun in the school is a different matter. Someone who uses a knife or other weapon on another student, granted, I can see that. But in the heat of the moment, sometimes…"

"Was she hurt?"

Skyler stopped his tirade in mid-sentence. "W-what?"

"Was. She. Hurt?"

"She who?"

Sherman's patience seemed to be wearing thin. "I know this was about Elei Sapani. Was she hurt in the altercation?"

Skyler wanted to laugh. But under the low, thick brows of Mr. Sherman's displeasure he was easily able to choke it back. "You got it all wrong, Mr. Sherman. Um, it was *Elei* who took a swing at…Alex Ryan, not the other way around."

He frowned. "Wait. Are you telling me that Elei Sapani decked Alex Ryan?"

"Well, in so many words, yes."

The principal stared at his desk for a moment before he burst out with a guffaw and quickly stifled it behind his hand. "I would really have liked to have seen that," he muttered.

Skyler remembered how much trouble Alex had been prior to Skyler's coming to the school. Alex had been in and out of the principal's office for fighting his freshman and some of his sophomore years. It was Skyler who had gotten him on the football team to begin with, and the teen had turned his life around. At least, Skyler had thought so.

He guessed Mr. Sherman was getting back some of his own.

Shaking his head, the principal lifted his brown eyes to Skyler's. "That's, uh, still serious business."

"I know. But I wanted them to have a chance to work it out and not lose football. It's so important to the both of them. Alex was baiting her, pretty much telling her she didn't belong on the team. I was really surprised at Alex's attitude, especially after he completed the Teen Police Academy certificate this summer."

"I saw that in his file."

Skyler had made sure it got in there.

"But it still doesn't excuse…"

"They're doing detention with me during lunch for the next week."

"Do you think that's enough?"

"I…hope so. At least it will give them a chance to talk about it. Alex was having trouble with a girl on the team."

"I hate to say it but so am I."

"I don't think Keith was wrong in taking her on. She's qualified."

"I know. But *you* know and *I* know that if she gets hurt or harassed it will be all over the news and we just don't need any more negative publicity."

Skyler felt affronted…for only a moment. Until he realized that Mr. Sherman was probably referring to the murders and other illegal activity at the school, not two gay teachers. What's two teachers being outed to that?

The man looked even more haggard than he had last year. A lot had been put on his plate, and not just the running of a school with fluctuating budgets, parents' demands, and the school district's ever-changing policies. Skyler hoped that he and his wife were finding some sort of normalcy after the loss of their son. But with the one year anniversary of that looming, it couldn't be easy.

Skyler scooted to the edge of his chair. "Look, Mr. Sherman, I'd do just about anything for those kids. They just need a chance. Sometimes you have to confront your biggest fears before you can overcome them. God, I know that sounded like an inspirational poster, but it does seem to be true. Can you give them a chance? And, uh, me for trying it?"

"You aren't quite in trouble, Mr. Foxe, but I'm glad you were a bit worried. We can't have teachers going off on their own. We do have rules at this school for a very good reason. Mostly for the safety of others."

"I do understand that, Mr. Sherman, but believe me, they were both stricken afterward. They really do know now how much trouble they were in."

"All right. I just hope it doesn't get back to the district."

"I will do all I can to make certain it doesn't." Breathing a sigh of relief, Skyler rose. "So…everything's okay, Mr. Sherman? I still have my job, right?" It was a joke. Sort of.

"Yes, Mr. Foxe. All is well. But uh, this is only the first day. Can we manage to get through at least the first week without any more drama?"

At the doorway, Skyler saluted. "I'd like to say 'yes', but you know me."

"I'm afraid I do."

Skyler slipped out the door and passed Pauline's desk. "You can't get rid of me that easily," he said out of the side of his mouth.

She smiled. "I certainly hope not."

❖

When Skyler came in the front door at home, he didn't expect to see Keith there, especially pacing back and forth and yelling into the phone. But when Keith took one look at Skyler he clicked off the phone and stuffed it in his pocket.

"How was your day?" said Keith hurriedly, distracting himself by fetching a beer from the fridge.

"Uh…different." So Keith hadn't heard. Good so far. "But, uh, it didn't sound as if you're having a good day."

Keith knocked back the bottle, swallowed down the beer, and licked his lips. "Nothing to worry about."

Okay. That's it! "Keith…if that was Ethan…then I know what it's all about."

The beer bottle stalled halfway to Keith's mouth. "What do you mean?"

"What do you mean 'what do I mean'? I know about your…kid."

"How did you…?"

Skyler held his hands up. "Now, don't get mad."

Keith lowered the bottle and narrowed his eyes. "Why would I get mad?"

"Because…I had Jamie steal your phone and hack into your texts. I'm sorry!"

"SKYLER!"

"I'm *sorry!*" Keith stalked toward him and Skyler backed away into the living room.

Keith's eyes were furious. "I…I don't even know where to begin. You…you *hacked* into *my* phone?"

"You wouldn't talk to me and I could tell it was important."

"That's an incredibly weak excuse. How dare you!"

He didn't expect a "how dare you". That made him feel like a complete turd. "I'm really sorry."

"Jesus Christ, Skyler. What about my goddamned privacy? How can I ever trust you? Partners don't do that."

"No, they don't. They talk to each other about their problems. They don't keep it bottled up, especially when it can affect the both of them."

Keith huffed like an angry bull. Skyler bit his lip and cautiously approached. His palms were still up in front of him defensively. "I know I hurt your feelings…and I know I had no right to do what I did. But we're supposed to share stuff like this, right? Help each other. I'll never do it again…"

"Yes you will. Of course you'll do it again. You lie to me all the time."

That hit him like a gut punch. He swallowed. "I'm a terrible person. I know. I just wanted to help."

The steam seemed to go out of Keith's murderous expression and he stared at the floor. "You're not a terrible person."

"Yes, I am. I got into your private correspondence and that is a terrible thing. I didn't even think twice about it."

"It's not a nice thing."

"I know."

Keith scrutinized the beer bottle before he lifted it to his lips and finished it in one long draught. He twirled the empty bottle in his fingers. "I suppose the whole damned SFC knows about this."

"No! No, I swore Jamie to secrecy."

"Christ. Jamie."

"No, he hasn't told anyone. I'm sure his brain is bleeding with the strain, but I did tell Sidney."

"Fucking great."

"Because I had her checking up on Ethan. Has it ever occurred to you that he might be a thief and a murderer?"

Keith emerged from his thoughts to give Skyler a skeptical look. "What?"

"He's Jerome's boyfriend. The both of them could be up to no good. If he's willing to blackmail you…"

"He can't blackmail me. It isn't illegal to have a kid out of wedlock."

That took the wind out of Skyler's sails. The whole thing was no longer speculation. It was out there, real. "So…is he yours?"

Keith ran his hand up through his hair. "I don't know."

"Can you…tell me about it?"

Keith turned on his heel, left the bottle on the kitchen counter, and grabbed another from the fridge.

Skyler gestured toward the open refrigerator. "Can I have one, too?"

Keith took another from the six-pack and without seeming to think about it, also grabbed a glass from the cupboard. Even in his agitated state he knew Skyler preferred his in a glass. Skyler felt doubly shitty.

He took bottle and glass gratefully, poured it in, and took a swig of it through the foam. They both retreated into the living room and settled in, Keith in his recliner, Skyler in his wing back.

Keith crouched forward, absently peeling the label from the beer bottle. "So…it was about eleven years ago. I was about your age. And the guys I hung around with were jocks. I was out, mostly. We went out to a few bars around campus and got a little…okay, a *lot* drunk. I was just getting over Ethan, you know. But he was still around. Knew the same people I knew. And then there was this girl in one of my classes and we kind of hit it off in a friendly way. I was pretty smacked from having to give up football and from my course load for my doctorate work and really needed to blow off some steam. Well...she was at the bar, too, and my buds bet me I couldn't get her to go home with me."

"Keith! That's horrible."

"I know! I was drunk." It was hard to imagine Keith young and stupid once, but there it was. Skyler tried to picture Keith at Skyler's age. He was probably handsome as hell, same as today. "It's not one of my prouder moments, believe me," Keith went on. "I guess she liked me more than I thought she did and she took me back to her place."

Keith took a long drink and set the bottle on the chair arm.

Skyler gestured. "And? Then what happened?"

"What do you think happened?"

"I mean..." A stab of panic ripped through him. He thought Keith was his. He never thought there was a possibility of anything else threatening their couplehood. Breathing hard, he asked, "Are you bi or something?"

"No, Skyler. I was *drunk*. And what she was doing...felt good. And then I...you know."

It was disarming this embarrassment on Keith's face. His whole demeanor changed. His cheeks were flushed and his eyes darted everywhere but at Skyler.

Skyler suddenly had a lot of questions he didn't want to ask. Did he like it? Would he want to do it again with a woman?

Was it better with her than with Skyler?

Keith fiddled with the bottle. "And when we finished...I threw up and passed out. It was a real triumphal moment for me."

Skyler's hands covered his mouth. "Oh my God." Well, he supposed that answered those questions.

"Yeah. So in the morning I apologized profusely to her and that was that. I soon got my doctorate, and I never saw her again. I was too embarrassed to even speak to her. Until recently. Because of fucking Ethan."

"What did she say?"

"Not much. I asked for a paternity test just to be sure but she refused."

"Oh boy. So…it's possible?"

"The timeline is right. It's possible."

"And if it…if *he's* yours, what are you going to do?"

"Skyler, I just don't know." He laid his head back, twirling the bottle on the chair arm.

"Why won't she do a paternity test?"

"She doesn't want to share custody."

"But if she doesn't, then…"

Keith raised his face. "If it's my kid I feel an obligation to try to be a father."

"'Course you do." That was his Keith through and through. "Then…you have to convince her."

"I'm working on it."

Skyler looked down into the golden beer as the foam dissipated in paisley swirls. "I wish you would have told me in the beginning."

Keith set the bottle down and leaned forward, taking Skyler's free hand. "I really should have. I'm sorry."

"Don't apologize to me. I'm not done feeling guilty about what *I* did. What I had Jamie do."

"I'm still sorry," he said, thumb painting circles on the back of Skyler's hand. "You were right. I had no business keeping that from you. From now on we both talk to each other, okay?"

Skyler nodded. This was one of those grown-up moments. Often he felt like an adult, doing adult things, teaching his classes as the only adult in the room. But other times, he felt so new, so adolescent. Especially compared to Keith. Skyler knew that he was rarely the adult in this relationship but sometimes he had to step up.

Could there be a miniature Keith running around out there? What was he feeling about that exactly? Jealousy? Anger that he didn't have Keith all to himself? Which was stupid because Skyler had certainly had a life before Keith. "Catting around" as his dad put it. There was certainly a little of that feeling, though, that Keith hadn't been waiting around in a sealed jar until Skyler came along. And would he have wanted that? A little part of him did. But it was time to put that aside and have some empathy for his man and what he was going through.

He turned his hand around and grabbed Keith's wrist and pulled him in. His mouth found Keith's and he kissed him. Not heatedly, but with enough passion that the man would know that Skyler had his back. He pulled away and looked at Keith close up. "You can count on me when you need me, you know. I'm on your side. And whatever happens we'll deal with it together. Because we love each other."

Keith's strained features relaxed and his smile said it all. "Okay. I do love you."

Then Keith leaned in and kissed Skyler back.

❖

As they prepared dinner together, Skyler knew that the adult thing to do was tell him about his day, even if it cost his students their chance on the football team. So he put down the carrot he was peeling and leaned his back against the sink. "I think — in the spirit of our new openness — that I should tell you what happened in class today...between Alex Ryan and Elei Sapani."

Keith, crouching over the broiler, smiled up at Skyler. "You mean when she punched him?"

Skyler slapped him with a towel. "You knew!"

"I was wondering if you were ever going to tell me. You think something like that can stay a secret?"

Skyler sighed and slung the towel back over his shoulder. "Fine! So...are you going to do anything about it? Do you think I did the right thing?"

"Your heart's in the right place. I know you care about Alex and Elei." Keith fiddled with one of Skyler's cooking gadgets sitting on the counter. "And I understand you are meting out discipline."

"I am."

"I'm keeping them out of the scrimmage on Friday night's game."

"Ouch. That's harsh. Especially after your interview and all."

"Yeah. Tell me about it. If I'm asked, I have to just say it's a disciplinary act but I can't say what for. You know, her parents are pretty much in my face all the time. They won't like this turn of events."

"What did they say about it? The kids, I mean."

"Alex brooded as usual, but Elei seemed to take it in stride. She's pretty mature for her age."

"They say that girls mature faster than boys."

"So when's it happening for you?"

"Ha, ha. I owned up. Eventually. You wouldn't love me if I was just like everyone else, now would you?"

Keith offered an enigmatic smile but said nothing. Skyler frowned.

Getting in bed later that night, Skyler laid awake. Now that he and Keith had talked it out, it didn't feel quite as stressful. Keith told him he was meeting with the girl...*woman*, he supposed—Laurie Henderson—tomorrow night. She lived in Los Angeles now and he was going to be late coming home. It seemed the perfect opportunity for Skyler to concentrate on the museum thief and murderer. And he knew just who to call for help.

Chapter Sixteen

"I REALLY DON'T SEE WHY YOU ALWAYS CALL US to be involved in these things," said Philip from their booth at Taquito Grill. "We have a business to run. Two businesses, with a shop to get rebuilt and decorated, and the idiot contractor never seems to be there."

"Don't worry, Philip, it will all work out," said Rodolfo with a particularly purring voice. "You always worry so much. You'll lose your hair."

Philip grabbed at his scalp and relaxed when he felt the reassuring locks. "Bite your tongue."

Rodolfo slid closer to him. "I'd rather suck on yours."

"Alright boys, calm down." Jamie set the fork and napkin in front of him with meticulous grace. "Now then. We are all here as the Scooby Gang to do our duty for Skyler."

Dave sipped his beer from the bottle. "This really is what you guys do."

"No, it isn't," said Philip. "It's just something that always seems to happen on the side. As we interrupt our lives to put ourselves into danger."

"It's not always that dangerous," said Skyler. "Besides, last time it was Keith who was in danger. Now he's safely off doing something else."

"And he's the only one who actually knows what he's doing. How convenient."

"You know, Philip, you don't have to come."

"Yes I do. Rodolfo always wants to do this and I can't let him do it on his own. I keep remembering that time he was almost killed. I couldn't stand the fact of leaving him on his own and something happens."

Rodolfo smiled a full grill of white teeth. "Isn't he cute?"

"Yes, I'm downright adorable."

Skyler grabbed a chip and crunched it. "Well, I appreciate you all coming."

Jamie settled both arms on the table. "So what's the plan, Skyboy?"

He shrugged. "Don't know. There are so many unanswered questions. Even Sidney is stumped."

Dave sat back, beer poised near his face. "Then I don't know what you expect us to do." He took a swig.

That detective spark ignited in Skyler's chest and he leaned into the table. "Well...I had this idea..."

Jamie clapped his hands. "I *love* it when Skyler gets an idea!"

"Since I don't work at the museum now that school started I can't keep an eye on the day to day of it. I mean, I still have the cameras, but I can't check up on it 24/7. So I thought that maybe you guys, in tag-team fashion, could check it out. Get up close and personal."

"Do you still suspect the nephew?" asked Jamie.

Skyler sighed. "He and his uncle were pretty close. I'm really surprised that Mr. Huxley told the board that Jerome wasn't his pick. It seemed like a sure thing to me and everyone there. But if he was the one stealing from the museum and Mr. Huxley knew it, then he'd have to stop him somehow."

"But maybe Mr. Huxley was stopped first," said Dave.

"Yeah. I hate to think that but...I've got nothing else."

Philip stirred his straw in his drink. "Then what do you want us to do?"

"The docents don't know you. You could reconnoiter the place, see that things are still in place, report any suspicious behavior."

"Like, on the hour every hour? For a day? A week? How long can we do this for and to what end?"

"Oh. Well…"

"As usual, you haven't thought it out."

"Now wait a sec," said Dave. "It isn't a bad plan, overall. But it has to be figured out. Now from what you said, Sky, this Jerome fella stormed out of there when that other guy was named director, right? How do you know if he ever came back?"

"I saw him on the museum cam, see?" He tapped on the app on his phone screen and showed it to them. The screen was divided into the nine camera views. It was night now, so no one was there.

Rodolfo raised his hand like one of Skyler's students. "If the board thinks he's stealing, why is he allowed to continue to work there? This I do not understand."

"Hmm. Good question. Out of respect for Lester?"

"No offense to the dead," said Philip, "but it's not as if he'd notice. I don't think that's the reason."

Dave tapped his lip with the spout of the beer bottle. "Maybe the board *didn't* know about it. Maybe Lester didn't tell them the details."

"Denise was pretty insistent that Mr. Huxley recommended *against* him being director."

"Maybe you should talk to her again. Get more details. In the meantime, I'm sure between the four of us, we can work out a schedule to spend time in the museum."

"Do we have to?" sighed Philip.

"We're on the case again!" said Rodolfo, nudging his boyfriend with his elbow.

"Lucky us," he muttered.

After a vigorous exchange of Rock/Paper/Scissors, Philip was up first for museum duty. "So what am I looking for again? I don't have to break into any offices, do I?"

"No," said Skyler. "Just kind of keep an eye on Jerome. And at the gift shop counter."

"Now how can I do both?"

He patted his shoulder. "You're clever. You'll find a way."

Skyler was in bed reading when Keith finally got home around one in the morning. "You shouldn't have waited up for me," he said as he passed through the bedroom doorway.

"I wouldn't have slept anyway worrying about you. So?" He closed his book and set it aside. "What happened with Laurie Henderson?"

"She was cautious at first. And then remarkably nice about it. She's not a big fan of Ethan Cooper, as it happens."

"Only Jerome Williams is, and God knows why."

Keith sat on the bed next to Skyler and Fishbreath jumped up to join them. He stroked the tabby that had come to look on Keith as his personal god. "So we talked...for a long time. She was actually glad to hear about how my life turned out. And I apologized again for what happened. And I met Josh. He's a sweet kid."

Skyler's hand curled around the edge of the quilt. "And...does he look like you?"

"Not really. He looks more like Laurie. But that doesn't mean anything. The upshot is that she agreed to the paternity test. Because she honestly didn't know if it was me or someone else."

Slut, thought Skyler, but he knew how uncharitable and misogynistic that sounded. The same could certainly be said of him...and often was.

"So maybe it's not your kid."

"Maybe. We're going to this clinic together tomorrow afternoon, so I'll be late again."

"Okay. Um...do you want me to go with you? I will, you know. As moral support."

"You don't have to do that."

"I know, but this must be weird for you."

"I'm sure it's weirder for you."

"A little. Kind of an instant family."

"Laurie was concerned that I'd want joint custody. I told her I didn't. That I wouldn't put her through that. But that I'd want to be part of his life. And I told her about you. Showed her a picture. She, uh, thinks you're cute."

"She does?"

"Everyone thinks you're cute."

Skyler flushed, perplexed at the confusing emotions roiling through him.

"Let's just leave it as it is for now," said Keith. "It will be a few days before we know anyway." He sat a moment in thought before he rose to get to the bathroom for his evening routine.

"Keith?" He stopped and turned toward Skyler. "What's the outcome you're hoping for? I mean, I'll support you no matter what. I'm just wondering...what do you want to happen?"

His face turned aside and he shrugged. "I don't know. I want kids. Maybe not like this, but I do want them. I don't honestly know."

Skyler left him to it and sat back against the pillows. He bit his lip thinking about it all, and what it might mean to the two of them as he listened to the water running in the bathroom sink.

❖

He didn't see much of Keith at school and he knew he'd be home late again, which was just as well. Skyler had other fish to fry. It was decided that Philip would head over to the museum around two.

Every spare moment during the day when Skyler wasn't worrying about Keith, he kept his eye on the museum cams. "Too bad they don't have sound," he muttered.

His phone chimed, notifying him of an email. He clicked on it and saw that his reimbursement check from the museum had bounced. "What?" There had been plenty in the ledger, if the written balance had been anything to go by. How could it have bounced?

He sent an email to Ron at the museum (even though the address still had Lester's name on it) and in a matter-of-fact sort of tone, explained about the bounce, that it was no big deal, and whenever it could be dealt with would be fine. He didn't voice his concern. Come to think of it, his paychecks from the museum had been coming to him later and later, but that was a moot point now that he was off the clock there.

The Nutrition bell rung, and Skyler stayed at his desk, trying to get in some extra work before the next class. The James Polk Podcast came up on the school speakers and Skyler was surprised to hear that it was Keith being interviewed. He set his work aside and sat back in his chair to listen.

"This is Lauren Swansen, your junior class correspondent and I'm here talking to biology teacher and football coach extraordinaire, Keith Fletcher. Thanks for talking with the Polk Podcast, Mr. Fletcher."

"Thanks for having me, Lauren."

"It's been a little exciting lately with your newest recruit to the football team. This is JPH's first girl on the team, am I right?"

"That's right, Lauren. We've had some great teams at James Polk and this year is certainly no exception. But additionally this year, Elei Sapani came to the tryouts and she excelled."

"It's certainly a controversial move. I know there are factions of boys and girls at the school who think that a rough sport like football isn't the place for a girl. But there are many others who think it's probably about time to integrate the team."

"Interesting that you should put it quite that way, Lauren. I do view this move as 'integration' of sorts. But let me make it clear. If no girl qualified to be in the scrimmage, I wouldn't have put any in. Same thing with boys, really. Sapani is a good player and she deserved the chance, just as anyone who tries out for the team. They need strength, agility, and a real feel for it. Those are the only qualifications as far as I'm concerned."

"But as I understand it, Coach, there was an altercation yesterday and Sapani was accused of punching a fellow football player. Is it true she'll be sitting out the first game of the season?"

Skyler heard Keith's hesitation. Boy, that sure got all over the school fast. He bit his lip, listening.

"There was, uh, a situation. And it is true that Sapani will be sitting out the game as would any student who engaged in inappropriate behavior."

"Can you confirm that Elei Sapani beat up Alex Ryan?"

"No one was beaten up, Lauren. Those kinds of rumors need to be quashed right here. There was an incident and discipline was meted out. End of story."

"There has been rumor of preferential treatment of Ms. Sapani on the team."

Keith expelled an exasperated breath. "I can assure all your listeners out there that there is *no* preferential treatment for *any* member of the football team. The whole point of Title IX is to even the score, so that there is no preferential treatment of boys over girls, and girls over boys. That's it really."

"But Alex Ryan—"

"I have nothing more to say on that subject. Except to remind everyone to come to the game on Friday night."

The reporter seemed disappointed that she couldn't draw out any more controversy, but Keith made it plain that he was done talking and made a hasty exit.

Cringing, Skyler sent off an encouraging email to Keith, and he only half-listened to the other stories she and her male counterpart on the podcast discussed, before classes resumed.

The lunch bell, and his students gathered their things and exited the room, leaving Skyler alone to settle in. He grabbed his cooler from under his desk. It didn't take long for Elei to arrive with her lunch bag. She was already getting comfortable at her desk when a sullen Alex shuffled in.

"Your extra assignments are on the board in the upper right hand square," said Skyler as he dug into his sandwich.

Alex said nothing, but Elei looked up to the board before unwrapping her own sandwich. "We aren't playing in Friday's game," she said. "My dad is pretty pissed about it."

"Well, I hope you told him why."

"Yeah, I did." She looked back slyly at Alex but didn't turn all the way around. "He told me what I did was right."

Skyler was about to open his mouth but she cut in with, "But I also told him that you said it was wrong and I shouldn't settle my differences with violence. And I agree." She turned back toward Alex this time. "And I'm sorry, Alex. It was sort of a gut reaction."

He stuffed his sandwich into his mouth and shrugged. With his mouth full, he said, "I've been told never to play the PMS card. By *lots* of girls."

Elei chuckled. "Yeah, bruh. Nothing gets chicks madder than that."

"I can tell."

"Okay you two," said Skyler, "finish up your lunches so you can get to the work. And Alex, if you have any questions, don't hesitate to ask me, okay?"

"Okay, Mr. Foxe." He stuffed what remained of his sandwich into his mouth and got out his notebook. He sipped at his Coke can as he scribbled down the instructions from the board to his paper and then sat staring at the sheet. Skyler didn't wait. He got up and walked to the back of the room and leaned on the boy's desk explaining what Alex needed to do for the assignment. Alex seemed to understand and opened his workbook to read.

Skyler took the opportunity to read and correct his many students' class assignments. Everyone worked quietly for some time, in fact, and well before the lunch bell rang, Elei handed in her papers. Skyler took them and began to read, his red marker only swiping a few marks across her page. "Good job, Elei," he said, and handed them back. She sat at her desk for the rest of the time, drawing on her backpack with a marker while Alex continued to work, head down, pen moving along the lined paper, up to the bell.

Elei got up, waved to Skyler, and left while Alex gathered his things. He stuffed his notebook, workbook, and pen into his backpack and thrust his wrinkled sheet of lined paper toward Skyler. "I did the most that I could, Mr. Foxe."

"Thanks, Alex. I'll take a look. See you at sixth period."

Alex waved hastily as he rumbled out of the room.

Those kids. Having these same students year after year was an interesting psychological experiment, he mused. He could almost track the arc of their understanding of the world as new experiences opened their eyes and minds. He hoped that the books he chose for his classes might help in small ways with that. It certainly couldn't hurt.

He threw out his sandwich wrapper and zipped up his lunch cooler before stuffing it away again and remembered to check his phone for anything Philip, before he realized it wasn't two yet. Sighing, he got up and wiped his white board clean, readying for the next class.

❖

During class, Skyler snuck a look at his phone, checking the museum cams, and sat up as he saw Philip walk in right on time. The man was looking as suspicious as a detective in a bad TV movie. The way he slunk around the room, looking over his shoulder, might have been comical under other circumstances. Though somehow, he got Jerome to engage with him. They talked. Jerome showed him exhibit after exhibit, talking the whole time. Finally Jerome left him to it and Philip rolled his eyes walking around. But then Jerome seemed to have gotten a phone call and stepped into a corner of the rotunda to answer it. Philip tried for nonchalant to move closer to him, presumably so he could eaves drop, and ended up unconvincingly reading book titles off the spines in the glass cases.

Fortunately, Jerome never noticed. His conversation appeared to get heated and finally he angrily shut it down. Skyler followed him to the next camera as Jerome approached Ron in the office, telling him something Ron didn't look too happy about. Jerome spun on his heel and headed out the door, nearly running into Philip who had been lurking outside the office. He pushed past him and left. Philip watched perplexed until he seemed to decide something and went after him.

"Mr. Foxe?"

Skyler startled and looked up. He had been so absorbed that he completely forgot he was teaching a class. What sort of example was he setting?

Fortunately they were all supposed to be engrossed in reading silently. But the freshman standing in front of his desk had a piece of paper in her hand. "Sorry, Mr. Foxe. I didn't mean to scare you."

"You didn't. What is it, Ms. Walters?"

"I have a doctor's appointment. I'm supposed to go now."

"Oh. That's fine. Go ahead. Did you get the homework for tomorrow?"

"Yup. Bye."

The freshmen seemed to be getting smaller every year. But to be fair, she was a pretty petite girl, after all.

He looked down at his phone. Where the hell had Philip gone? He couldn't call him now. He did a quick text and kept looking at his screen for a reply. None was forthcoming.

Fifth period ended, and finally it was his favorite class again. But still nothing from Philip.

He was writing on the white board when he saw Alex stomp in. He had a pretty murderous look on his face, so much so that Skyler turned away from the board to watch him take his seat at the back of the room. That was certainly not the situation at lunchtime. What had happened between then and now? A moment later Rick sauntered in, and it didn't look like they had been walking together. Rick didn't even acknowledge Alex in the back as he lounged into his front row desk, sticking his long legs into the aisle.

Uh oh. Trouble in paradise.

Then Amber and Heather came in, thick as thieves with their heads close together. Amber was talking a mile a minute in hushed tones, while Heather scowled.

Drew pushed his way in and the usually jovial teen merely took his place and opened his binder without looking around.

What was going on here?

Elei came through the doorway last. She looked exhausted...or defeated. He couldn't tell which, and simply dropped into her desk, her backpack forgotten as it pooled on the floor beside her.

"Hi, everyone," Skyler said cautiously. "Uh...everyone having a good afternoon?"

Mostly noncommittal grunts. But even the quick-witted Rick had nothing to offer but a sour expression.

Skyler gestured toward the board with his marker. "Today, we're going to 'craft persuasive topic sentences that transition and reveal the main idea of the paragraph.'"

"In plain English?" asked Alex from the back of the room.

"In plain English, Mr. Ryan, we're going to focus on topic sentences. Who can tell me the function of a topic sentence?"

Amber raised her hand. "The topic sentence gives the main idea."

"Correct! In plain language, Mr. Ryan, the topic sentence gives the main idea, but we want more than just a basic sentence. We want A+ topic sentences. Please take down the notes I wrote on the board and then we'll begin."

They scrambled for their notebooks and three-ring binders. Pens worked busily until Skyler thought they were ready for the next part.

"So, I want you to write a paragraph for the following situation: You are the Empire and you are trying to persuade the citizens that a Jedi rebellion would be a bad safety issue. You've got five minutes. Go!"

"But..."

"Alex, just pretend you're an Empire Stormtrooper. What would be best for the Empire? Your argument is safety. Got it?"

A small flame of an idea gleamed in his eyes. "Oh," he said, and actually leaned down over his desk to work.

Skyler walked slowly down each aisle, reading over shoulders, offering suggestions here and there, before he looked up at the clock and called, "Time! Okay, can I get a couple of people to share what they wrote?" Amber had her hand straight up, but he turned away from her to pick someone new. "Emily, would you read yours?"

The teen held her notebook in both hands, leaning almost her entire body on her desk as she read out her paragraph.

"Good argument," he offered. "It detailed the salient points. How about adding more critical reasons for each bullet point, rather than just a listing? Good job for a start. Anyone else? Stewart?"

The lesson went smoothly and the roughness of the students' earlier attitudes seemed to fade into the background...until Heather dropped her pen and it rolled under Drew's desk.

"O'Conner," she said, "could you grab my pen for me?"

"I don't know," he said gruffly. "Am I qualified to make that move?"

"Just give me my pen, a-hole."

"I think I'm too opinionated to get it for you."

With a sneer of disgust, she got up from her desk and dove under his, shoving it back and nearly dislodging him.

"You gonna beat him up, too?" asked Tyler, the stringy-haired boy. "Seems like the football team is made of wusses who get beat up by girls."

Alex spun in his seat to face the boy. "Shut the hell up, Tyler."

Tyler sniggered and turned back to his paper.

"Alex," Skyler warned.

Mouth squeezed tightly shut, Alex scowled at his paper.

"And you, Tyler, keep your opinions for the appropriate time. This isn't it."

Heather, with retrieved pen, sat back down, muttering about idiot boys.

The only way to shut it down was to move on into the lesson. Skyler proceeded to instruct them on the next part of the procedure. He answered questions, let more students share their progress, and finally ended the lesson with just about everyone understanding what their homework should be.

"We'll take a look at it tomorrow. Good job, everyone. I mean it. You're doing splendidly. If you have any questions, you know you can email me. You're outta here."

They gathered their things, binders stashed in the crooks of arms, notebooks stuffed into backpacks, and then the shuffle toward the door, chattering with one another or plugging themselves into smartphones.

He began stuffing his own homework papers—essays and sheets to correct—into his satchel, and when he looked up, Amber stood in front of his desk, clutching her binder to her chest. Alone.

"What's up, Ms. Watson?"

She shook her head. "It's not good. I'm sure you heard the Polk Podcast today. Well, Alex is being teased mercilessly about what happened."

"Oh? I wasn't aware of that."

"He is. And I don't think he and Rick are speaking to each other right now."

"Why not?"

"Because of Alex's attitude about girls on the team and some of the things he's said that kind of come off racist."

"Oh dear. I thought that the Teen Police Academy would be good for him about that."

"It was! At least for a little while. And now Heather and Drew are arguing because he tried to be a mediator between Alex and Elei and Heather got jealous or something. It's a mess."

"Well, maybe we can sort it out at the GSA on Friday, huh?"

"I guess. I just thought you should know."

"Thanks, Amber. A lot of these things sort themselves out, too. We'll see what happens by Friday."

"Of course Alex is peeved that he doesn't get to play in the game."

"Consequences, Amber."

"I know. And Elei, too. But Heather is talking about dropping out of the cheerleading squad."

"If she's not enjoying it…"

"But she's really good."

"It isn't for everyone."

"I know." She heaved a world-weary sigh. "Thanks, Mr. Foxe."

"Have a good afternoon, Amber." *And the drama continues*, he thought.

He gathered his things and *finally* got a text from Philip.

> *Overheard Jerome arguing with, I presume, Ethan. They have a storage locker. Followed him and found it.*

Holy shit, Philip!
What shall we do now?
Meet up later. Jamie and I have class. Shakespearean at 8:30?
OK. Agent Philip out.

All through his hasty dinner, Skyler wondered about this storage locker. But what was there to wonder about? It had the stuff, he knew it did. Shit. He was ashamed of Jerome for his uncle's sake. Why had he done it? And did he kill his own uncle? And for what? So he wouldn't get caught? It was all for nothing if Jerome didn't get the directorship anyway. What a mess.

He met Jamie at the foot of the stairs to the community center and he pulled Skyler aside before they went up. "So how did Keith react? Is he mad at me?"

"Well, he wasn't happy about it."

"Who would be? Why do I let you talk me into these things?"

"Because you are a good and loyal friend?"

"Well...I am that. But what did he say? Is the kid his? And did he really have sex with a girl?"

"He did have sex with a girl but he was drunk at the time."

"I would have to be almost comatose. No kidding. I just can't even."

"He was with his jock friends and they dared him..."

"Oh my God! That does *not* sound like our Keith."

"It was over ten years ago. He was young and stupid then. His words."

"Wait." Jamie rested a hand on his hip. "If that was ten years ago, that would make him…your age now."

Skyler raised his chin primly. "Do you want to hear this or not?"

"Dish, dish!"

"Okay. So he…um, fulfilled his bet and then felt like an idiot cause I guess she sort of had a crush on him and he never saw her again."

"Men are such pigs."

"He didn't know she was pregnant."

"So is it his?"

"They don't know. *She* doesn't even know. She finally agreed to a paternity test."

"This is serious, Sky. Does he want custody or something?"

He turned toward the stairs and began climbing. "He says he doesn't. She was afraid of that very thing but he did say if it is his, he wants to be in the kid's life."

"And how do you feel about that?"

"I don't really have a say in it, do I?"

"That's not what I asked." He stopped Skyler with a hand to his arm once they reached the doors. His gaze was earnest. "Do you want to be an instant family?"

"I…don't know. *No*, I guess, if it comes down to it. But what can I do? It's Keith's life."

"And yours, too."

"But don't you have to compromise on things when you're a couple?"

Jamie's expression slowly morphed to a smile. "My little Skyler's growing up."

"Shut up. Let's go in, already."

All the same women were there, and the instructors Steve Larson and Federico Rojas, the latter without his padded suit this time.

Larson clapped his hands, getting everyone's attention. "Today, we're going to try some throws."

Jamie elbowed Skyler hard. His grin was wide. "I was looking forward to learning this!"

Larson looked their way and smiled. "Skyler, want to continue to be my Guinea Pig?"

"Sure, why not?" He slipped off his shoes as the women encouraged him with catcalls and whistles. He rolled his eyes. Honestly!

"This time, Skyler, I'll have you be my attacker."

"It's about time," said Skyler to the women's laughter.

"You're going to come at me from the front. Try to grab me."

Skyler, hands out in front of him at hip-height, ruminated on what exactly to do. "Uh…"

"Just come at me. Grab me."

Skyler lunged, grabbing him at the shoulders. Quicker than he could blink, he was tossed ass over teakettle onto the mat. He shook his head, stunned.

"You okay, buddy?" asked Larson, looking down at him.

"Yeah." He took the offered hand to help him up.

"Let's go through it slow motion like we did before. Grab hold of my shoulders, Skyler."

Skyler did. Larson showed how he pushed his arm over Skyler's and pinned it while grabbing his tricep. "Then you bring your other arm underneath that same arm of his and crook your arm so you're clamping his armpit."

Skyler felt fairly trapped at that point. And when Larson pivoted so his butt was facing Skyler, Skyler could see that when Larson knelt and curled his back, it was a physical inevitability for Skyler to simply follow through and fall over him. Which he did in slow motion.

"Want to try it on me, Skyler?"

"With all my heart." He faced Larson, and when the man grabbed him, he was able to slip his arm down, clamp his other arm as instructed, pivot, kneel, and voila! Larson was down. "I did it!"

"You sure did, buddy. First time, too. Now. Let's everyone line up. Get your partners. It's a throw down!"

Skyler watched Jamie get thrown and do his own throwing of the ladies present, even as they giggled the whole time.

Skyler was able to do it each time and he wondered if he could finally throw Keith if given the chance.

Pumped after the class, he and Jamie made their way to the Shakespearean to meet up with the rest of the SFC.

"You should have seen Skyler tonight," gushed Jamie, settling on his chair next to Dave. "He was throwing like a pro-wrestler. All we needed were the folding chairs."

"It seemed really easy once I got the hang of it." He preened, pushing his beer mat back and forth.

"I'm so happy for you," drawled Philip. "That will come in so handy when you meet your next bad guy."

Dave frowned. "Let's hope Sky never has to use it."

"So let's get our drinks and Philip can fill us in." Skyler signaled for the waiter and he took their orders. "Philip? What happened?"

"I went to the museum this afternoon and talked briefly to Jerome. He's quite knowledgeable, by the way, and it's a very interesting collection. I don't know why I haven't been there sooner."

"Philip." Rodolfo sighed. "We don't need a tour. Get on with the story."

"I'm getting there. I'm just saying that he talked lovingly about everything. It seems so unlikely that he would have a hand in fencing the stuff."

Everyone paused as the waiter brought their beers and set each pint in front of them. Dave picked up his and drank through the foam. "Who knows what motivates a person? If his financial situation was dire, for instance, he might just have to do the unthinkable."

"It was strange to think of him as a possible murderer," Philip went on. "It was all very surreal, actually. But then he wandered away to answer his phone. And I gathered it was from the dreaded E-person. They argued. I could only hear snatches of what Jerome was saying. He kept telling E-person—"

"You can say his name," said Skyler with an exasperated scowl.

"All right, then, he kept telling *Ethan* to stop doing what he was doing and not to touch one more thing, that he would be right there to discuss it. Sounded mighty suspicious to me. And then he went into the office and told that preppy fellow he was leaving. Some kind of emergency. I didn't know what to do so I followed him. I tried to keep him in my sight, got to my car, and drove after him."

"Did he see you, *minino*?" asked Rodolfo.

"I really don't think he noticed anything. He was spitting mad."

"Seems to be his natural state these days," said Skyler.

"Well, with that *polla* of a boyfriend…"

"*Anyway*," said Philip interrupting. "I managed to follow him to a storage place."

Rodolfo speared his finger into the air. "Aha!"

Jamie made a face. "Didn't you already hear this story?"

"It's better every time my *minino* tells it."

"ANYWAY," said Philip, louder this time.

"We're all listening, Philip," said Dave, taking another long drink.

"I followed him to this storage place and found which locker or whatever they call it was. And they're open till nine."

Skyler checked his watch. "It's almost nine now. Maybe we should go."

Everyone rose except Jamie. "I didn't even get to drink my beer."

Dave tugged on his arm. "Come on, Jamie! The SFC waits for no man."

Jamie lunged for the table, grabbed his pint, and pounded two thirds of it down in one go. He gasped and licked the foam from his lips. "Fortified! Now we can go."

They all piled into Dave's new black Cadillac CT6. Skyler brushed his palms against the beige leather seats. "Nice, Dave."

Jamie settled in the front passenger seat and buckled in. "His car talks to him. Tells him the weather and how the brakes are doing. I swear, if it starts giving blow jobs I guess he'll get rid of me faster than Nicole Kidman runs out on a Scientology picnic."

"Hon," said Dave, resting a hand on Jamie's thigh, "you are one-of-a-kind-irreplaceable."

"That's a relief."

Skyler consulted his watch again. "Can we just go?"

Dave pressed the button to start it up and peeled away from the parking space. He drove as per Philip's instructions and pulled up to the storage facility just as they were locking the gate.

"Shit," said Skyler. "We're too late." He stared at the fence through the car window. "Where was it, Philip?"

"Just around the corner to the right. Number one fifty-six."

Skyler studied the fence and opened the car door. He stood on the sidewalk looking up at the metal bars.

Philip scooted along the seat, opened the window, and hung out of it. "What are you doing, Skyler?" he rasped. "The gate is locked."

Skyler walked along the fence. It was some kind of painted metal where the top curved outward to sharp, discouraging points. "I bet we can climb that."

Philip scrambled out of the car followed by Rodolfo. "We most certainly cannot."

"Sure we can. If you'd give me a boost. I can pull myself over that curved bit and jump down to the other side."

"Skyler!"

"What?"

"Are you insane?"

"He's got the museum exhibits in there! He has no right to them. And he might have murdered Mr. Huxley to get them."

"Then maybe you should call Sidney?"

"And that will take forever and he might get rid of all the evidence by then." He grabbed the fence and looked up. "I'm gonna climb it."

But Philip grabbed him. "Don't be ridiculous. You're not thinking. You'll get caught. Don't you think this place has cameras?"

They both turned their heads and spied one aimed at the front gate. "It's looking at the gate, not over here."

Dave slammed his door and joined them just as Jamie came up beside him. "We could get into big trouble, Sky," said Dave.

"Which is why I'm going alone. Will someone give me a boost?"

Everyone looked at each other.

"Come on, guys. SFC? Scooby Gang?"

Dave shook his head. "What are you gonna do when you get to the lock-up?"

"Well, I'll…" He glanced at the other metal roll-up doors. They all seemed to be secured with padlocks. "Oh. Um…"

Dave sighed and turned back toward his car. But instead of walking around to the driver's side, he opened the trunk. He took out something and returned to the fence. "I suppose we're gonna need this."

Jamie blinked at him. "What is that?"

Dave rested the long, two-handled tool through the fence's bars. "It's a bolt cutter."

"And why do you have a bolt cutter in your car?"

"In case I come across a fire and have to get through something. Always be prepared."

Skyler grinned. "Dave, you're a lifesaver. Boost me?"

Dave swept the others with a glance, quirked a smile, and crouched to lace his hands together as a step.

"Dave!" screeched Jamie. "Are you crazy? Skyler could get into a lot of trouble."

"That's why I'm going with him. What about you, sweet thing?"

"Me?" He glared skeptically at the fence. "Climb that?"

"I'll help you."

Jamie sighed dramatically. "Good grief. Okay."

"Well if he's going, then I'm going," said Rodolfo.

"No you're not!" said Philip. "I am really putting my foot down."

"And it's so cute when you do that, Philip. But I'm going to help Skyler. It's what friends do."

"No, friends help friends stay out of jail. I swear, Skyler, sometimes you are too stupid to live. Oh for the love of… Fine! I'll stay on this side of the fence. Someone will need to bail you imbeciles out when you get arrested."

Rodolfo suddenly grabbed him, leaned him over, and gave him the wettest, loudest kiss, Skyler had ever heard. "You are my hero!" he declared and let Philip go.

Slightly dazed, Philip wiped at his mouth and took a staggering step back. "It's ridiculous," he muttered.

Skyler set his foot on the step Dave made and by rested his hand on Dave's shoulder. Dave managed to hoist Skyler up and boosted him higher. Skyler grabbed hold of the sharp curved fence along the top. Designed to keep people out, it hadn't looked all that impenetrable from the ground, but up close and personal, it was formidable enough. "Can you boost me a little higher?" he stage-whispered.

Dave put his back into it and Skyler threw a leg up over the curve. Those spikes were dangerously close to his groin, but he tried not to think about it as he rolled over it and grabbed onto the bars to slow his progress down to the other side. "Hey! Piece of cake. How about Rodolfo next?"

Rodolfo's sinewy elegance on a dancefloor did not seem to translate to climbing over fences. He squeaked and squawked his way over the top after much work by both Dave and Jamie. Philip muttered and wrung his hands the whole time.

"Okay, Jamie," said Dave. "You're next."

Jamie gnawed on his thumbnail. "It's really high. I don't think I can make it."

Dave leaned forward and bestowed a gentle kiss and they were lip-locked for quite a few moments. Jamie pulled back and gazed dreamily at his boyfriend. "Well why didn't you say *that* before?"

He dug his foot into the step Dave made and reached up. Being much taller than Skyler certainly helped, but he dangled precariously from the pointed ends before he was able to stumble over the fence, but not before tearing his shirt first.

"Fuck. That was a Dolce & Gabbana, and I didn't buy it at an outlet."

"Sorry, Jamie," said Skyler, grimacing at the tear.

"Here I come," said Dave, oblivious to the fashion disaster that had just occurred. He jumped up, grabbed the pointy part, and hauled himself up, arm muscles bulging.

Everyone stopped to watch him. By brute strength, he nimbly cleared the fence and landed superhero-style on the other side.

Skyler and Jamie exchanged a look. "My fire-fightin' man," murmured Jamie.

"What was the number again, *minino*?" asked Rodolfo of Philip, nervously bouncing on the other side of the fence.

"One fifty-six. And would you all please hurry?"

Dave grabbed the bolt cutters through the bars and followed as Skyler led the way. The place was brightly lit, so that was no problem. But he did worry about the cameras he kept seeing aimed in all directions over what looked like an endless compound of tiny garages.

They followed the numbers up to the one they were looking for and stood before it. It, like all the others, was sealed with a padlock.

Dave held the tool, what looked like a giant set of pliers, and cocked his head. "Shall we further break and enter?"

"Maybe you shouldn't." Skyler was suddenly feeling the weight of what they were doing. In the heat of the moment, it was all very exciting, but this was serious. They had already trespassed onto private property. Was he really going to break and enter, add burglary to any charges levied against him should he be caught? "Maybe I should do it, Dave."

Dave waved him off. "Skyler, there's no way you can work this thing. And we've already been spotted by about a million cameras. That safety ship sailed the moment we climbed that fence." He lifted the bolt cutters and placed the pincer end on the padlock's shackle. "Bye-bye, career," he said, before putting those triceps to good use again. The cutter seemed to cut through the lock's shackle like butter and it snapped in two.

"That's a pretty handy thing to have around...as is the man wielding it," said Jamie, leaning over to kiss him again.

Skyler waved everyone back. "Let me do it. I don't want your fingerprints all over it. Why don't I ever remember about gloves?" Delicately with one finger, he pushed the lock away, knelt, and threw the roll doors up.

It made a lot of noise in the quiet of the night, but once it was firmly set overhead, Skyler peered inside. Naturally it was too dark to see anything.

As if on cue, four phones were whipped out at the same time with flashlight beams spearing into the darkness.

"Ho-ly shit," said Dave.

Skyler expected to see Abe Lincoln's stovepipe hat sitting pride of place in the middle, with the rest of the missing museum exhibits around it.

"What's all this?"

Dave stepped forward, and careful not to get his fingerprints on anything, lifted a tag or two with the very tip of his finger. "Looks like lots and lots of sports shoes and equipment."

"And shirts and stuff," said Jamie.

"This is not from your museum, *amante*," said Rodolfo, stating the obvious.

Dave whistled. "Some of these have store tags. Looks like a shitload of stolen goods."

Jamie nodded. "Could even be counterfeit."

"What?" Skyler scanned the unit, looking for anything else that might be lurking in the background. But all the boxes and bags were strictly merchandise, looking like they came straight from the factory. Or out of the back of a truck. "This can't be right." He lifted his phone, but this time switched it to camera mode and took pictures.

Dave held his phone higher to shine his light into the back. Nothing more was there but the back wall. "What did Philip say Jerome was yelling into the phone?"

Jamie fiddled with his torn shirt. "Something about stopping doing what he was doing—Ethan, presumably. You think the two of them are in cahoots?"

"Yeah," said Skyler. "But not fencing museum stuff." Skyler reached up to the rope attached to the door and hauled it down, closing it up. "I guess we'd better…"

In the distance he heard the sound of dogs barking…and they were getting closer.

Dave stuffed his phone away and tucked the bolt cutters under his arm. "I think we'd better scram."

They turned and ran. The barking was definitely coming closer.

Shit! thought Skyler. *Torn apart by dogs, never to be seen again? Keith would never forgive me!*

They ran hell-for-leather back to the gate. Philip was as white as a sheet and grasping desperately to the fence bars. "Hurry! The dogs!"

"We know, Philip!" gasped Skyler. He wasn't quite ready when Dave hoisted him up, but there was no time to waste. Straddling the fence on his belly, Skyler was soon joined by Rodolfo. They both hastily turned as best they could but ended up tripping each other up and fell to the other side in a tangle of limbs. The something soft that broke their fall turned out to be Philip.

"Jesus, Philip, I'm sorry!" cried Skyler.

"*Minino*, are you all right?"

With the wind knocked out of him, Philip couldn't yet reply. Another body sailed past them, and Jamie bounced upright, shaking his head. "Come on, Dave!"

Dave shoved the bolt cutters through the fence. "Jamie, start the damn car!" He tossed his keys to Jamie.

He caught them and ran around to the driver's side, hitting the button on the key fob. "The car, the car. Oh I hope it listens to me." He cast open the door and the engine roared to life.

The dogs—German Shepherds—cleared the corner and with scrabbling of claws, ran full bore toward Dave. He leapt for the fence and climbed, feet walking up the metal bars. The dogs arrived and barked, jumping after him, nipping at his heels.

Skyler, Philip, and Rodolfo backed away from their snarling muzzles. Dave was at the top and leapt down. He looked back at the angry dogs and motioned toward the car. "What the hell are y'all waitin' for?"

Everyone piled in and before doors could be closed and seat belts fastened, Jamie tore away from the curb and with tires squealing, shot down the street.

Chapter Seventeen

THEY ALL SEEMED TO TRY TO SQUEEZE THROUGH the Shakespearean's door at the same time and when they popped through, laughing nervously, they returned to the table they had vacated. The waiter looked at them funny but came over and asked if they wanted the same round as before.

Skyler flopped into his chair with relief.

But Philip was a killjoy as usual. "Don't think this lets you off the hook. There were cameras everywhere."

"Philip's right," said Skyler. "We'd better start coming up with a story."

"A plausible one?" asked Dave. "I don't think there's any such thing."

"Okay, an implausible one."

Jamie looked mournful as he examined the tear in his shirt. "Do you suppose any of that stuff was legit?"

"I guess it could be," said Skyler. "But is it likely?"

Dave drank a dose of beer and set his glass down. "Sky, you gotta call Sidney."

"Yes, Skyler," insisted Philip. "Right now."

"Right now?"

"*Right* now. Or *I* will."

For once, he agreed. He took out his phone and hit her contact number.

"Hey, Skyler. How's my party planning going? Did you get a hold of everyone?"

"Hey, Sid. Yeah, it's fine. Everyone seems to be able to make it Saturday. Even some of Mike's family. We'll get the whole top floor."

"Good. How about the cop list I gave you?"

"It's all good, Sid. Um…doing anything right now?"

"Mike and I were just settling in to watch another hilarious episode of Law & Order."

"Okay. But maybe you could come over to the Shakespearean. The guys are here."

"I'm too bushed for that."

"I think you might want to. Um—*okay, Philip, I'm doing it!* Sidney? There's sort of something I need to talk to you about."

"Can't it wait? It's…what, almost ten?"

"For God's sake," groused Philip. He grabbed the phone out of Skyler's hand.

"Hey!"

"Sidney, Skyler and friends just broke into a storage facility—all so very illegal—and he needs to talk to you about what he found." Philip held the phone away from his ear for a moment, but everyone heard the blue tirade. Jamie looked intrigued with some of the expressions he had, no doubt, never heard before.

"Just get over here." He clicked off the phone and handed it back. "You were taking too long," he said in a half-hearted apology.

"Thanks, Philip! I can make my own explanations, you know."

They drank quietly, no one saying much, until after about fifteen minutes, the door burst open and Sidney stood in the doorway. Dressed in a black tank top and khaki shorts, she stomped inside and stood above their table. Mike sauntered in after her and swept them all with a look that seemed to say, "You're in for it now."

"Skyler, what the living fuck did you do?"

"Could you keep your voice down and just sit. Hi, Mike."

"Hi, Skyler." Mike pulled out a chair for Sidney and sat in the one beside it.

"Is she armed?" he asked

"I made sure she wasn't."

"Good."

"Shut up, both of you. So who's going to tell me what you did?"

Skyler looked around at the blank faces and lowered his face. "It's on me. I'll tell."

The waiter approached but Sidney whipped her head up with a face so full of vitriol that he spun on his heel. "I'll be back in a bit," he muttered and returned to the bar.

"Talk!" she ordered.

"Okay. So…so Philip overheard Jerome Williams— you know, from the museum—he heard him talking to that asswipe *Ethan* on the phone about a storage locker and when Jerome left to go to the locker Philip followed him."

She held up a hand and shook her long curls over her shoulder. "Wait. Why was Philip eavesdropping on Jerome? Do you know him?" She turned toward Philip.

"I got caught up in Skyler's recognizance of the museum. I went in posed as a simple patron just so I could spy on the place."

"Okay—idiot. Then what?"

"Me or Skyler?"

"Skyler."

"Yeah, so Philip followed him and saw him at one of those storage units. And then he texted me and I gathered the guys."

She scanned their faces again, but they were all ducked into their beer glasses or were suddenly fascinated by the soccer playing out on the TV screens.

"And then we went over to the storage place but they were closed. So...I...suggested—just for myself, mind you—to...climb the fence."

Her long fingernails drummed on the table. He watched the manicured nails click one after the other.

"So...so...then the others came over...except Philip...and then we all went to look at the locker. Oh! And Dave brought his bold cutters."

She and Mike turned as one toward Dave. "You what?"

Dave rubbed his eyebrow. "Yeah, I think I was hypnotized or something. I plead the fifth."

"You think this is funny? Trespassing? Breaking and entering? Possession of stolen property?"

Skyler jumped in. "We didn't take anything!"

"Oh. What a relief. Go on."

"We found the locker and cut the lock off— you know, when I say it all like that, it does sound pretty bad."

"That's because it *is* pretty bad."

"I know. And then we opened it up."

"So were the museum exhibits in there?"

"No. But a shitload of stolen sports stuff. Look." He turned on his phone and showed Sidney the pictures.

She grabbed the phone out of his hands and scrutinized it. She showed it to Mike who nodded.

"Looks like stolen stuff to me," said Mike.

"So then we closed up the locker and left. We were chased by dogs. It was really scary. Dave almost got bitten."

"And where is Superhunk through all this?"

"Keith? He's out of town. I mean, he'll be back late."

"Did he know you were doing this? I thought he was supposed to be regulating your activities."

"Not 'regulating.' Just…helping. And no, he doesn't know. The place was closing. I wanted to get to it before Jerome got rid of the stuff. Except I thought it was museum stuff."

She heaved a sigh and dropped her face in her hand, massaging her temples. "Okay. We'll play it like this. We'll call that storage place, say that it was reported that there was suspicious activity near locker number — what's the number?"

"One fifty-six."

"That number, and we're going to investigate. We notice the lock is off, the door is ajar — somehow — and we spot something suspicious inside. We call for a warrant, yadda yadda and go from there."

"Skyler?" asked Mike, leaning on the table. "Were you guys seen?"

"Well…there were a lot of cameras there."

"Did you ever look directly into any of the cameras?"

Jamie raised his hand. "I might have. It was irresistible. Like telling someone to clear their mind and all they can do is fill it with things…and then they can't help it."

"Not true," said Sidney. "I don't believe for one minute any of your minds are filled with *anything*."

"*I* stayed *outside* the fence," said Philip.

"Next to the getaway car?"

"I…" Philip closed his mouth.

"I will do what I can to staunch this menstrual flow of jerkiness…"

"Ewww," said Jamie.

"…and the rest of you will lay low. Do you all understand me?" Then she smacked Skyler upside the head.

"Ow!"

"*Mashugana*! Stay out of trouble, goddammit. I've got enough on my hands with our real detective work."

"Well you haven't gotten very far on Lester's murder. Someone had to step in."

For once, Skyler was in real fear that she was ready to haul off and punch him. He cowered back but she only narrowed her eyes. Mike interjected before she could.

"We're doing our best with what we've got, Skyler. And this really could help. We'll see where it takes us. In the meantime, you *have* to stay out of the way."

"Okay. I know."

Sidney and Mike rose. "So we're going to go over there now," she said. "And I will inform you of our progress just so you don't meddle again. But I am telling Keith what you did, because I want him to know what's going on."

"I'll tell him, Sid."

"No. I can't trust you. And I want him to know. Have a trouble-free evening, gentlemen."

Skyler watched her leave and he glared into his beer.

Dave rose. "Well it has been a slice, but it looks like it's time for me to turn in." He was smiling at least, and it seemed genuine.

"I hope we don't get into trouble."

"I was banking on Sidney getting us out of it. It's kinda nice having the cops on our side to get us out of fixes."

"But you simply cannot rely upon that," said Philip.

"Sure I can. We're the SFC! And Skyler's homonista has our back."

"Oh God," said Philip. "Another true believer."

"Dave's right," said Rodolfo. "I do not worry because I know Sidney will come to the rescue."

Philip jolted to his feet. "Let's go. I'm afraid if you stay any longer you'll be thoroughly brainwashed."

"What does washing a brain have to do with anything? And why would someone do that?"

"Come *on*, Rodolfo!"

With eyes rolling, Rodolfo threaded his arm in Philip's, waved to everyone, and hurried his steps to keep up with Philip out the door.

"You coming, Jamie?" asked Dave.

"I guess."

"My place?"

"Oh. I didn't know if you'd be up for it."

"Actually, this high-adrenalin stuff turns me on." He grabbed the growing bulge in his crotch. "I'm 'up' for it right now."

Jamie gave Dave the once over. "I see! Well, good-night, then, Skyboy. Go straight home."

Shoulder to shoulder, they exited the tavern and Skyler sat alone. He finished his beer, left a tip, and slowly walked out to his Bug. He sat in the car, staring out the windshield, hands draped over the steering wheel. What was Keith going to say?

❖

Plenty, as it turned out.

Keith paced back and forth across their living room. "I leave you for a few hours and what happens?"

"No one got hurt. Sidney's covering for us. We found out something important."

"That's not the point. Stop pretending it is. You're an adult. Act like one."

"I wish you wouldn't talk to me like that. You do dangerous things all the time."

"I'm trained. I have a badge. I stay within the law, Skyler. All those measures are there for my safety as well as the public's."

"No one got hurt."

"This time. What about the next time?"

"I'm taking those self-defense classes you made me take."

Keith flopped down on the sofa, cradling his head in his hands.

Skyler stood over him. "You said you'd be on my side. You said I could still investigate."

"I thought I would be with you when you did."

"It couldn't wait."

"And what if you get hurt?"

"What if I do?"

Keith merely looked at him before he lowered his gaze to the floor. "I promised."

"Yeah, you did."

"Shit. That was probably the dumbest thing I ever said."

Skyler wanted to point out that agreeing to that bet to take home that woman was probably first in line as the dumbest thing, but he held his tongue.

Instead, he sat next to him. "So if all the yelling is out of the way...what do you think? Of the situation, not me and my investigating habits."

Keith scrubbed at his cheeks before angling his face toward Skyler. "Truth? It sounds fucking fishy to me."

"Sidney said she'd call me back. Do you think Ethan is the collaborator...or instigator?"

"God I hope it's the latter. How I'd love to see him behind bars."

"There now. Doesn't all that make you feel better?"

He leaned in until his mouth was close to Skyler's. "I worry over you."

Skyler lifted a hand to cup Keith's stubbly cheek. "Don't." He leaned in the rest of the way and kissed him, lips warming on lips. They kissed for a while. Skyler hadn't even noticed when he'd pivoted and ended up in Keith's arms, fully encompassed and chest to chest, breathing in Keith's musk. "Wanna take this to the bedroom?" Skyler whispered.

"Love to." Absorbed in kissing, he nearly carried Skyler the rest of the way and Skyler was happy to let him.

Keith's stubble burned Skyler's smooth cheek, but he loved the feeling, loved holding on and sucking on the man's mouth. He kneaded those hard biceps. Fingers massaged up that taut neck before slinging up around it. Keith's lips were full, moist, and soft. They didn't devour, but explored and gently caressed, even when Skyler sought for more. But though Keith didn't press or hurry, it seemed just the right thing to Skyler. He savored those lips, their contour, their taste, relished the gentle moans Keith uttered as the man seemed to fall utterly lost into their kiss.

When they got to the room, Keith slowly drew away, trailing his hand all the way down Skyler's body, from his neck down to his groin and then pinching Skyler's hard cock through his trousers. He stepped back, taking in Skyler with dreamy eyes, and stripped.

Skyler never got tired of that view, of broad chest and that forest of trimmed hair that led down to a defined six-pack; strong thighs, also dusted with hair; bulging calves; feet worthy of a Michelangelo sculpture.

Keith moved toward the bed — giving Skyler that luscious view of muscled ass — and laid down, his erection jutting proudly above a trimmed thatch of dark hair. "Why don't you get naked, babe, and come on up?"

Sounded good to Skyler. He quickly stripped off his shirt and kicked his shoes aside, watching them fly. His trousers were next and then socks and underwear. Naked, gleaming from sweat and anticipation, Skyler climbed on the bed and straddled Keith's body on his hands and knees. His kissed that chest, rubbing his nose through chest hair, and then took a side trip toward a nipple and latched on with his lips. Keith moaned and Skyler sat up and positioned his butt over Keith's dick, waiting for Keith to give him a sploosh of lube, but Keith seemed to have other plans.

"Uh-uh," he said. "Come closer."

"Oh?" Skyler walked forward on his knees till he bestrode the man's chest.

Keith was staring at Skyler's cock with a hungry expression. "Feed it to me," he said.

Amused but now achingly hard, he scooted even further toward Keith's face, lifted his cock with his hand, and placed it on Keith's opened lips. His hot mouth enclosed him and Skyler threw back his head in silent bliss. *Yes!* Warm lips and wet tongue wrapped around him, undulating, sucking, causing magnificent pressure. His balls grazed Keith's fuzzed chin with an erotic tap-tap rhythm as he sucked, as Keith kept pulling him deeper into his mouth. Skyler watched his dick slide in and out, wet from Keith's tongue. And Keith was staring up at him, eyes half-lidded, enjoying his meal. Skyler held himself back...until he couldn't, and began thrusting into that eager mouth beneath him.

Keith's hands steadied Skyler with a squeeze to his butt cheeks. One hand crept closer to his crease and fingers dipped, exploring, teasing at his hole.

Skyler shoved his butt back against that finger. His thighs quivered, holding himself above his man. Sliding his dick into Keith's mouth made him feel both powerful and humble, the things that Keith always made him feel. Breathing hard, he watched as Keith brought a hand to his mouth, shoved the finger in alongside Skyler's cock, and wet it good before returning it to Skyler's ass.

The wet finger prodded. Skyler opened himself and Keith pushed in the digit releasing a mutual moan from Skyler and a muffled sound from Keith's throat. The sensations were building. Skyler leaned back, trying to keep his balance. Keith was dipping his finger in earnestly now, circling, thrusting. With his other hand, Keith stroked his own dick with hard pumps.

The ache in his balls, the fullness in his ass, kept Skyler taut on the edge until he couldn't help but tip over, and a blast of aching want rushed upward and he came with his vision blurred by white-hot sensation. Keith sucked his release down and soon after spattered up Skyler's back. It dribbled down to Skyler's butt crack—he felt the tickle of it—but was incapable of doing anything about it, still suspended as he was in bliss and coming down from it like a feather on the wind. Keith still had him in his mouth until he popped his lips open and Skyler slipped out.

He slid bonelessly to the man's chest and lay there. Keith's cum cooled on his back but he didn't care. His whole body rose and fell with Keith's quickened breaths. His ear listened as the man's heartbeat slowed from its clamouring rhythm. Kissing the chest through the hair he sighed. "Well, that was good...for starters," he slurred dreamily.

Keith chuckled.

❖

Thursday was a blur of bells ringing, students with problems, classes full of laughter, excuses about homework not turned in, whining about grades received, and Alex looking angrier than the day before. Skyler had heard the jibes all day, about how Alex Ryan was beaten up by a girl. That certainly would not help the equality cause. And it didn't look as if he and Rick had patched up their differences either, though Heather and Drew seemed to have come to some sort of detente.

He asked Elei to stay after when everyone else was dismissed.

"I wanted to ask you something," he said. "Fridays at lunch I host the Gay-Straight Alliance in my classroom. Now, you're welcome to come, but I can't force you to do your detention during that time. You have your choice. You can come on Friday like always and sit in on the GSA meeting with a really great bunch of kids, or you can finish up your detention with me at lunch on Monday."

She folded her lips inward in thought. Finally, she shrugged. "I don't mind going to the GSA. People call me a dyke anyways."

"Um...I think most of them prefer the term 'lesbian.'"

"Whatever. See you tomorrow, Mr. Foxe."

"Oh, one more thing. Is Alex getting harassed on the team for...for what happened in class?"

"I don't know what happens in the locker room, but Coach shuts any of that down at practice. But as for the rest of the school, yeah, he's getting slammed."

"Shoot. I was hoping that would cool off by now."

"People like the story. But it's pissing the boy off."

"I can tell. Okay. Thanks, Elei."

Well, there was nothing he could do about that. It wasn't as if he could police all of the school. Maybe they could talk it out at the GSA. At least he knew Alex would have to be there. He hoped Rick would stay, too.

Skyler decided to hang around and grade papers instead of going home to do so. He was so involved he hadn't noticed the time, until his phone dinged. When he pulled it out to look, another museum check had bounced, this time his paycheck. "Now this is ridiculous!" He glanced at the clock. Keith would be at practice at least another hour. The museum would be closing any minute. Maybe he could go over there after everyone left and check the computer to see what was up with the money situation. It would also give him the opportunity to look around, see if anything had been stolen. He was out of the loop, after all, once he had stopped working there.

But Keith would surely want to go with him.

He was sure he'd be fine. He'd go there and be back home in no time, before Keith ever missed him.

Packing up his things, he locked his classroom and headed down the stairs.

There was a bit of traffic moving through town but he parked behind the museum around five fifteen, well after everyone had gone. He walked with purpose to the back door. It was still daylight and he didn't fear that the neighbors would make a fuss.

The code still worked and so it was an easy thing to go inside. He moved around the desk and switched on the desk lamp before powering up the computer. If everything was normal, no one would have changed any passwords. When the computer was booted, he typed in the login and sure enough.

Clicking on the bookkeeping program, Skyler looked it over. Everything seemed all right, added up. He went to the internet and to the bank website and logged into the bank account. "What the...?" A negative balance, lots of messages and alerts. What was going on? No wonder his checks bounced. He wondered if the others were in similar straits. Scrolling he looked at the dates of deposits and withdrawals. Looked like the withdrawals were right after the deposits. He scrolled further. The withdrawals looked to be coming in greater amounts, but in the distant past they were smaller, maybe even unnoticeable. Someone was obviously skimming off the top and then it got out of hand. Was it really Lester?

He looked at the date of the latest withdrawal. The day before Lester died.

Lester had told Skyler there were no checks, but that was a lie. That's why he hadn't written him a reimbursement. He hadn't wanted to issue one to Skyler that wasn't any good. He knew. Either it was him doing it or it was Jerome. He supposed Sidney could check to see if Jerome had any deposits of the same or similar amounts around the same time. He guessed she would likely have to check Lester's account as well.

His phone rang. Skyler got it out and looked at it. Shoot.

"Hi, Dad. Do you think I can call you back?"

"Look, son, your mom felt kind of bad how we left it last time we saw you. She, uh, she wants to make it up to you."

"She had every right to say those things to me. I have been acting like a...a shit to you, Dad, and I'm sorry. Maybe I do have an Oedipus complex...but right now, I really can't talk."

"Okay. But your mom wants you and Keith over for dinner next week. Call her back, will you, Sky?"

"Okay, Dad. Love you. And love to Mom.

"And I love you, too, son. Bye."

Wow, it had just slipped out. He didn't recall saying lately that he loved his dad *to* his dad, but there it was. Old habits, he supposed. But also...new chances. New...

Skyler snapped his head up. Someone was fiddling with the door! He shut off the light, shut off the computer, and scrambled away from the desk. The door was opening! Where to go?

He slid around the other side of the bookcase and cowered down in the dark. If they turned on the light they'd be sure to find him.

A hooded figure slipped through the door, lit in silhouette before the door shut again. Fortunately, they didn't turn on the light. Skyler assumed it was their thief come to get more museum goods...but he surprised Skyler by coming around the desk and taking the seat Skyler had hastily vacated.

Skyler tried to breathe quietly, shallowly. The computer fired up again and the person sat at the chair, tapping impatiently at the desk as the computer — shut down improperly — took longer to boot.

Skyler watched from his crouched position as the person went through the exact maneuvers he had only just performed himself, first looking at the bookkeeping software and then online to the bank account.

The only sound in the room was the soft whirring of the computer fan, the gentle tapping of computer keyboard, and a soft tinkling, like a chain or keys. The person stopped to read.

Skyler tried to keep himself still, tried to keep his breathing shallow, but as he coiled tighter, his foot slipped and banged a trash can.

The person at the desk shot to their feet and turned. The chair rolled away and slammed into the bookcase. Skyler sprang upward. The thief ran around the desk to flee but Skyler was having none of it. He leapt forward to cut off his avenue of escape but he underestimated the thief. The hooded figure turned and jerked his elbow back to jab Skyler in the gut. Skyler flung himself back out of the way. But the figure advanced and grabbed him.

Without thinking, Skyler slipped his arm down, shot the other across and hooked the figure's arm, pivoted, and threw him over his back. The thief hit the ground with a sharp release of breath.

"I did it!" cried Skyler.

But that was enough for the person to spring to his feet and lunge for the door. He threw it open and darted onto the street, running for all he was worth.

Skyler took off after him, but the thief was fearless and ran right into traffic. Tires squealed, cars honked and skidded out of the way, and Skyler stopped dead at the edge of the pavement, not daring to pursue.

"Shit!" He caught his breath and when he couldn't see the running figure anymore, he trotted back to the museum to lock it up. He sat in front of the computer again, shut it down properly, and pushed the chair back in. But something skidded along the floor under the chair's caster wheel. He ducked under the desk and felt around for it, bringing it up. A set of keys.

Nothing on the ring was identifiable. Just several silver keys. They each read "Schlage" and "Do Not Duplicate" across the top.

Chapter Eighteen

AT HOME SKYLER FIDDLED WITH THE KEYS (*THE clue!* he said in his head) and got out his phone. Days ago he'd meant to call Denise and ask about Jerome. He had to know just what Lester had told her. Maybe she didn't know about the shortfall... Hell. He needed to call it what it was. Someone was embezzling the museum funds. It was as simple as that.

The phone rang and rang and finally voicemail picked up.

"Hey, Denise," said Skyler. "Um, I was just wondering about exactly what Lester might have said about Jerome. My friend the detective may have a few ideas and she was interested in knowing, so give me a call back. Thanks."

He stared at the phone's screen a moment before he scrolled down the contact list and came up with another board member, John Rawlinson. He dialed his number and waited for the former Marine to pick up. The gruff voice answered and Skyler unconsciously sat up straighter.

"Hi, John. This is Skyler Foxe."

"Hey, Skyler. School back in session? I'm sure the guys at the museum are missing you."

"Yeah, we're back. Busy as always. So listen, John. I was trying to get a hold of Denise but she's not answering at the moment. I was told how Lester came to the board and recommended *against* Jerome Williams taking over his post as director, and I just wanted to know if Lester shared with you why? I know you can't tell me specifics of what was said in private consultation but I am helping local law enforcement get to the bottom of Lester's murder and I—"

"Wait a minute, Skyler. What did you say?"

"Oh, sorry. I heard that Lester told the board that he didn't recommend his nephew to replace him."

There was a pause and then that gruff voice returned. "As far as I know, Lester never told the board any such thing."

"What?"

"No, I think I'd remember something like that. He's always given glowing evaluations of Jerome. Frankly, I was surprised when Ron Harper was put forth for that position. Nothing against, Ron, certainly, but I think everyone assumed Jerome would be taking over."

Skyler stared into space, mouth hanging open before he pulled himself together. "So...let me get this straight. You have no reports, no written evaluations that say Lester specifically said that Jerome was *not* to succeed him."

"That's correct. Now, mind you, I went along with the other board members as they seemed to know something I wasn't aware of."

"And you didn't ask? Sorry, John, it's just that my friend the detective is bound to ask that question."

"I see what you're saying. I, uh, think I'll root around a little. See what I can come up with and call you back."

"Yeah, thanks."

Rawlinson hung up and Skyler rolled his phone over and over in his hands. "That's weird." Maybe the problem with the books stemmed from Lester, not Jerome. But maybe they thought Jerome was in cahoots.

Could Lester really have been embezzling? That seemed so incredibly unlike him.

Biting his lip, he looked down at the phone again. He opened it, scrolled through the contacts, and dialed Jerome.

Before Skyler could say anything, Jerome got in a clipped, "What makes you think I want to talk to *you*?"

"Look, Jerome, I don't know how we got off on the wrong foot, but there are some things I need to talk with you about. Can you meet me somewhere?"

"And why would I do that?"

"Because I want to talk to you about the possibility of Lester…cooking the books."

There was a pause and a long low breath released through the speakers. "Where do you want to meet?"

The Shakespearean was as good a place as any and Skyler waited, turning his sweating pint glass around and around before Jerome pushed his way into the front door. Jerome sat opposite and simply stared at Skyler.

It was fairly early yet, and the smell of the fryer was busy with fish and chips. The bartender clattered behind the bar, and a waitress was running a carpet sweeper over the rug in the front door portico.

Jerome hunkered over the table and got in close, and Skyler leaned in to listen. Quietly, Jerome said, "Lester didn't do it, but he did know about it. He told me. And before you say anything, I didn't do it either…or I wouldn't be sitting here talking to you. I'd be gone to Ibiza, looking for another boyfriend."

Uh oh. "What, uh, happened with Ethan?" He tried to keep the acerbic tone out of his voice but he wasn't certain he succeeded.

"The bastard had all sorts of shit going on on the side. Counterfeit sports stuff and the like. Took out a storage locker in *my* name. I shut that down and kicked the boy out. And then lo and behold, the police come calling asking about that locker. And now *I'm* in the shitter."

Skyler squirmed. "You can probably prove it, right? That it was Ethan who did all that?"

He ran a hand up over his short-cropped hair. "I don't know. I sure as hell hope so."

Not knowing what else to say, and aware that he was responsible for the latest in Jerome's troubled life, Skyler gulped his beer, choking a little. Jeez, *now* what was he supposed to think? Had it been Ethan all along? But someone was stealing the stuff from the museum.

Skyler cleared his throat. "Jerome, you don't think Ethan might be responsible for the museum thefts, do you?"

"Instead of me, you mean? I know everyone is thinking it. But as far as Ethan…" He shook his head. "No way. He didn't have a key and he didn't have the code."

Skyler felt the presence of those keys in his pocket. Why hadn't he checked them in the museum door? *Idiot!*

"I don't suppose you have any idea why the board would suggest that, um, that Lester spoke against you."

Skyler was prepared for him to blow up. He braced himself but was surprised instead by the man's sagging shoulders and defeated tone. "I have no idea. When I spoke to my uncle last, everything was fine. He never said a thing to me. We discussed it often. The only person he trusted just as much as me...was you. And I'm sure you might have noticed that I have a little... jealousy where that is concerned."

"I hadn't noticed," Skyler said with all the sincerity he could muster. But Jerome saw through that with the squint of his eyes.

"Sure you didn't. Well, I was an asshole to you and I want to apologize."

"Oh. Okay."

"And I'm real sorry for kicking you out of my uncle's funeral. I saw red and there wasn't a soul who could have talked me out of it. My mama gave me what for afterward, if it's any consolation to you."

It was but Skyler never indicated it by expression or posture.

"I should have known it was all *Ethan's* fault."

It was funny how everyone who knew the guy referred to him that way, Skyler mused. It made him feel better about Keith's past association.

Jerome's tune seemed to have changed. Perhaps it was Ethan who was the crappy influence. He was calmer without him, that much was clear. And yet the board had decided against him. Why? Rawlinson didn't know. Denise never called him back. It was Skyler's guess that the board probably thought Jerome *did* have something to do with...what? The thefts? The embezzling? That's why they didn't want him in charge, though Lester didn't trust him either. Or his judgment. After Ethan, maybe he didn't blame him. Unless all that was a lie as well.

"Who do you suppose is responsible for the, uh, loss of funds? And the thefts?"

"And my uncle's murder? Skyler, I just don't know. It's not lost on me that I've become the prime suspect.

But someone is pulling a scam and trying to put the blame on me. And when I find out who... Well. That's just one more worry in a long line of them. I gotta find another job. I need a career with a future. I don't have one at the museum anymore. If I have a future at all."

"Ah Jerome. I hate to see you leave."

"What choice do I have?"

"This really sucks."

They sat in silence for a time until Jerome raised his head. "So what's between you and Ethan anyway. I couldn't help but notice that you look a lot like him. Are you related?"

"No, thank goodness. It's just that he...well, about ten years ago, he was Keith's boyfriend. They broke up because he cheated on Keith."

"DAY-AM!" Jerome looked like he was considering that. Skyler wondered if Jerome might be thinking about Keith inappropriately, and by the look in his eye he was sure of it. Time to change the subject.

"My friend the police detective will likely be talking to you."

"The woman with the long curly hair, brash attitude?"

"That's her."

"Yeah, she's already talked to me. I was wondering why I wasn't already arrested."

"Sidney's fair. She really goes over all the facts. She won't treat you badly."

"I kind of thought you already decided I was guilty."

"I guess I didn't have all the facts either."

"Do you believe I'm innocent?"

Skyler thought a moment. "I...can't say for certain either way."

He nodded. "Fair enough. You've always been fair, Skyler. I don't think that if I were in your shoes, I'd be able to dismiss it all either. I don't blame you."

"Then help us."

"I would if I could, believe me. I just don't know anything. That's God's truth, Skyler."

"Then where is Ethan now?"

"At his place, I imagine."

"Could you...could you give me his address?"

"Sure." Skyler got his phone and punched in the information as Jerome recited it.

"I'm not interested in talking to that man anymore. So keep me out of it."

"I'll do my best. I'm sure Sidney will, too."

"Okay." He looked around. "Nice place. I never been in here."

"Oh, I like it. It's pretty quiet, generally. Except karaoke night on Saturdays."

He rose. "I'll try to avoid that then." He reached out his hand.

Surprised, Skyler skidded his chair back and stood, grasping Jerome's hand and pumping it once. "Good luck, Jerome. I'm rooting for you." But to himself he said, *Don't disappoint me. Or your uncle.*

❖

Keith was there when Skyler walked in their apartment. He was bent over his biology binders for a change. Skyler knew that football was all-encompassing to him but he also taught classes in biology and had his own homework of correcting papers and notebooks to do.

"Wondered where you were," said Keith, never looking up from his work at the kitchen table.

"So I have stuff to tell you."

"Oh?"

Skyler pulled out a chair and sat down. "After school I went to the museum to take a look at the computer. My paycheck bounced."

Lifting his head at last, Keith pushed aside his work. "Your *paycheck* bounced?"

"Yeah. Earlier, a reimbursement check bounced but I thought maybe someone made an accounting error, so I didn't make a big fuss. But with the paycheck I knew something was up. And when I went I saw that the bank account was not only drained but in arrears. And then…I was attacked."

Keith nearly leapt from his chair before Skyler motioned him back down. "I'm fine. I actually used some of that self-defense you made me take and I threw the guy." He preened a little before he sagged. "But then he got away."

"Did you see who it was?"

"No. Whoever it was had on a hoodie. I tried to chase after but they dodged in and out of traffic. Believe it or not I wasn't willing to risk myself that way."

"Thank God. So…" Keith gestured loosely. "What happened? Did they take anything?"

"No. Funnily enough, they sat down at the computer too to do the very same search. Weird, huh? But they left this." He dug the keys out of his pocket and dropped them on the table.

Keith picked them up and examined them. "Do they fit to the museum?"

"Like a dummy I didn't check at the time, but I compared them to my own keys and they aren't the same."

"Without gloves, right?"

"Yeah. Fingerprints are a little late in the game now. Oopsy."

Keith looked them over again before setting them down. "They look more like master keys."

"Master keys? The kind that open anything?"

"Not anything, but a lot of things.

"Hmm. I'll have to think about that."

"When you give them to Sidney."

"Yes. And then I had a meeting with Jerome."

Keith sat back and hooked his arm around the back of the chair. "How did that go?"

"Well, you'll be pleased to know that *Ethan* is spreading the love everywhere he goes. Jerome claims that it was Ethan who procured that apparently *counterfeit* sports stuff *and* took out the storage locker in Jerome's name."

"Sounds like Ethan to me," he grunted.

"He has since kicked Ethan to the curb. I'll be sharing all that with Sidney, too, by the way."

"I certainly hope so."

Skyler nabbed the keys and played with them. "Jerome seemed a lot different from what he's been lately. Calmer. And he is adamant that he hasn't done anything illegal. And get this; he says that he and his uncle were on good terms and he had no reason to believe he'd be cut out of the museum gig. He doesn't understand what happened, and neither does one of the board members I just talked to. He said that he never heard that Lester bad-mouthed his nephew."

"That's odd."

Skyler crossed his arms and shook his head. "It's all odd. None of it makes sense. I'm just trying to figure out if I can pin all of this on Ethan."

"Why does that guy bother you so much? It's been over a long time ago."

"He's made everyone's life miserable. Whatever he touches turns to shit. And…he didn't deserve you."

"I'd like to think *I* didn't deserve *him*," he muttered.

"I have a mind to send the SFC over there and stalk him."

"Just leave them out of it."

"Why? They've always got my back. Philip was being kind of a slug, but even Dave is stepping up to the plate like a champ. But boy, *Ethan*. I'm so tired of hearing about him. I can't wait till he's out of our lives for good."

Keith's eyes narrowed. "Are you really that jealous?"

"I'm not jealous. But him, looking just like me…"

"For Christ's sake. *That's* what's got your goat? What about me? From every nook and cranny of Redlands and all of Palm Springs, I've had to endure the *parade* of your past conquests. You think that's been easy for me? And here you are, encountering *one* guy from my past whom I didn't even   like—"

"And one woman…"

"It *does* bother you."

"Okay. It does! It scares the hell out of me. Maybe some woman who looks like me might—"

"Jesus, Skyler. I am not *bi!*" He shook his head. "SFC. You know how tired *I* am of that whole idea? Don't get me wrong. I love your friends. They're great. But sometimes when I think about where they all came from it drives me crazy. Not that I think anything will happen with them again. So I get it, okay. I get your thing against Ethan. But it was the past, a guy I did *not* love and who cheated on me in the worst possible way. So get over it."

Keith's words finally hit home. "Okay. Jeesh. You don't have to... It's just that we'd be even if you had your own SFC."

"A KFC?"

Skyler held it in for a full three seconds before he burst out with a laugh. "I think that one's taken."

Keith seemed to realize what Skyler meant and chuckled before a full blown guffaw left his lips. "Well, according to you, I do like my share of chicken."

"Now, now." Skyler smoothed his hands over the polished wood of the table. "I get it," he said quietly. "I guess I *was* jealous."

"You have nothing to worry about."

"I know. And neither do you."

"I know. Now if you're done with your hissy fit I have some news of my own." He took a paper out of his pocket, unfolded it, and handed it to Skyler.

Hissy fit? It was a printed copy of an email. Skyler forgot the slight and frowned. "What is this?"

"My DNA analysis. Turns out that Josh...*isn't* my son after all."

Immense relief washed over Skyler, but he carefully schooled his face. "How are you feeling about that?"

"A little disappointed. A little relieved, to tell you the truth."

"Relieved? Really?"

"I know *you* are."

Right. He could never hide how he felt around Keith.

"Relieved," Keith continued, "because I guess I'd like to have a little more control over how and when I have a kid."

Skyler stiffened. There it was again. Keith wanted a kid. Keith wanted to get married. These were things that Skyler wasn't even sure *he* wanted. He said nothing, trying not to hurt Keith's feelings with his facial expression or body language. He handed back the paper.

Keith took it, read it over again, and stuffed it in his pocket. "So that's that."

Was it? Skyler knew that someday soon, this would all rear its ugly head again and what would he say then?

Friday. The first game of the season for James Polk High was going to be a home game. Everyone was gearing up. A pep rally was planned for the late morning, and the players walked around in their jerseys to get everyone riled up.

Skyler spotted Alex on campus, and though he was wearing his jersey he looked anything but happy about it. He wasn't going to be playing in the game, after all.

He ran into Amber in the hallway as he was making his way to the office to check in. "Hey, Amber. I see you're in your motely."

She looked down at her cheerleading uniform and gave him a withering look. "I hardly think I'd call it that."

"Where's Heather? Did she decide to stick with it?"

"Barely. That girl is causing me to get wrinkles. Well, gotta go. See you at the pep rally and at the GSA!"

He'd almost forgotten. He watched as she tried to look nonchalant as she ran into Ravi Chaudhri. He suddenly perked up from his zombie walk and engaged her in conversation, eyes scanning her long legs and short skirt. Looked like another boy had fallen for the charm of a cheerleading outfit. Not that Skyler hadn't fallen for a man or two in a thong...

Walking purposefully down the corridor, Skyler lit up the stairs. He had a lot on his mind, from Jerome's seemingly sincere assertions, to Ethan (*asshat*), to Laurie Henderson and her son (who was no relation to Keith, thank goodness), to today's GSA meeting, to Sidney and Mike's party he was coordinating for Saturday, to museum thieves, murderers, and embezzlers. Something was ready to break, and he certainly hoped it was a clue and not his mind.

Midmorning, his second period class was cut short so everyone could go to the gym for the pep rally.

Skyler sat with Trish Hornbeck and they whooped and cheered with the best of them. For a little while at least, Skyler could forget all his other troubles and concentrate on being a teacher, on all the activities that centered on school, *his* school. He was a young Polk Panther again, and though he might have cheered on the football team for entirely different reasons back then (his crush on Handsome Hanson the quarterback who didn't know he existed), he was all in now. Each member of the football team was introduced and they ran up to the center of the gym and lined up to the cheering crowds. Skyler got to his feet for Drew, Alex, and Elei, screaming himself hoarse.

Trish shook her head and laughed at him. Maybe it was old hat to her. After all, she was older and had taught longer, but to Skyler it was new and fresh and full of promise. He wanted his kids to have every chance they could to enjoy this time of their lives but also to grow from it.

He was just as pumped as some of the kids after the pep rally was over. Some kids, of course, rolled their eyes and slumped off to class as usual, no worse for wear but certainly not amped. But once Skyler got to the main building, he bounded up the steps to his classroom and cast open the door, humming the school fight song as he erased the white board and hastily wrote the next period's assignment.

"Someone is a real school nerd," said a voice behind him.

Skyler turned. Ravi Chaudhri stood behind him, long-fingered hands toying with his backpack strap over his shoulder.

"I happen to be full of school spirit. What about you, Ravi?"

"I guess the usual school spirit," he said distractedly. "Do you have a moment, Mr. Foxe?"

Glancing at the clock, Skyler nodded. "A very brief one. Especially as you have to get to class, too."

"Okay. I was...wondering about the GSA meeting today."

"Oh?" Geez, was Amber out of luck again? Not that Skyler was ever in her ballpark.

"I'm not gay or anything," he was quick to add, a panicked look on his face. "It's just that...Amber...you know, Amber Watson from comp class—"

"I am acquainted with Ms. Watson."

"Yeah. Well, Amber invited me to come to lunch. At the meeting. And I didn't know if it would be all right. Or if I should. Or...if I'd feel..."

"Comfortable there? Well, Ravi, I don't know you too well yet, but that is a bunch of great kids. Probably a few you already know, like Alex and Rick and their friends, Amber, Heather, and Drew. They aren't gay either but we call them allies, people who are gay-friendly, people who have an open heart and an open mind."

The boy still looked nervous. "What happens at the meetings?"

"We design clothes, do flower arranging…"

Ravi's dark eyes widened.

"I'm *kidding*! The kids just talk about their lives, their parents, issues with how they're treated. That sort of thing. Actually, it's the same kinds of things any student might need to talk about."

Ravi let out a long breath. "Okay. Sounds all right."

"It *is* all right." Skyler pointed toward the door. "Now scoot. You're going to be late for class. I'll see you at lunch, then. Won't I?"

Ravi smiled. The guy was cute. No wonder Amber had fallen for him. He pointed at Skyler. "You got me good. You're funny. Thanks, Mr. Foxe."

Students began filing in, and for the next hour, it was all about Jane Eyre and The Martian Chronicles.

The bell. Lunchtime. And soon the students would arrive for the GSA, Skyler's first as host in his classroom without Ben Fontana. He begged Trish Hornbeck to come and she had promised she would. Skyler wondered if he should move the desks into a circle, and then changed his mind and began moving them back, changed his mind again, and pushed them, scraping in screechy noises across the old linoleum, into a crescent.

"Good Lord, what's going on in here?"

Skyler smiled as Trish entered with a Tupperware with what looked like salad, and a bakery box with something that smelled like chocolate chip cookies.

"I couldn't decide if I wanted a circle or keep it as it is. Now I'm halfway through a crescent and I'm still not sure."

"Crescent," she said, setting down the salad and box on his desk. "It breeds conversation."

"Okay, majority rules." She helped him organize the desks and then he sat at his desk and she took a student desk of her own. She opened the bakery box.

"To share," she said.

"Those will be gone in no time."

"I hope so. I can't have those around for the sake of my thighs."

Skyler chuckled and dug into his sandwich. Slowly, the rest of the GSA began trickling in. Evan was first, the long half of her dark hair falling over her face, while the other side of her head was shaved. She had a silver nose ring and a matching ring in her eyebrow.

Lisa (whom he had always referred to as "Shapeless Dress") was wearing bike shorts today with an oversized flannel top with cut off sleeves over a black tank top.

Kevin who usually wore Doc Martin's was wearing chucks today with shorts that hung below his knees.

Rob was grace itself in his usual frat boy garb and swept-over hair. Skyler doubted he ever broke a sweat.

Then Joyce and Stephanie entered, wearing their cheerleading uniforms (Go Panthers!), and Reese was in his rocker t-shirt and cut-offs as always.

Even Stewart was there. He had started attending after his mother's problems, though he rarely said much.

Elei sauntered in wearing her jersey, trying to look as if she belonged, though she stopped at the door when she noticed the desks in a circle. Seeming to think about this for a moment she finally took a desk in the back of the room.

"Elei," said Skyler. "You can sit in the circle if you'd like."

"I don't want to take up someone else's space." She curled her brown bag in her fingers.

"You won't be," said Evan.

"I'm just here doing detention. I'm not really here for the meeting."

They all turned to Skyler skeptically.

He shrugged. "Up to you, Elei. But your insights are always welcomed."

She gave a half-hearted grin and thrust her hand into her bag and fished out a sandwich.

Amber arrived in mid-conversation with Ravi. He winked at Skyler as he came through the door with her and sat where she indicated.

Skyler hid his grin behind his sandwich.

Rick finally arrived. By himself again. *Calm down, Skyler. You are not their fairy godmother. They have to work it out for themselves...or not.*

Drew came in with Heather, though they still seemed a little stiff with one another.

Glancing at the clock, Skyler tapped out the time with his foot...and Alex arrived at literally the last second.

"Sorry, Mr. Foxe. I couldn't find my lunch. Had to buy one at the lunch window."

Skyler wiped his mouth with a napkin, took a swig from his aluminum water bottle, and faced the group. "Thanks for coming, everyone. Looks like we have a few new people, too. Welcome! As you know, Mr. Fontana didn't have a sixth period and because he thought it important that I be at the meetings and because I didn't think it was fair that he stick around school for an extra hour, I offered to do the meetings here on Fridays at lunch. I hope that works out for everyone. So here we are! Do the new people want to introduce themselves? You don't have to."

Ravi waved. "Hi, I'm Ravi. I was invited here by Amber. And that's it, really."

Another pale freshman introduced himself as Jacob. And then as one, they all turned toward Elei.

When she noticed she looked up at them with widened eyes. "I'm just here for detention."

Rob laughed. "Because you beat up Alex."

Alex clutched both sides of his desk so tightly he was liable to break it. "She did NOT beat me up."

"I heard what he said to you," said Evan toward Elei. "Good one, girl."

"She did NOT beat me up!"

Rick was trembling with the effort to stay where he was, to say nothing.

Drew faced the crowd. "Elei was only defending herself."

Heather was in his face. "And you're defending her *again*?"

"What? What is your problem, Heather? I thought you liked a guy who stood up for women."

"Maybe you're standing up too much."

Rob rested his chin on his hand with a wide grin, watching it all like a ping pong match.

"You guys!" said Skyler. "We are not here to sow discord. We can go anywhere else for that. Here is where we stand together."

"But you were there, weren't you, Mr. Foxe?" asked Joyce. "The way I heard it, Alex said some pretty dumb things."

"Like girls don't belong on the football team?" said Kevin. "They don't."

The room blasted into pandemonium.

Skyler was momentarily stunned by the shouting matches going on and who was shouting at whom.

Trish stood up and banged her empty Tupperware tub with her fork. "Hey! Quiet down. You should all be ashamed of yourselves. Did you actually hear what you were saying? Girls don't belong here or there. Isn't that the same thing people say about LGBT people? We wouldn't even have this GSA club if that attitude was allowed to prevail. We wouldn't have girls' volleyball or softball if it wasn't for Title IX protections. We wouldn't have a lot of our rights if good people didn't fight for it and fight against all those very attitudes. I'm ashamed of you guys."

She sat again and everyone looked at their desks or their hands.

After a while, Kevin spoke. "I didn't mean anything by what I said. I just meant girls can get really hurt. They have…" He motioned vaguely to his torso. "Different equipment, know what I mean."

"I have protection…for my *different* equipment," said Elei bitterly. "And what the hell do *you* care? You don't even like football."

"I beg your pardon," he said, hand to his chest. "Now who's stereotyping?"

"Most queers don't like sports," she said matter-of-factly.

The room exploded again.

Skyler fell back to his chair. It rocked back and swiveled away, as he longed to do. But he knew he had to bring order. He turned it around again and shouted above them until they quieted. "Now look! This has got to stop. LGBT men like sports as much as the next guy. Alex and Coach Fletcher being the example here. And some girls who are not LGBT people also excel at sports, as Elei exemplifies. Can we just cut the crap, ladies and gentlemen?"

"Yeah, we can," said Drew. "'Cause I'm outta here." He slipped from the desk, grabbed his pack, and stalked out the door. Heather, stunned in his wake, seemed to be debating whether to go after him or not.

When she glanced at Skyler he gave her a subtle head jerk toward the door. And as nonchalantly as she could, she gathered her bag as well. "I think I should leave, too. Catch you all later."

Joyce and Stephanie didn't even say anything as they left.

Rick rose, sighed toward Alex without actually looking at him, and ambled out the door. Alex raised an arm toward him, "Rick! Goddammit."

"Sit down, Mr. Ryan. You're doing detention, remember?"

"Shit," he muttered.

The others seemed to feel that the magic had gone out of the meeting, and made their apologies and left, too. Rob was last. He saluted Skyler. "A most enjoyable meeting, Mr. Foxe. We must do it again, sometime."

"I sincerely hope not, Rob."

Skyler sat back in his chair and cast a forlorn look toward Trish. She burst out laughing and didn't stop for a full minute.

Later he told Keith about his disaster of a meeting, but Keith only half-listened, rushing around the apartment as he was. "Look, babe. I gotta go. We'll talk later, okay. You coming to the game?"

"Of course."

Keith leaned in and kissed him on the cheek. "For good luck." And then he grabbed Skyler unexpectedly and planted a good one to his lips. "And that one…was for me." He smiled, grabbed all his gear, and hurried out the door.

Skyler threw up his hands. Nothing for it but to go to the game as well.

Buying a bag of popcorn from the Scholarship Federation booth, he looked up at the stands already full of kids. He climbed the concrete steps and squeezed into a spot on the first row nearest the player's benches. He wanted to cheer on his kids and Keith.

Though he never understood all the details of the game no matter how many times Keith tried to explain it, Skyler was nevertheless caught up in the excitement. The bright lights flooding the field, the hum and chatter of the audience of students, the smell of popcorn, the flag girls, the cheesy Panther mascot, the cheerleaders, the band. Yeah, he got it. He understood at least that much of it.

He crunched his popcorn and when the cheerleaders began their sets to get everyone ready for the game, he did the cheers with the rest of the crowd. Amber, out there in her uniform and pom-poms, winked at him. Heather was there, too, and she was darned good. He hoped she would stick with it. A variety of activities was always good for a students' CV.

Joyce and Stephanie pom-pomed their way through the cheers as well, and offered extra waves to Skyler.

Embarrassed, he looked around, and the students beside him giggled.

Finally, everyone stood for the national anthem that the band pumped out with a few discordant notes, then their school song, and then the football players were announced from the sound booth.

One by one they ran onto the field. And there was Keith! Skyler shook his head at himself. He was like a kid again, excited by the pomp. Keith wore his Polk Panther polo shirt, with a lanyard sporting the silver engraved whistle Skyler had given him last year at Christmas. The sight of it made Skyler a little gooey inside and terribly flattered, especially after Keith had declared it his lucky whistle and vowed to wear it just for the games.

But tonight, Keith had eyes only for his team and the field.

Skyler was staring so much at Keith that he missed the kick off and suddenly the game was on. But when he scanned the bench, there was Alex and Elei, sitting with the water boy and a few other players. Both of them looked much larger and fiercer with their shoulder pads. Elei's wild hair was caught up tight in a bun squashed flat to her head.

Skyler turned to the girls beside him and offered them the rest of his popcorn. They took eagerly it with thanks, and he excused himself through the crowd and made his way down the stairs. He didn't know if he was supposed to be on the field or not, but he had started on instinct and before he had a chance to consider it, he was there. He crept toward the bench and sat down between his two students.

Alex looked aghast. "Mr. Foxe! What are you doing here? I don't think you're supposed to be here."

"I don't know if I'm allowed here either but I thought you two needed some moral support."

Elei glanced at him mildly. "You're really a hands-on kind of teacher, aren't you?"

"Yup, I guess so. But I really want you guys to get along. You have two years left together on the team and I'd hate for you to end up on this bench for most of it."

"Talk to *him*," she said, turning back toward her teammates on the field.

"No, actually, I'm talking to both of you. After all, Elei, you're the one who hit Alex."

"And I apologized for it, did detention, and I'm sitting out my first game. So I think I did enough."

She had a point. It really was Alex who needed that attitude adjustment. "But to be fair, Elei," he said aloud, "it's Alex who is getting a hard time for it from the rest of the school."

"Thanks for reminding me, Mr. Foxe," he muttered.

"And it's a blow to one's ego. Boys have a harder time with that than girls do."

She shrugged. "Fragile male ego," she said.

"Yes. So can we at least acknowledge that Alex is getting doubly punished?"

She gave Alex a look. "Yeah. I'm sorry for that, too. Really. And though we don't have to be bosom friends, I'd appreciate some respect."

Skyler turned toward the agitated teen. "How about it, Alex? What must Elei have sacrificed to get where she is? How much extra training must she have done to be even as good as the boys? How much taunting? Way more than you're getting."

By the look in his eye, Alex was slowly comprehending.

"And you know, Alex, if you were a cop and there were two teens getting into fights, you'd have to talk to them like I'm talking to you. And I'm pointing out these things because I'm able to imagine what it's like to be in the others' shoes. Do you understand what that means?"

"Yeah," he said, the idea dawning on his features. "We talked about that in the Teen Police Academy. It's called 'empathy'; understanding how someone else might feel, about what might be happening in their lives, not by what you see on the surface." Skyler got the sense that he wasn't parroting back a series of facts, but had truly internalized the message. After all, that was Alex in a nutshell. Alex's backstory was deep and filled with controversies. He was likely especially aware that he could well be judged by his own past indiscretions.

He got up and stood in front of Elei, who looked up at him skeptically. "Dude, I didn't do my own homework. I studied this shit and I totally forgot it." He put his hand out. "I'm sorry for what I said. And I *do* think girls should be on the team. As long as they work as hard as you."

It took her a moment but she finally put her hand in his and shook it. Some of the kids in the stands noticing their exchange, wolf-whistled and cat-called but Alex seemed to be able to ignore it. He nudged Skyler aside to sit next to her, and began talking about the game and what he would have done on a play, asking her opinion.

Feeling proud of himself, Skyler sat and watched the game, too. And then he noticed Keith looking his way and grinning. He winked and turned his attention back to his players.

The bench wasn't the most comfortable of places to sit, and that lump in his pocket did him no favors. He took it out—the keys—and remembered again why he had them. He toyed with them until Alex spoke.

"Those look like the keys our sergeant had at the Teen Police Academy."

"What's that you said, Alex?"

"Those keys. Our instructors had keys just like them. See. The Schlage name and the 'Do Not Duplicate.' Everyone seemed to have them at the station. I noticed those things. I'm trying to notice stuff like that. As a cop, you know?"

Skyler looked at the keys again. Police station? Why would someone from the police station be breaking into the museum?

All his ruminations were cut short when a tall shadow fell across him and his benchmates. He looked up and spied Rick standing awkwardly on the field in front of them.

"Rick?" said Alex. "Dude, you aren't supposed to be on the field."

"I saw you shake hands with Elei. Are you done being an asshole to her?"

"I don't think he's ever done being an asshole," said Elei with a grin. She elbowed Alex good-naturedly. "But he's done being an asshole to me."

"Yeah," he said sheepishly. "I finally remembered about empathy. And it's true, dude. She got me good. And if I were the rest of the school, I'd rag on me, too."

"Wow, homey. You're taking this police thing to heart."

"I want to be a good cop, Rick, not one of those guys who ends up in a YouTube video. But I'm learning, okay?"

Rick was smiling from ear to ear. "Okay. Get together after the game?"

Alex was smiling, too. "Yeah. We'll have a wrap up with coach and stuff and if we win there's a party, but...yeah. Stick around, okay?"

Skyler got to his feet. "My work here is done. Come on, Rick. Let's go back to the stands before we cause more of a scandal."

He followed Rick out and gave him a friendly shove when he kept looking back at Alex with a goofy grin on his face.

Everyone seemed excited for the halftime entertainment. The cheerleaders outdid themselves. Skyler was impressed by their gymnastics, the mascot's antics, and the flag girl routine with the band's rousing and slightly off-key rendition of Beyoncé's "Freedom." Their marching formations were inspired, and there was a projection of the music video in the middle of the field that made everyone cheer especially loud.

The Panthers were already ahead and Alex and Elei couldn't seem to contain their excitement when the game resumed. They yelled and clapped, rooting for their teammates.

It was the last half of the last quarter and Keith must have felt sorry for the two. Skyler saw him trot over to the bench and speak to the both of them. Their faces burst with amazement and gratitude and they grabbed their helmets and jogged out to the field.

"We have a change of line-up," said the announcer from the sound booth. "Looks like number forty-nine, Alex Ryan, will be taking his place as tight end. And…yes, yes, number fifteen, Elei Sapani is taking to the field. Ladies and gentlemen, this is James Polk High's very first female football player. We are making history tonight, folks. Sapani is a wide receiver. I've watched her during practice and all I can say is the Citrus High Blackhawks had better be on their guard."

Skyler stood and grabbed the railing in front of him. "Go, Sapani! Go, Ryan!" he screamed.

The team got into a huddle, no doubt changing their tactics with the presence of their new players. They broke huddle with a unison clap and got into their starting positions. They were marching toward the end zone, around the twenty yard line.

Skyler couldn't tell if the player on the opposing team directly in front of Elei was giving her a hard time, but by the rolling of her shoulders, he might be.

"You can do it, Elei," he murmured. She looked even bigger with those shoulder pads, and she was pretty big on her own. "Just ignore the jackass."

Alex wasn't too far from her, and Skyler *could* tell that he was saying something and gesturing to one of the other team's players. The player facing Elei looked back once at Alex before he dismissed him with the flick of his hand.

The snap! Elei immediately zig-zagged forward toward the goal post. The quarterback fell back, feinting with the ball. Another wide receiver ran out to the open field and the quarterback cocked his arm, ready to throw. The Blackhawk defense took off after the receiver, but at the last minute, the quarterback faked it and chucked it instead toward Elei.

She leapt high to catch it. Pivoting, she turned toward the goal post.

Out of nowhere, a Blackhawk offensive lineman dove, nearly sliding along the grass to grab her legs. She had nowhere to go but down gripping the ball to her chest. Alex leapt toward her before the pile on, a particularly brutal one as far as Skyler could tell. He twisted on the railing and clenched his teeth in sympathy.

Whistles stopped the action, yellow flags were thrown, and two refs hurried toward them. Everyone slowly climbed out of it, with Alex lifting off last. But Elei was down and not moving.

"Oh crap," said Skyler. The stands fell quiet, with only the barest of murmurings. Alex stood protectively over her while the refs double-timed it over there. *This was just what Keith feared*, he thought, biting a fingernail.

As soon as the refs arrived, Alex leaned over and offered her a hand. She rose stiffly and took it, rising to her feet.

"She's all right!" blared the announcer. "And look at that. Eight yards from the goal. Excellent catch for Sapani. First down, Panthers. And a penalty for the Blackhawks."

Skyler screamed. Alex had protected her. He had used his body to shield her from the worst of the impact. "Ryan! Whoo hoo!" he screamed again.

"That's my homey!" cried Rick proudly, even as Alex limped back toward the huddle. "That's my boy!"

And so it went. The Panthers crept closer by increments to the goal. Skyler didn't sit for the rest of the game. He and Rick clung to the railing, with Skyler biting his nails. They were going to win their first game of the season with Alex *and* Elei. He grabbed Rick's sleeve. "They're gonna do it!"

"I know, Mr. Foxe." He laughed and shook his head at his crazy teacher. Skyler didn't care. All at once, he understood why Keith loved the game so much, and Skyler was all in, too, white-knuckling it on the rail.

The snap, and all the players scrambled. Skyler tried to follow who was who in the mad dash, but he couldn't quite make out the numbers. This time Sapani and Alex were out of it, but the receiver ran over the goal line. It was over. Panthers twenty-seven, Blackhawks twenty. Game!

Students flooded the field and surrounded the team, jumping and cheering. There was no stopping the celebration. He knew he wouldn't see Keith till late tonight, but he left the school to it. In the parking lot, he texted a congratulatory message to Keith that he knew the man wouldn't see for hours, and threaded his way through the cars, now free to ruminate about what Alex said about those keys and what it could mean.

Chapter Nineteen

KEITH CAME HOME LATE AS SKYLER SUSPECTED he would, and he didn't seem tired in the least. He was still pumped from their win, elated about the Josh situation...and horny. Skyler, needing to let off his own steam, relieved Keith of his condition in a rather energetic session that left Skyler feeling it the next morning with aches and pains. He remembered a day when he could stretch and flex in all kinds of positions, but he supposed his muscles weren't as pliable as they used to be.

Even Keith was feeling it. "Are you as achy as I am?"

"I'm probably sore in a few more places than you are."

He rolled over and grabbed Skyler into a hug and nuzzle. "Sorry, babe. I might have gotten a little carried away. I hope I didn't hurt you."

"You didn't. Just...a little sore is all."

"I was just so proud of that team of mine. And Alex and Elei."

"I hope you didn't celebrate with them the way you did with me."

He gave Skyler a withering look and slowly rose from the bed, massaging his lower back. "Could I be getting this creaky at thirty-six?"

"What can I say? I'm your best work-out."

He eyed Skyler from head to naked foot. "You sure are. I never had this much fun in a gym."

"Honey, you aren't going to the right gyms."

He gave Skyler the eye until Skyler held up his hands in surrender. "And I'm not either…anymore."

Keith rolled his eyes and walked unsteadily toward the bathroom.

Skyler lay back. "I'm so glad you relented and put Alex and Elei into the game."

"I wasn't going to," he said around his toothbrush. "But I guess I'm just a softie."

"That's not how it felt to me last night," murmured Skyler, rubbing his ass. Now that the drama of the game was over it was time to think of Sidney and Mike's party tonight, but even though he would ordinarily be stressing about that, his mind shot straight to the problem of the museum. And he wondered a little bit about his most recent encounters with the museum stalker. And those keys. Police station, Alex had said. What about the police station might be connected?

He was still lying in bed thinking when Keith emerged from the bathroom in a cloud of steam. Hair wet and tousled into shape, Keith stood in front of the bed in all his naked glory. Skyler's brain just about shut down to all but that.

"Hey, mister, eyes up here," said Keith, snapping his fingers in Skyler's face.

"I'm paying attention," he muttered half-heartedly.

"Sure you are. It just occurred to me. The video off the cameras in the museum. What did you find when you looked at them? And what did Sidney say about it?"

It took a second for Keith's words to penetrate the clutter of Keith/naked/chest hair/cock in Skyler's brain. Skyler sat up. "Hey. I forgot all about that!"

He fumbled for his phone on the side table while Keith retreated to the closet to cover all that naked loveliness. Skyler sighed and sat back against the pillows, calling up the app. "Now let's see," he murmured. "That first attack was last Friday." He ran the video in fast forward. He saw the place to enter a time stamp and set it for before he entered the museum. And there it was, the stalker in the hoodie. "Hey Keith! I got it."

Pulling on his t-shirt, a shorts-clad Keith hurried from the closet and sat beside him on the bed, watching Skyler's phone with him.

The hooded figure moved through the darkened museum, from camera to camera. Then Skyler entered.

"I look terrible," he sighed.

"Shush."

"There's no sound."

"I can't think when you're talking."

They both watched as the figure froze once Skyler's presence was detected. He seemed to move slowly and carefully along the edges until Skyler got closer, then wham! Trash bag over the head. He dashed into the office, hid behind the desk as the cops ran through, and then he was out of there.

Skyler crossed his ankles. "Not one of my prouder moments."

"Let's see the latest one. When was that? Wednesday?"

"Yeah. Just a sec. There." The app played the newest video. Skyler was at the computer when he looked up at the door. He slapped the light off, switched off the computer, and looked like a cartoon character, snapping his head back and forth before he dove for the bookcase.

The door opened seconds after that and the hooded figure entered. The door shut and they went directly for the computer, tapping their fingers impatiently as it took a while to boot up.

Skyler's foot silently hit the trash can, the figure jumped up from their seat, and scrambled to leave, but Skyler foolishly tried to cut off his exit.

"Little idiot," said Keith shaking his head. "What if they were armed? Never try to stop a felon, Skyler."

"My blood was up."

The figure grabbed Skyler and almost faster than Skyler could see, he handily threw the thief over his shoulder to the ground.

"Holy shit," said Keith.

"See that? Let's watch it again." Skyler rewound and re-watched his triumph of self-defense skills.

"Good job, Skyler." Keith held up his hand and Skyler smacked it with his own.

When they both tore out of the office, Skyler stopped the video. He frowned. "I couldn't see anyone's face."

"There are other clues, you know. Let's see that first one again."

Skyler queued it up and hit play. They watched it for a bit until Keith pointed to the screen. "Pause it."

Skyler hit the button.

"See that?" Keith's finger pointed to the hooded head.

"See what?"

"In the office shot, the hooded man comes to this height on the bookshelf. Now run the other one."

Skyler did.

"Okay," said Keith. "Now this person only comes to here on the bookshelf."

Skyler squinted at the screen. "Oh yeah." He looked at Keith. "They aren't the same person."

"Nope."

"Well shit. Now what?"

"Let's see that first one again."

Skyler played it. He watched the taller hooded man struggle with Skyler and then high-tail it out of there. A flash of white. Skyler paused it and rewound. He played it, slower. Sure enough, as the assailant turned to flee, his foot came into view of the camera. A white running shoe. Just like the ones...

"I know who this is," said Skyler.

He and Keith got out of the car in front of the building. Skyler led the way through the tangle of green landscaping, up some stairs, up to the townhouse apartment. It read number thirty-four on large brass numbers on the jamb. He knocked. They waited. Skyler was trying to breathe evenly but it was tough what with his adrenalin pumping and his heart beating a tom-tom in his chest. Finally the door opened.

Ron smiled, holding the door, and looked from Skyler to Keith. "Hey, Skyler. Keith. What's up?"

Skyler looked to Keith for confirmation and the man nodded. "Ron, you know why we're here."

Ron shook his head, his smile frozen on his face. "No, I don't."

"Yes, you do. Will you let us in or shall we do it out here?"

The smile on Ron's face faded. Horror replaced the cheer in his eyes. He turned away from the doorway, leaving the door open. Skyler stepped in first.

Ron sank to his sofa and dropped his head in his hands. Suddenly he heaved a great sob. "I wouldn't have done it. I would never have done it if I had known I'd be the director." He wiped sloppily at his face. His speech was broken by more crying and more tears that he continued to wipe at. "I was at the end of my rope. I was never going to get a decent museum job. It's so hard to find them, you know, Skyler? And I needed money. This stupid apartment costs so much and the cheaper ones are in dangerous neighborhoods. I have six years of school, Skyler. Six years I'm still paying for. My degree is worthless!"

He fell to sobbing again.

Skyler crossed his arms over his chest and shuffled his feet. "You tried to deflect me toward Randi and Seth. That was very uncool, Ron."

"I know. I'm sorry. You obviously never fell for it."

"Where's the stuff? Is it all gone?"

"I tried to sell it on eBay...but I couldn't. I couldn't sell any of it. It doesn't belong to me. It belongs to the public. Oh God! What have I done?"

"Well...that's something." He looked to Keith, but Keith subtly shook his head.

Ron raised his ruined face again. "I thought you were on to me. I saw that message on eBay and I panicked. I took my page down."

"So...where are they?"

"Spare bedroom. Second door on the right down the hall."

Keith left them to investigate. Skyler watched him stalk over the carpeted floor, enter the dark hallway, and open the door. He just stuck his head inside and looked around. When he closed the door he nodded toward Skyler. "You'll have to take a full inventory but it looks like it's all there."

"Oh, it is," said Ron. He sniffed. "Do you have to call the police?"

Before Skyler could answer, Keith cut in with, "Yes. And you attacked Skyler."

"I didn't. I mean I didn't hurt you, did I? I tried not to hurt you."

"He tried not to hurt me."

"What he did was a felony. It's not up to you to decide, Skyler. You don't own these things."

"But...but if he just returned them and quit his job..."

"No, Keith is right," said Ron in a deadened and defeated tone. "I have to make this right, Skyler. I did this and I have to let justice take its course."

Biting his lip, Skyler pleaded with his eyes again but Keith was adamant. He was already getting out his phone. And Skyler could no longer ignore the other possibility.

Quietly, he asked, "What about Lester, Ron? Did you kill him?"

"Lester? Oh God no! I'd never hurt Lester. Why would I?"

"Because he caught you stealing maybe? Threatened to go to the police?"

"No! No way. And poison? I don't even know how to find poison. I couldn't hurt anyone."

Skyler remembered the keys in his pocket and took them out. "Ron, are these your keys?"

Ron wiped at his eyes again and looked. "No. Never saw those before."

"Are you sure? They don't belong to some secret lock-up, do they?"

"For what? I kept all the stuff here."

"Poison, maybe?"

"I told you. I couldn't hurt Lester. And why would I keep poison to incriminate me?"

"You kept the museum stuff."

"That's different. Those are exhibits. Artifacts. You can't just...toss those away behind a vault where no one can see them and appreciate them. They have to be available for seeing, for research. That's why I...I couldn't sell them. Some rich guy putting Lincoln's hat on display in his private atrium. It sickened me. I couldn't do it. And then I didn't know how to return it all."

Skyler could relate. He knew, even if he was on his last dime, he couldn't sell some of his more prized books. They'd have to go into poverty with him. Some things just couldn't be sacrificed.

"What about the museum bank account? Were you stealing from that?"

"How? Believe me if I could have done that, I wouldn't have stolen the exhibits. *And* my paycheck bounced. If I wasn't in the shitter before I sure am now. So...what? Was someone embezzling money, too? I suppose everyone will blame me for that as well. But I didn't do it. I don't have access. No one gave me the power to even write checks on the account yet let alone steal from it."

Something Sidney could check out. Skyler watched him sob some more and wondered if he believed him.

After talking to the police for a few hours, Skyler was ready to go home. Keith took him home.

"He didn't kill Lester," said Skyler. "He didn't." He moved toward the living room and plopped down on the sofa.

Keith stood above him. "That's for the police to decide."

"He couldn't even sell them. All those things he took and he couldn't even sell them."

"He would have made a good curator. If it wasn't for all the larceny."

"And now he'll never be a curator. He's blown it. He'll go to jail and when he comes out with a tattoo on his face, he'll be in a gang or something. He'll have to become a rent boy."

"Skyler, aren't you getting a little carried away?"

"I've known him for years. What's he gonna do?"

"Maybe he'll get time served."

"It's all so horrible."

"I know. Breaking the law is always pretty horrible. There are always victims. Sometimes the victim is the criminal themselves."

"That was so After School Special, what you just said."

"All right, you're feeling better. I have to go."

"Go? Where are you going?"

Keith headed for the door. "I told you, I have a meeting with Elei's parents."

"Jesus. Can't they do that on a weekday?"

"I know. But they want to talk about her detention and the reasons for it. I thought I already talked to them but obviously they have more to say."

Skyler gave him a weak smile. "Aren't you glad you gave her a chance on the team?"

"Yeah, I'm ecstatic. I'll see you later."

"What about the party tonight? You aren't going to be late, are you?"

"Absolutely not. I will *be* there, Skyler."

"On time!"

"On time." He returned to Skyler, bent over, and kissed him. "I'll be back to change. Love you. And don't obsess over this. There was nothing you could have done."

"But he could have reached out…"

"Skyler…do *not* obsess. Instead, obsess over this party. Surely you need to check the arrangements a few hundred more times."

"Ha, ha! Have a good meeting with angry parents!"

Keith scowled and shuffled out the door.

Skyler *could* obsess over the party…but he'd rather obsess over Ron. The man was right. If Ron could have drained the bank account as clearly someone had, he wouldn't have had to steal the museum stuff, and that had continued even after the money was gone from the bank. So it likely wasn't him.

"Wait! The other video." He got out his phone and called up the app. He passed over the video with Ron and clicked on the other one. Okay, so this person was a lot shorter. Shorter than Skyler? No, almost the same height, but that didn't mean anything since he was pretty short. What had he felt when he threw the thief? Heavy, light? Girl, boy? He closed his eyes and tried to remember. It had all happened so fast, almost on instinct, so he couldn't really recall of any details. All he could think at the time was his surprise that it had worked so well.

He opened his eyes again and watched the video. He let it run over and over. There must be something distinguishing, something different.

He got out the keys again and looked at them.

And just as he turned away, something flashed in the video out of the corner of his eye. He rewound and watched it again. Maybe it was the keys falling. That would make sense. But even as he made the video go slowly, something snapped into place in his head.

The keys. He turned them over his palms, his fingers.

"It's not the police station. It's the city hall." And as the video slowly rolled along, he saw it. He sat back with a moan. Shit. He didn't want it to be true. But there it was.

Skyler still had plenty of time before the party. He wrestled with himself, thinking that it could wait one more day. Have the party, do it tomorrow. But then he thought about Lester taken out before his time, and none of it mattered anymore.

He pulled up in front of the modest 1960's home. A low manicured pine tree sat on the perfect lawn, like an oversized banzai. The ranch style house stretched out before him, and when he got out, he walked along a stone path to the front door, hidden behind a living bamboo screen.

He knocked on the door and waited. *Don't answer*, he told himself. Then he could put it off. But he heard footsteps and then the door opened.

"Skyler? What are you doing here? Dear me, where are my manners? Come in."

He walked over the threshold and followed his host into the living room of tasteful mid-century furnishings.

He was offered a seat and he took it, folding his hands together.

"I was just about to pour myself some tea. Let me get another cup."

"That isn't necessary."

"It's no trouble."

Skyler waited until they returned, set the cup and saucer before the pot on the glass coffee table, and poured. "Sugar? Cream?"

"Just a little sugar."

He took the offered cup. The aroma of strong, fragrant tea filled his nose and he lifted the cup to his lips.

"What can I do for you, Skyler?"

Skyler sighed. "Well...I know about the embezzled funds. And I'm just speculating here, but I think Lester Huxley knew about them and knew who did it and was about to turn them in."

Silence.

"So..." He set his tea cup down. "That's why I'm guessing he was killed. That...*you*...killed him."

She raised her hand to scrape the hair from her face. Her bracelet lightly tinkled, catching the light, as it had caught the light in the video.

"That's a lot of speculating."

"Yeah, I know," he said sadly. "But since you're the only one of the board members to say that Lester told you not to promote Jerome...I figured that you thought Jerome would have spotted something wrong with the books right away. The other board members didn't understand why Jerome wasn't promoted, never heard of any controversy. Never heard from Lester. Because Lester never said any such thing. It all came from you and you alone. I guess you didn't know that *I* had access to the bank account and the checkbook already, have had for years."

She sat back and crossed her legs. She was wearing a tasteful pair of dark capri leggings and flats. "No, I didn't know that. Well, what a shame."

"Yeah." His anger was mounting. "A shame you had to kill such a nice guy for something as stupid as stealing money. What's wrong, Denise? Isn't your salary enough? Here's your keys, by the way." He tossed them to the glass table. They clanged inharmoniously, skidding the teacup and saucer a few inches away from him.

"No, the salary is barely enough for all the work I do. For all the work I've done for this city all these years. Do you think this lovely house is paid for? Taxes keep rising, expenses keep rising, but the salary doesn't. I'm one paycheck away from disaster, like most middle class people I know."

"You *killed* him, Denise, and tried to ruin another man's career."

"Two men. Killed two men."

"Two?"

"You. Do you think that was only tea I put in your cup?"

Skyler shot to his feet. "You bitch!"

She rose, too. "Let's just let this take effect and it will soon be over."

Skyler kicked the teacup from the table to the floor. The shards flew everywhere.

"That was my favorite set," she said without emotion.

"Good. And the joke's on you. I didn't drink it."

Emotion on her face at last!

"Do you really think I'd walk into your house—a known poisoner—and eat or drink anything you had to offer?"

"I know you're here alone."

She moved quicker than he realized she could. But of course, he *had* chased after her and she had gotten away from him.

A heavy-looking art piece was in her hand and she lunged for him. He grabbed the wrist holding it even as she tried to bash him in the head with it. She was stronger than she looked and Skyler was struggling.

He yanked it out of her hand and tossed it as far away as he could. She went for his face with her nails. Grasping her wrists, he twisted them away, but now she was after his neck.

With a force Skyler didn't know he was capable of, he crossed his arms over, pivoted, and threw her over his shoulder. She landed hard on the glass coffee table, shattering it and upending the hot teapot. She screamed as the liquid hit her and the shards of crockery and the glass table cut her.

The door burst open.

"Hold it right there!"

Skyler sighed in relief. "Officer Carey. What took you so long?"

Chapter Twenty

SIDNEY STOMPED ONTO THE SCENE, PUSHING techs and police aside. "Skyler Leslie Fucking Foxe! Where the hell are you?"

He rushed up to her with placating hands. "Keep your voice down. What are you doing here?"

"It's my case. Someone from the police station called me. Funny how *you* didn't."

Skyler looked at his watch. "Because you are having a party in less than three hours and I didn't want you to miss it. I thought Officer Carey and I could handle it."

"It's *my* case."

"Whatever. But you'd better not be late. Or make me late."

"I won't. It's my case, after all."

"So I've heard…from somewhere."

She shoulder-nudged him. "You all right?

"Yeah. That self-defense class is really paying off."

She glanced behind her to the shattered coffee table. "Holy shit. Did you do that?"

He rocked on his heels with a smug expression. "Yup."

A large man bullied his way through the doorway holding his badge up. "Skyler!"

"And there's Keith right on cue."

"Skyler are you all right?"

"I'm fine. I can take care of myself. See?"

Keith looked at the ruined table and tea things with widened eyes. "Holy shit."

Looking down at himself, Skyler ticked his head. "But I did get tea stains on my shirt. By the way, one of those cups had poison in it. She tried to poison me, the beyotch."

Sidney and Officer Carey talked with Skyler for a long while as Keith looked on. It was decided that Skyler's shirt would also have to be taken in as evidence, in case the tea that spattered him was the poisoned one.

"My shirt? But...but...it's a nice one."

"Take off your shirt, O Pale One," said Sidney, crooking her finger at him.

"What? Now?"

"Yes, now. Chain of evidence. Come on."

Embarrassed, Skyler glanced back at the techs eyeing him and unbuttoned his shirt, slipped it off his shoulders, and handed it over. Sidney's gloved hands took it and handed it to Carey, who bagged it and marked it.

Standing naked from the waist up, Skyler self-consciously folded his arms. "Can I go now?"

"Yes. And don't be late to the party."

"*You* don't be late. It's your fucking party."

"I know. Hey!" She turned to the officers and techs in the room. "Are you all going to my fucking party?"

"Hell yes!" some cried. Others laughed.

She raised her hands like Evita. "I have the power to make crime stand still."

"I bow to your magnificence," muttered Skyler as he scuttled out the door with Keith following.

❖

The party had been in full swing for some hours. People brought gifts, which Skyler dutifully stacked on a table next to a two-tiered wedding cake that Rodolfo had whipped up. The figurines on the top were both in cop uniforms. Officers and friends played pool, darts, and foosball together, mingling Filipino, police, SFC, and men from Trixx within the private space upstairs at the Shakespearean.

But after cake was consumed, after Skyler played the host and made a humorous toast for the bride and groom—for which Sidney gave him the finger—Skyler got down to some serious drinking with Sidney, the kind they used to do in days gone by when they were both single and hanging out in bars.

Skyler leaned his numb chin on his hand, but it kept slipping off. Sidney downed another tequila shot.

"Did you ever imagine yourself married?" he slurred.

She licked her lips as if wondering whether they were still there or not. "Not in a million, million years. While other girls were imagining their perfect weddings and perfect dresses I was playing war with the boys."

"I know. I was the one planning the imaginary party."

"What about you, Skyboy? What if Keith pops the question?"

"The question? What question? Ooooooh! *That* question. Oh no, no, no, no, no."

"You'll say no?"

"He won't ask."

"But look at him."

They both turned. Keith looked as fresh as when he emerged from the shower. He had on a stylishly tight t-shirt, and the sparkle in his eyes came from cheer not alcohol. "God he's *gorgeous*," said Skyler, smiling sloppily.

"Yeah, he is. Be a shame if he walked."

"He's...he's not gonna walk. Jeez. Why do you always think the worst of people? He loves me. He's not going anywhere."

"Let's hope so. Oh! You were gonna tell me about the board. What did they say when you broke the news to them?"

"They were pretty shaken up. But they did decide to give Jerome the directorship. I'm sure he's over the moon."

"That's nice."

"It *is* nice. I think it's going to be okay for him. Especially now that *Ethan* is out of the picture."

"He's in jail," she said, sucking on a lime wedge. "Probably for a long while, with all that counterfeiting and fraud and stuff."

"Good. Serves him right."

She sat up. "Oh! The girls are dancing. I'm gonna join them."

She staggered away from the table, blew him a kiss, and meshed with a gaggle of giggling women from the police station who were dancing with some drag queens from Trixx, while some of Mike's family, whom he had taken as calm and sober, were whooping it up in the far corner near the dart board. He forgot that Catholics liked their drink.

Out of nowhere, Mike slid into the bar stool next to him.

Skyler smiled. "Hi, Mike." Throwing an arm over Mike's shoulder, Skyler got in close. "You got a really great girl there, you know that?"

Mike nodded enthusiastically. His eyes were bright with alcohol, too. "I know! She's really great."

"I know! We've been friends since we were nine years old. Did you know that?"

"I think I did know that."

"I don't want anything bad happening to her, okay? So you'd better be a good husband."

"I promise."

"You'd better. Or I'll...I'll throw you, or something. 'Cause I know how to do that."

"So I heard."

"That's right. I can do it." He belched. "'scuse me. So Mike, Mike. Mmmmmike... I like that name. It's a good cop name."

"A good Irish name."

"Yeah. But you don't look Irish."

They both cracked up, leaning over each other.

Skyler recovered first, wiping at his eyes. "And Mike, you know what?"

"What?"

Skyler got in even closer and poked him in the chest. "I think you're really cute and Sidney is very lucky."

"Thanks, Skyler."

"No, I mean it. You're cute. And I want to kiss the groom."

Before Mike could say anything, Skyler grabbed him by both cheeks, dragged him in, and planted a wet sloppy one to Mike's lips. It seemed to hold on a bit long, but if anyone were to ask him later, Skyler would tell them that Mike had kissed him back.

A shadow fell over Skyler. "Okay, mister, that's enough partying for you."

"Keith! God, you are sooooo good-looking. Mm-mm. I was just kissing the groom."

"Yeah, I noticed. Come on, lover boy. Time to go home. They'd like to close this joint soon."

"Awww, do we have to go?"

"When you start kissing the straight guys? Yes. It's time."

"Okay. Bye, Mike, Mike, Mike! G'bye, Sidney! Where's Sidney?"

Sidney had her phone out and a group of people were surrounding her chortling at something on the screen.

"What's she doing?"

Keith laughed. "I think she's sharing a humorous video she just took of her best friend and her husband."

"Really? I wanna see."

"See it later. Come on home, sweetheart. I've already taken care of the bill."

Skyler allowed Keith to direct him carefully down the stairs and to his truck. He laid his head back against the seat and closed his eyes as Keith drove. "It was a good party, wasn't it?"

"The best. Very memorable."

"You're laughing at something. What are you laughing at?"

"Nothing, babe. It was a good party."

"It was a really good party," he agreed.

The next morning Skyler had a bit of a headache and more of one later when Sidney texted him the link to the video she shot. Embarrassed, he tried to hide most of the day from Keith, who snorted a laugh each time he saw Skyler try to creep unnoticed into the room.

Skyler took it easy the rest of the day and was finally able to laugh at his foolishness the night before. He was glad Keith hadn't been jealous about it.

Later that night, they made love. Flushed, sticky, and satisfied, Skyler turned to gaze at his lover, the man who had come into his life out of the blue and filled it full like a water glass. How had it happened? How had love snuck up on him and overtaken his life so completely? How had this man become "home" to him?

Sidney had surprised him most of all. She had always played it like she didn't care, like relationships were just one of many things on a shopping list one could check off. But she had fallen hard, just as hard as Skyler had. He never imagined she would ever want to be married. Was she being honest? Would she have given up Mike if he hadn't wanted it, too?

Did Keith want to marry more than simply staying with Skyler as they were? Sometimes he didn't know what went on in Keith's brain. The man didn't talk much about his past. And this woman, this Laurie Henderson, seemed like a pretty important moment. Anyone would have shared that, wouldn't they? Unless…

Skyler's insides squirmed with strange discomfort.

"Keith?"

Keith crooked a smile, reached out, and stroked Skyler's cheek with heartbreaking tenderness. "What is it, babe?" It was more of a rumble than words, that deep baritone of sounds that made Skyler shiver.

"I…" He huffed a breath. "It's just that…I was thinking about that woman, Laurie Henderson."

Keith's stroking hand stopped and fell away. "Yeah? What about her?"

"It's so stupid, I know. But I keep turning it over and over in my head. That it was maybe this deep dark secret fantasy of yours. That you…liked it more than you let on. And that's why you never told me about it."

"Are you kidding me?"

"Well…"

"Skyler...I can't believe this. You, who have had hundreds of lovers...I mean literally *hundreds* of encounters with all those men...and *you're* insecure?"

"You don't have to put it like that..."

"I have to put it *exactly* like that." Keith sat up, the blanket falling to his lap. "Skyler, I thought we already went over this. That was *one* time over ten years ago. *Once* with a woman in all my life, and I was so drunk at the time that I can barely remember the details. It never honestly occurred to me to mention it to you. I'm sorry. I would have said something much earlier had I even remembered it." He took Skyler's hand and Skyler looked up into those intense eyes. "I am here with you because I am so terribly in love with you that I can hardly breathe sometimes. Do you know how much joy and love you've brought into my life? Do you have any idea?"

His anxiety began to thaw again. "Yeah... Because you've brought that same love and joy into mine."

"Come here, you little idiot." He grabbed Skyler and slid him the short distance across the sheets against him. Arms encircled and lips pressed against his temple. "Are you still drunk or something? How can *you*, of all people, be insecure about how *I* feel?"

Skyler snuggled against Keith, feeling foolish, basking in his warmth and love, clutching a hard bicep. "You do realize," he said against Keith's chest, "that you didn't actually answer the question."

Keith roared and Skyler ended up beneath him suddenly, giggling away the rest of his apprehension. Keith looked down and shook his head. "There's something wrong with you, you know that? Too many blows to the head. Okay, for the record; you are better than the woman, better than hook-ups, better than all my wet dreams. I have no secret fantasy about women. None. At. All. Does that satisfy your greedy little heart at last?"

Skyler smiled. "That will do." He rolled to the side and Keith spooned up behind him. The brush of warm lips on the back of his neck made him shiver, as did the calloused fingertips at his stomach, teasing lower. There was a long moment of lips kissing his tingling skin. And even though they had just coupled not more than a few minutes ago, Skyler's cock stiffened as Keith's hand closed around it, touching, squeezing in excruciating slowness. The breath at his neck, the lips, the hand, had Skyler squirming pleasantly.

There was the briefest of pauses for getting lube and Keith settled down behind him once more. Skyler shivered again at the slow caress of his butt cheek, the hand sliding, dipping. Then a finger gently circling intimately, wetting him, finally working inside, easing him open. Hands, lips, finger, all operated in concert, and Skyler writhed back against the hard body behind him.

Kissing Skyler's neck and moving around to his face, chin, and finally his mouth, Keith jostled Skyler onto his back. The kisses intensified, rubbing soft mouth to soft mouth. And the finger at Skyler's crease was soon replaced by Keith's cock, nudging his entrance. Keith drew back at last and they stared into each other's eyes as Keith slowly pressed deeper. One hand was cupping his bottom, cradling him, and at the same time drawing him closer, while the other hand hadn't stopped working on Skyler's erection.

Skyler couldn't go anywhere. It's wasn't as if Keith had pinned him to the bed. It was nothing like that. His body was held in place by the "V" of Keith's hairy thighs, by the grip on his butt cheek, by their physical connection, and the long slow strokes of Keith's cock inside him. He didn't want to be anywhere else but right there.

Such complete bliss! This is what it was like to be with the perfect person. He knew it. It was more than just fucking. He'd done plenty of that enough to know. Fucking was great. But this? This was beyond great.

But it could all slip away from him — the sensations of warmth and life and something he couldn't even name — if he didn't *do* something …

He kept his eyes open on Keith's, even though he wanted to close them from the dizzying sensations threatening to overpower his senses. His heart was beating madly and his stomach swooped from an undefinable emotion. He gasped out his surprise as his orgasm took hold. Arching his back, he took Keith deeply. The man's eyes darkened and he clutched Skyler's ass painfully as he drove home, grunting through his teeth like a bull, and unloading with shuddering force.

But Skyler *had* blurted it out at the last moments of his release. And Keith, those eyes that had always captured Skyler's with their calm blueness, looked down at him now with a layer of awe and disbelief.

After Keith's release had subsided, the man managed a half-hearted smile. "I wasn't *that* good," he said with a chuckle.

"It wasn't that," said Skyler, trembling suddenly. "It wasn't only that. I meant it."

Keith held Skyler's hips tightly, firmly. They were still physically connected. "Skyler…w-what…?"

Skyler basked in the sensation of Keith still inside him. "I mean it, Keith," he said as earnestly as he could. He licked his lips and said it again. "Will you marry me?"

AUTHOR'S AFTERWORD

I PROMISED I WOULDN'T DO IT. AFTER THOSE FIRST three Skyler Foxe books, I promised you, dear Reader, that I wouldn't end the books in a cliffhanger ever again. And I apologize for breaking that promise, but…it was a really good place to end the book! What can I say? I mean, what do you seriously think is going to happen? Are they gonna break up? Really? Would I do that to you?

All that aside, I wish I had known about Redlands when I first moved to the Inland Empire. We might have moved there instead. It's a cute little town with lots of old Victorian and Craftsman homes, charming shopping streets, and a thriving artistic community. The Lincoln Shrine and the Redlands Bowl are real. Only those involved in it in this book are fictional, and there is *no* relation in this book to *any* person that has *ever* had *anything* to do with the Shrine or the Redlands Bowl living or dead. I made ALL those people up.

So now that *that's* out of the way…

Really, the only reason I even know about the city of Redlands is because of the fabulous Redlands Bowl. We've been going every summer for over twenty years, enjoying concerts, dance, and theater there. And now that I put Skyler in Redlands, I have the feeling he and Keith are somewhere on the lawn having their picnic just like we do. It's weird, actually. And it's well worth going to (but go early to set up your place). The Redlands Bowl survives alone on donations so if you would like to donate to the Redlands Bowl go to this link http://redlandsbowl.org/how-to-donate/ If you ever find yourself in the Inland Empire in the summer, you should really check it out. We might run into each other there!

Now I realize that docents in a tiny museum like that are volunteers and don't get paid, but for the purposes of this book, just flow with me here, okay? Still, the Lincoln Shrine is an amazing assemblage of Civil War memorabilia and has an awesome collection of books on the subject and from the era. Go check that out, too. It's free!

As always, do go to my website to see new things. I've also started a quarterly newsletter and there's always a contest with giveaways. You can sign up for it there. Find me also on Facebook /skylerfoxe.mysteries, and chat. I'm always around. And thanks so much for reading! The next Skyler Foxe Mystery is STONE COLD FOXE, with romance and murder on the high seas with Skyler and the gang! Be on the lookout for that. Cheers!

Made in the USA
Middletown, DE
29 October 2020